Get hooked on the Loon Lake mysteries from Victoria Houston . . .

Dead Frenzy

"Houston has a way with words. . . . Her humor is well rationed. . . . The good doctor is a pleasant, witty voice. The description of a fishing experience is well done, depicting the Northwoods to a 'T.' The mystery is plotted well, and there is enough action to keep the reader engaged to the end. The Loon Lake series holds great promise for a pleasurable reading retreat." —*Books 'n' Bytes*

Dead Water

"*Dead Water* is her best yet . . . [Victoria Houston] puts me right there in the Wisconsin heat and cold, lets me know what the fish are biting on, lets me spy on the interesting characters of Loon Lake, and most of all, spins an intelligent and captivating tale. I look forward to more and more." —T. Jefferson Parker, author of *Silent Joe*

"Victoria Houston's love for her Wisconsin setting—and her wonderful characters—is evident on every page of her fine series. . . . A great getaway, even if it does keep me up at night." —Laura Lippman, author of *The Sugar House*

Dead Creek

"Fans of a well-drawn regional police procedural will want to read this novel. All the subplots smoothly return to the main theme and there are plenty of suspects to keep the audience guessing about what is going on and who is the mastermind behind the mysterious events. With this fine novel, Victoria Houston will hook readers and make them seek her previous stories." —*Painted Rock Reviews*

continued . . .

"What a great story! A book that fishermen of all ages (and species) are sure to enjoy."

—Tony Rizzo, legendary Northwoods fishing guide and author of *Secrets of a Muskie Guide*

"Murder mystery muskies! *The X-Files* comes to Packer Land."

—John Krga, dedicated Northwoods "catch-and-release" muskie fisherman

Dead Angler

"Who would have thought that fly-fishing could be such fun? Victoria Houston makes you want to dash for rod and reel. [She] cleverly blends the love of the outdoors with the thrill of catching a serial killer." —*The Orlando Sentinel*

"As exciting as a fishing tournament—and you don't know the result until the end."

—Norb Wallock, North American Walleye Angler's 1997 Angler of the Year

"Houston introduces us to a cast of characters with whom we quickly bond—as fly fishers and as good citizens—in the first of what I hope will be a long series."

—Joan Wulff, world-class fly caster, and cofounder of the Wulff School of Fly Fishing

"A compelling thriller . . . populated with three-dimensional characters who reveal some of their secrets of trout fishing the dark waters of the northern forests."

—Tom Wiench, dedicated fly fisherman and member of Trout Unlimited

"Should net lots of fans . . . a good catch." —*The Star Press*

Titles by Victoria Houston

Dead Hot Mama

VICTORIA HOUSTON

BERKLEY PRIME CRIME, NEW YORK

This is a work of fiction. Names, characters, places, and incidents either are the product of the author's imagination or are used fictitiously, and any resemblance to actual persons, living or dead, business establishments, events, or locales is entirely coincidental.

DEAD HOT MAMA

A Berkley Prime Crime Book / published by arrangement with the author

Copyright © 2004 by Victoria Houston.
Cover design by Jill Boltin.
Illustrations by Dan Craig.

For information address: The Berkley Publishing Group,
a division of Penguin Group (USA) Inc.,
375 Hudson Street, New York, New York 10014.

ISBN: 0-425-19332-2

Berkley Prime Crime Books are published
by The Berkley Publishing Group,
a division of Penguin Group (USA) Inc.,
375 Hudson Street, New York, New York 10014.
The name BERKLEY PRIME CRIME and
the BERKLEY PRIME CRIME design
are trademarks belonging to Penguin Group (USA) Inc.

PRINTED IN THE UNITED STATES OF AMERICA

10 9 8 7 6 5 4 3 2 1

For Madeleine,
So glad you made it, kid

*Where did that dog
that used to be here go?
I thought about him
once again tonight
before I went to bed.*

—SHIMAKI AKAHIKO

one

For the listener, who listens in the snow,
And, nothing himself, beholds
Nothing that is not there and the nothing that is.

—Wallace Stevens, *The Snow Man*

Head down, shoulders braced, Osborne plunged through the wall of aspen. With one bird in the bag, all he needed were two more and he would be happy.

It was December 22. Grouse season closed in nine days, and he was eager to have a few more tiny bodies wrapped tight and tucked into his freezer. Nothing tasted better than mushroom-smothered partridge on a frosty winter night.

Right now, the crisp cold of the forest was invigorating, felt good, and took his mind off Mallory's pending arrival. Her announcement a week ago that she wanted to spend the Christmas holidays at his house had caught him off guard. While his feelings were changing towards his oldest daughter, he wasn't sure how the two of them would survive a full week in close proximity. And if Mallory were there, would Lew be reluctant to spend the night?

Oops! His right foot slipped down a hillock hidden by

the snow, which was nearly a foot deep in some spots. That's enough of that, thought Osborne to himself, time to pay attention, watch where I'm walking—and try to avoid shooting my foot off.

He wished like hell he had Mike along. Could that dog flush birds or what? Not to mention retrieving any he brought down. But news that bear hunters were training their dogs in the area had forced him to hesitate. Those damn packs wouldn't know a black lab from a black bear, and he didn't need to see one of his best friends torn limb from limb. Even now he could hear baying off in the distance. It crossed his mind to wonder if the goddam dogs would know a retired dentist from a black bear.

Nah. He forced that thought from his mind, too. One blast from his twenty gauge would answer any questions. And it wouldn't be a warning blast either. Osborne hated bear hunters, hated the idea of treeing an animal with dogs, then taking pot shots from below. That's not sport. In fact, it is so unsporting that all you have to do is mention someone hunts bear, and you know exactly what kind of moron you're dealing with.

The aspen gave way to a logging trail. He stepped down, deciding to walk the trail for a few hundred yards. Recent use by logging trucks had exposed the ruts down to fresh dirt, which suited Osborne fine. It was just that time of day when grouse are apt to leave their cover to scout gravel for their gorgeous little gullets.

Butt resting under his right elbow, finger near the trigger, the safety on, he moved ahead in near silence, eyes and ears alert. The stroll down the rutted lane was as easy as moving through the dense, young aspen had been hard. Also noisy. Warmer days and colder nights had glazed the snow, producing an icy surface that crackled underfoot. At the same time, multiple early frosts had stripped the aspen, birch, and maple of their leaves, making it much easier to spot a grouse in flight.

A sudden flutter to his right, and Osborne's shotgun

was up and firing. Yes! He got it on the wing. Osborne watched the bird fall. Oh, he was a happy man. Then off the trail and into a stand of balsam—he had a pretty good view of the bird's trajectory about forty yards ahead and to the right.

Trudging forward, eyes focused on where he was sure the bird had landed, he felt his right foot give way too far and too fast. Down he went, down and back, bouncing along on his rump as he struggled to keep his shotgun up and out of the snow. To his surprise, he landed in a very comfortable position cushioned from behind by a snowy hillock and snuggled up against a decaying tree stump.

Leaning to his left, against the stump, he fished around in the pocket of his hunting vest, hoping to hell he had something he could use to wipe the snow off the butt of his gun. He found a packet of Kleenex. After wiping the wood dry, he was reaching back with the Kleenex, when his eye caught a flash of white inside a hollow in the stump. Mushrooms? At this time of year? He bent forward to take a closer look.

Thirty-two teeth greeted him: a full set of dentures. The upper set carefully on the lower.

Osborne stared at the disembodied grin. Now that was damn strange. And they were set so carefully, too—not like the wind had blown them into place or an animal had stashed them. No, some human had set these dentures down quite carefully.

Osborne looked overhead and all around. Had there been a deer stand here? Flat-line winds two years ago had reconfigured the forest, and he knew many hunters who had lost their stands in the blowdown. Losing a deer stand was one thing, losing your teeth was another. He hadn't heard of any locals with *that* kind of bad luck. But then, he was three years into retirement and out of touch. The more he thought about it, he decided maybe he shouldn't be so surprised.

For one thing, this region was heavily hunted, starting

with bird and bow hunters in the early fall, then packed with deer hunters into mid-December and now stragglers like himself. Several hundred had probably cruised through here, many stopping to eat or grab a quick nap. And this was a comfy bowl where he had landed. If it were early in the fall when temperatures were in the seventies, he could see a hunter, older than himself of course, deciding to remove his dentures for a short snooze. Add to that forgetfulness. If you wake up, relieve yourself, then start hunting again only to remember you forgot your teeth—well, once you've walked fifty feet in this well-logged terrain, all stumps look alike.

Something else he was aware of: More people over age fifty misplace their teeth than lose their eyeglasses. One of those little-known facts that allow dentists to retire early.

Osborne reached into the hollow. Even without his reading glasses he could see the teeth were finely made. Not his work; he knew that the instant he felt them. He had never had a patient who would pay for materials of this quality. He'd bet anything they were imported.

Again, he looked around—this time checking the snow cover for signs of recent visitors. But all he could see were the paw prints of a large dog. Damn bear hunters.

Osborne turned the dentures over, tipping them this way and that, but the light was too dim for him to make out either the owner's name or the Social Security number, which he knew he would find somewhere inside each.

Oh well. He took out the Kleenex packet again and wrapped each section with care, then tucked the dentures into the upper left pocket of his vest. He could check for the identification at home, then get in touch with the owner or their dentist. Someone would be very pleased.

Grabbing the branch of a nearby balsam, he pulled himself to his feet. The sun was dropping fast, and he'd better hurry if he wanted to find that bird and get out before dark. He scoured the shallow ravine in front of him but no sign of the grouse. Maybe he could see better from the rise behind him.

Osborne turned to start back up the hill. Looking up, he was startled to find he wasn't alone.

two

The best part of hunting and fishing is the thinking about the going and talking about it after you got back.

—Robert Ruark

Topaz eyes bored into his, their brilliance heightened by a setting of ebony fur.

Osborne had never been so close to a wolf. He had never wanted to be so close. The animal could not be more than twenty feet away. The forest that had felt so familiar, almost cozy, moments ago was now stone silent, watching.

He stepped forward with his right foot, praying the wolf had the instincts of a deer and would bolt. Not even a flinch—nor did the eyes leave his. Osborne raised his gun, knowing he wouldn't fire but hoping the broader movement might frighten the animal.

No such luck. He remembered now that the Department of Natural Resources had recently reported a pack moving into the region, but he never imagined one would stalk a human being. Still, he had no urge to argue the issue. He backed away slowly, moving to the right until he felt hidden by the stand of balsam. When he reached the logging trail, he ran. Ran hard.

Ran until he was safe in his car with all four doors locked. Breath held, heart pounding, Osborne waited, eyes fixed on his own tracks in the dusk-gray snow. No sign of the wolf. He let a solid sixty seconds pass before he let his shoulders relax. Only then did he reach back for his gun case.

Whoa. Osborne cranked his ignition. Would he have a tale to tell over morning coffee at McDonald's. First the teeth, then the wolf. His buddies wouldn't believe it. Osborne made a mental note to check his wallet—the guy with the best story buys the coffee. Of course, he knew darn well what one of those razzbonya pals of his would likely say: "What's your problem, Doc? You got a gun—all that wolf's got are two canines."

As he drove home, he started to rethink what he had done. Maybe he should have left those dentures right where they were. The more he thought about it, he couldn't be sure that someone had actually *forgotten* their teeth. No, chances were better that someone had hidden them deliberately. If he had learned anything in his thirty-three years as a small-town dentist, it was that people do strange things with teeth.

More than one patient had saved the dentures of their dear departed. Now that he thought about it, he could see a bereaved widow or friend—in lieu of scattering ashes—carefully tucking away a loved one's dentures near their favorite hunting ground. He'd better put those teeth right back where he found them.

Tomorrow. No need to challenge a wolf guarding a fresh kill.

And why on earth had he locked his car doors? Wolves may be capable of acts of violence, but breaking into cars is not on their list of canine felonies.

By the time Osborne was nearing his driveway, he was feeling pretty silly. But he forgot everything when he saw his house—lights blazed from every window. The place was lit up like a Christmas tree.

"Grampa! Grampa! Can I walk Mike on the lake? Please, please?" Eight-year-old Mason was jumping up and down at the back door as he approached. Behind her, Mike levitated in unison.

"Better check with your mom first," said Osborne.

"Whaddya think, Dad? That ice is thick enough for her to walk the dog on, isn't it?" said Erin from inside the kitchen.

"Ray's been ice fishing for three weeks—had his truck out there the other day," said Osborne from the back porch, as he emptied the unused cartridges from the pockets of his hunting vest. The lakes in the region had frozen over by Thanksgiving, and Loon Lake already sported a solid twelve inches.

"All right with me, kiddo—you better check with Mike," said Osborne, ruffling Mason's light-brown hair as he spoke. "If it's too cold on his paws, he'll let you know."

"I know," said Mason. "If he dances on three legs, it's way too cold, and I'll bring him right back, Grampa." She spoke with such serious authority that Osborne had to hide a smile. He helped her pull a bright red and yellow stocking cap down over her ears and watched as she thrust her hands into matching mitts.

"Mason, you look like a sausage in that outfit," said Osborne, grinning at the sight of the little girl, her red parka zipped tight over quilted bib overalls. The combination of an ecstatic dog and a well-padded youngster heading out the back door jarred memories. How many times had his mother done exactly the same with one of Mike's predecessors? Life has a wonderful way of repeating itself, he thought as he watched Mason dash after the dog.

Entering the warm kitchen, Osborne found both his daughters seated at the kitchen table, mugs of hot coffee steaming in front of them. Mallory looked up from a pad of lined paper in front of her, "Surprise, Dad. I got in earlier than I thought I would." She set down the pen that was in her hand and stood up to give him a hug and a light kiss on the cheek.

"Great, hon, how're you doin'?" Was it his imagination, or did Mallory pause for a split second? "Easy drive?" he asked. She would have left her new apartment in Evanston, a solid six hours away, early that morning.

"Not bad, but I'm glad I drove up today. Sounds like a major winter storm heading this way. I'll bet the roads will be icy tomorrow."

"Oh?" Osborne poured himself a cup of coffee. "The weather forecast must have changed since I heard it around noon."

"Dad," said Mallory as she sat down again, "Erin and I are planning Christmas Eve dinner—standing rib roast with Mom's wild rice casserole okay with you?"

It was obviously a rhetorical question, as the two women resumed making their list before he could answer. The sight of their heads bowed, one blond and one dark brown, made his heart feel full. A flash from the past reminded him how lucky he was that he hadn't lost his family.

As if she knew what he was thinking, Mallory lifted her eyes to his briefly. "Feels good to be home, Dad. We've ordered in pizza. Mark's bringing it out after he picks up the other kids. Is that okay?"

"Fine," said Osborne. "Excuse me a moment, would you? I almost forgot something." He hurried back out to the porch. From the back of the vest, he pulled out the breast of the one partridge that he'd dressed in the woods. Using the utility sink on the porch, he rinsed it and dried it with a paper towel. Then he took white freezer paper out of the drawer next to the sink and ripped off a sheet.

As he had since he was a boy, he tucked the ends of the paper neatly around the carcass and rolled it up, securing it with tape, which he kept in the drawer with the freezer paper A black marker was there, too, which he used to date the bird. After slipping the package into a small Ziploc bag, he set it carefully inside the freezer of the porch refrigerator: the fourth in a small stack of mummies.

Only four birds, but enough to offer an excellent excuse for dinner with Lew. Pleased with that thought, he smiled as he closed the door and walked back into the kitchen.

"More coffee, Dad?" Erin stood up to refill her mug.

"Just a touch. Now listen, you two, let me in on some of this planning. Lew's daughter is coming up from Milwaukee for New Year's, and I'd like you to meet her and her family."

"Oh ho!" said Mallory, rocking back in her chair with a sly grin on her face. She might be thirty-four years old, Osborne thought, but she looked twelve at the moment.

"Told ya," said Erin, two years younger than Mallory and just as devious. The two sisters chortled.

"Jeez, you razzbonyas. You don't make it easy on the old man."

Just then Erin stood up and walked off through the living room. "Excuse me, Dad, I want to check on Mason." She peered through the large window at the front of Osborne's living room. "What's that mound of snow out there?" she called back. "Two docks down on the left."

"The Kobernots are icing up a rink this year," said Osborne. "We had black ice, which makes it easy," he said, referring to one of the rare times that the lake froze over with no wind blowing. Craig Kobernot was a neurologist at St. Mary's Hospital. He and his wife, Patrice, had two boys in their early teens who were on the Loon Lake High School hockey team. "The kids will have to bring their skates out."

"Dad." Mallory laid a hand on his as he sat down at the kitchen table. She dropped her voice. "Would it bother you if I did my AA meetings with the group over in Minocqua?"

"Not at all," said Osborne, "so long as you don't mind the drive and keep an eye out for deer. You doing okay these days?"

"Pretty good. Every day isn't a great day, but you know . . ." Again, that pause.

"I know." Osborne gave her hand a quick pat. He was relieved that she wouldn't be joining his group in the room at the top of the stairs, the room behind the door with the coffeepot. Why he wasn't sure, but he was. Maybe because Ray was there?

"Dad, you don't have your tree up yet, why not?" said Erin, walking back into the kitchen. "That expensive one that Mom bought in Minneapolis that time? That's a pretty nice tree for an artificial."

"Nice, but fake," said Osborne. Both daughters caught the edge in his voice and gave him sharp looks. He curbed the impulse to tell them it wasn't the only thing about their mother that had been fake. "I've decided this year I want a *real* tree."

"Then you better act fast," said Erin, "the Boy Scouts are selling them down in the bank parking lot, and I know they don't have many left—not if you want something decent."

"A real tree is one you cut yourself," said Osborne. He turned to Mallory. "Got plans tomorrow? I could use a little help."

"D-a-a-d, I would love that. We haven't done that since I was a kid." Mallory's face was so radiant, Osborne felt like Santa Claus. A smart Santa to boot—he could find a Christmas tree and return those dentures all at the same time.

"Boy, I found the darndest thing—" He had just begun to tell the girls about his discovery, when the back door slammed.

Mason ran into the kitchen, her eyes wide with worry.

"Grampa, something's really wrong with Mike! He's

down by that big pile of snow where those boys are skating. He won't come when I call him. He just keeps giving these little barks—like something's hurting him."

A chill traveled down Osborne's back. He knew his dog. And it wasn't the dog that was hurt.

three

Muddy water, let stand,
Becomes clear.

—Buddha

"**Watch** the steps, they're icy," said Osborne over his shoulder. Erin and Mason were following so closely he could hear their boots crunching snow as the three of them hurried down the stone stairway to the lake.

Two doors down, the Kobernots' dock lamps were lit and angled out, throwing pools of light across the small rink. A snowmobile trail running along the shoreline made it an easy run, and they got there in a matter of seconds. As they arrived, one of the sons was slamming hockey pucks into a goal at the far end.

Some pucks made the net, others flipped up and over the snowbank and onto the snowmobile trail that wound around the back of the rink. That was an accident waiting to happen: A passing snowmobiler could easily take one right in the head. Even as Osborne noted the danger, he saw points of light bobbing towards them from across the lake.

Snowmobiles were out in large numbers this year due to the early and deep snow cover. While he hated the noise and the congestion on the lakes, even Osborne had to admit the Loon Lake economy needed these alien-looking riders with their cash-heavy wallets. The roar of the snowmobile was the sound of money.

"Your dog is acting weird, Dr. Osborne," said the boy as he bent down to dig an errant puck out of the snow behind the goal. Osborne stepped up and across the snowbank to where he could see Mike, his black coat barely visible in the inky shadows on the far side of the mounded snow.

Head high, nose up, and eyes intent on an area where a plow had pushed the snow much higher, Mike was air scenting. His tail whipped with an enthusiasm that signaled he wouldn't quit until he had his master's approval. As Osborne slid slowly down the bank towards the dog, the black lab trotted in his direction, then backed off with a bark ending in a yelp.

A yelp he recognized. Years of hunting together had forged an intuitive bond between Osborne and his dog. And though Osborne had heard that yelp only once before, he knew exactly what it meant.

Never would he forget the day that he and Mike had found the hunter, one of Osborne's partners in his deer shack. He had been missing since breakfast. Obscured by a clump of tag alder where he had fallen from his deer stand, the man was dead of a heart attack suffered hours earlier. Fifty yards before Osborne could even see the body, Mike had signaled the presence of death.

"Erin, sweetheart," said Osborne at the sound of boots scrabbling up the icy bank behind him, "why don't you and Mason stay on shore while I check this out." Keeping his voice level as Mason tumbled down the snowbank to land at his feet, he said with more emphasis, "I want you both to stay back . . . *way* back."

Erin grabbed at the sleeve of her daughter's jacket. "Mason! Stop, I want you here with me. Come on now, you heard Grampa—back on the dock." The little girl, sensing something was up, pulled away from her mother

and tried to peer around Osborne. "Mason, I mean it."
Erin gave her a yank.

Just then Mallory scrambled up onto the snowbank.
She had stayed behind to dig a pair of ski mitts out of her
suitcase. Her arrival was too much for the Kobernot kid—
he gave up on his hockey pucks and skated over to watch.
Osborne put up a hand, signaling both to stay right where
they were.

Then he began pushing at the snow with his gloved
hands. Drifting spray from the water gun used to ice the
rink had glazed the surface of the snow, but he was able to
break through with one thrust of his fist. Beneath the
glaze, the snow was airy and light: It had been mounded
recently.

"Mallory," said Osborne, pausing to look up, "would
you stand behind me and hold this so I can see what I'm
doing?" He handed over a flashlight he'd jammed into his
pocket as he rushed out of the house.

"Sure, Dad." She slid down, grabbed the flashlight, and
positioned herself behind him. "Does this work?"

"Yes, thank you."

When he felt his gloved fingers encounter resistance,
he took them off, reaching down and in with bare
hands . . . skin. After so many years of working in people's mouths, he knew the feel of it, fresh or frozen.

"Come closer," he motioned to Mallory. "Shine that
light right here." A swift intake of breath from his daughter told him she could see what he had felt.

He kept working. Fingers tender and light, he dusted
the snow back and back, exposing a slender wrist, then a
forearm, then a hand—a hand with long, graceful fingers
and nails—nails painted dark blue and silver.

Osborne looked up at the boy, who was watching with
worried eyes. It was the older of the two sons. "Is your father home?"

The boy nodded.

"I'd go get him if I were you," Osborne said.

"Erin," Osborne turned his head in the other direction,

"take Mason up to the house and give Lewellyn Ferris a call at the police station, would you please? Ask to speak to her directly, and if she's not there, let whoever is on the switchboard know it's an emergency and they need to patch you through to wherever she is. Tell Lew . . ." Osborne, aware of Mason's wide eyes, paused, ". . . tell her there's been an accident and a . . . casualty out here."

"A casualty? No ambulance, Dad?" Erin knew he was protecting his granddaughter from nightmares.

"Not on an emergency basis, but she'll want to alert Pecore—she'll need a coroner's report on this.

"Now Mason, your job is to call Mike," said Osborne. "He needs a reward, and I want him to stay in the house with you, okay? Can you do that for Grampa? Can you make sure that Mike gets two treats?"

Delight crossed Mason's face as she called the dog. With a hand signal from Osborne, Mike followed the little girl, bouncing happily behind her up the stairs and back to warmth.

Mallory waited until they were out of earshot before she said, "We don't want to do anything further, I guess, huh?"

"Not until Lew gets here. I just want to be sure no one moves anything or touches anything around this—"

"Holiday nails," said Mallory, interrupting.

"What?"

"You see them everywhere in the city." She pointed at the painted fingernails. "Acrylic and expensive. I can tell you one thing, Dad—this is no hockey player."

four

Regardless of what you may think of our penal system, the fact is that every man in jail is one less potential fisherman to clutter up your favorite pool or pond.

—Ed Zern, *Field & Stream*

Even as the police cruiser pulled into his driveway ten minutes later, Craig Kobernot was vomiting off his dock.

"God Almighty, I think I did it," he choked, wiping at his face. Osborne stood by, arms ready in case the neurologist slipped and fell. One body was enough for the moment. "I plowed late last night," said Craig, wiping at his mouth as he pointed over at a small shed. Behind it was parked an ATV with a plow attached.

"My night vision isn't real great, and I remember feeling something I thought were chunks of ice. Man, if that snowmobiler was alive when I plowed—my insurance is going to . . ." He couldn't finish.

"I don't think the victim was on a snowmobile—"

"Of course they were," Kobernot cut him off, "how the hell else could they get here?" He retched again.

"Well . . ."

Osborne paused, knowing anything he said would be ignored, "I wouldn't beat myself up until we know more."

What a self-centered pain in the butt. He never had liked the guy and now he had yet another reason to find him irritating. Tall and rangy with the insouciant smirk of a man who knows he's attractive to women, Kobernot had the opposite effect on Osborne and his buddies. More than one liked to poke fun at the physician, noting his resemblance to a raccoon, the sly forest thief with the perpetual smile, beady eyes, and brazen ways.

It didn't help that Kobernot was a known womanizer, that he had managed to build a million-dollar home in spite of two malpractice suits, and that he owned three extremely loud personal watercraft. Oh, and four snowmobiles. How many times had Osborne walked over and graciously requested that Craig and his sons tone it down a little only to hear, "I'll see what I can do, old man, but you know boys . . ."

As if that wasn't enough, Kobernot was a fisherman who couldn't tell a spinning rod from a fly rod: "Hey, Doc, I've got some friends coming up from Appleton—can you show me how these damn things work? Where do you buy worms?"

As far as Osborne was concerned, Craig Kobernot might be a professional man and he might have had enough taste to buy property on Loon Lake—but that could not hide the fact he was an out-and-out jabone. And now—to be more concerned about his insurance liability than the fate of some poor human being? High time someone wiped the smirk off that face.

The two of them stood alone on the dock. Craig had banished his son to the house, and Mallory had run back up to Osborne's to help Erin. Mark was due any moment with the pizza and the two boys, and Osborne wanted to be darn sure his grandchildren were kept far away from the disturbing scene behind the snowbank.

"Doc? Is that you down there?" A figure in a khaki-colored parka tripped quickly down the Kobernots' wood stairs and skidded towards them across the slippery rink.

"Sorry to take so long—you must be freezing." Dark and serious, Lew's eyes caught the light. Black curls fell in a tangle across her forehead, struggling out from under the circle of fur that anchored her hood.

The parka was new. After one of her deputies, wearing the traditional dark green, was nearly killed by a motorist who didn't see him in the dark, Lew had insisted the entire Loon Lake police force—all three of them—switch to lighter-colored jackets. Though the decision was made strictly for safety reasons, Osborne found her new uniform quite easy on the eyes—or maybe it was just Lew and not the uniform at all.

Every time he watched her approach, the tawny band of possum framing her face, he was reminded of a favorite story from his childhood: the tale of an ice princess whose sled sped along moonbeams. Not an image the chief of the Loon Lake Police Department would appreciate. No siree.

Tough-minded, gun-friendly, Lewellyn Ferris would be appalled to think she was making such a frivolous impression. Osborne, who did not always know the right thing to say around her, at least knew better than to share this observation. But that didn't mean he couldn't relish it in private. That and the fact that even though Lew had the demeanor of a quarterback for the Green Bay Packers, she had a way of making him feel sixteen all over again.

Right now, having stopped a few feet from where Kobernot was bending over and spitting into the snow, Lew clapped her gloved hands to keep them warm. She cut her eyes towards Osborne. "Is he okay?" As Osborne nodded, Craig straightened up.

"Chief Ferris," said Osborne, beckoning Lew forward, "this is my neighbor, Dr. Craig Kobernot. Craig is a neurologist at St. Mary's, and he just wasn't prepared for what you'll find over behind that snowbank."

"This your rink, Dr. Kobernot?" said Lew.

"Yes."

Lew acknowledged Kobernot with a quick handshake

before stepping off the dock. "So what do we have—a snowmobile accident?" She hopped up onto the snowbank. "Erin didn't say much when she called." Osborne followed her, then aimed his flashlight down into the snow.

"Oh . . . I see," said Lew, pausing at the sight of the bare forearm in the snow. "Any idea what happened here?" She dropped to her knees, and Osborne knelt beside her.

"No, Lew. Mason was walking Mike when the dog air scented the corpse," said Osborne. "Hoping I was wrong, I uncovered just this much. When I didn't see any sign of life, I thought I better hold off just in case . . ."

Lew reached for the flashlight. Osborne handed it over, then leaned in with her for a closer look. Glancing up, he caught a funny look on Kobernot's face. "The chief and I fish together," said Osborne, as if that explained their easy familiarity.

"I see."

Working as gently as Osborne had, Lew brushed away more snow, careful to leave it piled to one side. In less than a minute, she had exposed the head and shoulders of what appeared to be a young woman with spiked blond hair. The head was turned sideways, face tilted down into the snow, away from Kobernot's line of vision.

Lew sat back on her heels. "No blood in the snow that I can see in this light, no winter clothing on the victim—in fact, she appears to be naked . . . and no sign of a wound. I don't know if the body is frozen or still in rigor, but I can't move her," said Lew. She pulled off a glove and slipped her hand into the woman's armpit. "Cold. Very cold. Cold enough to say she's been dead awhile—and this is no accident.

"I better have one of the Wausau boys take a look. Since I have another situation over on Two Sisters Lake, we've already got someone in the area." She unzipped a side pocket in her parka and reached for a cell phone. She punched in a number and waited. As she waited, she looked at Osborne. "Is this a breakthrough or what?"

She meant the cell phone. Up until two months earlier, cell service in the northwoods had been lousy. Drive just two miles out of Loon Lake, and you lost your signal. While service was still spotty in areas, tonight, at least, it was working.

"Hello, Roger, you have one of the Wausau boys there?" Lew spoke quickly, giving directions to the Kobernot residence. Then she said, "Oh, really . . . that's strange. That's very strange . . . thank you."

"Who are the Wausau boys?" asked Craig as she slipped the phone back into her pocket.

"The crime lab from Wausau does our forensic analyses," said Lew, referring to the larger town located sixty miles from Loon Lake. "They're not the best in the state, but they're all we've got." The look on her face said it all.

Lew detested the head of the crime lab. That fall, while fly-fishing for smallies on the Wisconsin River, she had shared with Osborne the extent of her frustration with the man. He was an old-timer who didn't like seeing women in law enforcement and made it his mission to make her job difficult. His favorite technique was to demand that she fill out and fax a two-page questionnaire before he would take her phone call.

"C'mon, Frank, I've completed that damn form at least twenty times, and you are deliberately delaying my investigation," she would say. He would chuckle.

One thing about the guy that Osborne did appreciate, however, was his refusal to spend state funds on a full-time forensic odontologist. That encouraged Lew to call on Osborne for assistance when dental records were a last resort for identification purposes, not uncommon in a region dotted with hundreds of lakes, rivers, and streams—and peopled with tourists who thought wearing a life jacket was a negative fashion statement. "Boater today, floater tomorrow," read a T-shirt popular with Loon Lake locals.

While Osborne may have had limited forensic experience during a brief stint in the military while he was still in dental school, it was enough to make Lew's life easier. And his significantly more interesting.

They had met when she volunteered to teach him how to fly fish—in return for a new fly line from the owner of the local fly fishing shop who was too busy that weekend to take on a private student. Since that first night in the river, Osborne had pursued any excuse to see Lew—in, on, or off water.

"Dr. Kobernot, we'll have to secure the area, including the snowmobile trail and the skating rink, including your dock area—"

"But my son has to practice—"

"I'm afraid there's a five hundred dollar fine if you violate—"

"All right, all right." Kobernot raised his hands in surrender. "My family and I will cooperate in every way."

"Lew, that ATV up there," Osborne pointed on shore, "Craig used it to plow the snow where the body is."

"Okay, I need the ATV and the area around it secured, too."

"How long are we talking, Chief Ferris?"

"As long as it takes to secure all trace evidence."

Kobernot turned away, throwing his arms up in total frustration. "Honest to Pete. All right. Okay. Well, then— at the very least can you do whatever you need to do as soon as possible? We've got a winter storm due in tomorrow sometime, and if I don't keep my rink cleared, I'll lose this good ice."

"I'll do what works for the investigator out of Wausau, Doctor," said Lew, keeping her voice level as she made it clear she was not in the mood to take orders.

"Lew, what the heck happened on Two Sisters?" asked Osborne, sensing this was an excellent time to change the subject. He knew she'd been working overtime with the usual holiday influx of skiers, snowmobilers, and ice fisherman—actually more than usual thanks to the snow and frigid temperatures. Still, she never called on Wausau unless she had a serious crime.

"Late this afternoon, some fishermen pulled a snowmobiler out of Two Sisters Lake. Roger took the call. They told him it looked like animals had gotten to the body. I didn't like the sound of that, so I asked a few more questions. Turns out the body was found right over a sandbar—a *wide* sandbar where you can stand up and climb out if that's where you go in. Then, oddly enough, there was no sign of his vehicle. That's when I sent Roger to the scene and called Wausau."

"Any idea who it is?" asked Osborne.

"None whatsover. Roger checked with the neighbors to see if anyone had friends or family missing. Then I had Marlene call around, and we discovered Eagle River has had two riders missing for over a week! But about that time I got the call from Erin. So I left Roger waiting for Wausau at Two Sisters and hurried out here."

"Are you talking about Roger Adamczyk?" asked Kobernot. "He used to be my insurance agent. When you talk to him next, tell him to give me a call."

"I won't have time to do that. Dr. Kobernot," said Lew. "Roger's no longer in the insurance business, you know. He's been working for me for two years now."

She darted a quick look over at Osborne, who was repressing a grin. They both knew poor Roger's chagrin over finding himself more involved in law enforcement than he'd ever planned. When he sold his small insurance agency, he had planned on a few years emptying parking meters down Loon Lake's Main Street segueing into an easy retirement—then Lewellyn Ferris got promoted and changed his life.

"I know that, but he handled my property insurance—"

"Dr. Kobernot," said Lew, "your business is not my business."

Lew turned back towards the victim. Slowly, she ran her flashlight up and down the head and shoulders that lay outlined in the snow. "That face is not familiar to me, Doc. What about you?"

Even though he was retired, after thirty-three years of practicing dentistry in Loon Lake, Osborne still knew many of the people living in the region. He dropped to his knees for a closer look and brushed away more snow, better exposing the face and the line of the jaw.

"No, Lew, I don't think I've seen her before. I'll be happy to do the dental exam once the body is moved."

"I would very much appreciate that."

Lew waved her flashlight towards the dock, "Dr. Kobernot, please step over here and take a look. See if you recognize the victim."

"I hardly think—" said Kobernot from where he stood at the end of his dock, his hands on his hips. He exhaled with impatience as he let himself down onto the rink, then up and over the snowbank.

The moment his eyes fell on the dead woman's face, his gloved hands jerked involuntarily. "No!"

"'No,' you can't believe she's dead or 'no,'" you don't know her?" asked Lew.

"I've never seen that woman before in my life."

Osborne gave a quick glance at Lew, but her expression was opaque. Then he looked at Kobernot. The smirk was gone, the impatience, too. Craig Kobernot was scared.

five

Every healthy boy, every right-minded man, and every uncaged woman, feels at one time or another, and maybe at all times, the impulse to go a'fishing.

—Eugene McCarthy, *Familiar Fish*

"**The** legs are gone? What do you mean the legs are gone? Roger, settle down . . . what's the guy's name? Bruce? Okay, put Bruce on . . . that's okay, I'll wait."

Lew's cell phone had rung as the three of them were trudging up the stairs towards the Kobernots' house. Motioning Craig Kobernot to go on ahead, she had stopped to take the call. Osborne paused beside her. As she waited, they both looked back down towards the snowbank.

Osborne was concerned that snowmobilers might show up before Lew could close off the trail, although the lights that had been bobbing in the distance had since turned away, traveling northeast. And given that this was a weeknight, riders would be few and far between. Tomorrow—Friday before a holiday—it would be gridlock on the trail. Right now all he could make out were intermittent points of light where the windows of fishing shacks glowed in the distance. Glowed with the warmth of the bonfires and gas stoves and camaraderie that drew so many to ice fish-

ing. A warmth that would never touch the young woman
who lay naked beneath her crystalline coverlet of ice and
snow.

"Bruce," said Lew, "thanks for driving up. Now what
on earth is Roger talking about?" She listened, her eyes
fixed on her right boot, which was kicking repeatedly at a
chunk of ice. "Two, huh," she said after a long stretch.
"Two bodies but no snowmobiles anywhere, huh? Okay,
but what do we do out here on Loon Lake? I'm going
down to secure the area and close down the trail, but I
need direction from you on how to protect the scene and
the victim I have here." Again, she listened. "How soon
can you meet me?" A long pause. "Yes, I can arrange that.
Of course." She clicked off the phone.

"You won't believe this, Doc, but they found another
body in a snowmobile suit under the ice, not far from the
first one. Both are missing their legs."

Osborne was stunned. "Their legs?"

"Right. Bruce said the only animal that touched those
two was human—well-equipped with all the right tools."

"Whoa," said Osborne.

"Frustrating news is Bruce—that's the new guy they
sent up from Wausau—said he can't work this scene
tonight. Too risky to try to find trace evidence in the
dark."

"You're kidding. What do we do with—it's going down
to 25 below tonight, too cold for you or anyone to stand
out here."

"He's bringing a special type of tent for the corpse—
with this deep freeze, we won't lose anything as far as the
body goes. But you hit on the problem: Someone has to
be here tonight."

"Not me, not you, kiddo. You've worked late every
night this week, Lew, and I'm way past my days of winter
camping."

"You're right, Doc. I'll have Terry take over. He's
young, he can manage."

"Why don't I call Ray and see if you can borrow that

portable ice shanty of his? He hauls it to the Willow
Flowage in the back of his truck—no reason he can't
drive it over from his dock."

"Now that's a thought," said Lew. "With a gas heater
inside, I won't lose Loon Lake's newest police officer to
frostbite. Doc, are you available to do the dental exams on
all three tomorrow morning?"

"Of course." He could put off getting the Christmas
tree; the storm wasn't due in until late afternoon. The look
of relief on her face made any inconvenience for him
worth it.

As he followed her up the stairs towards the Kobernots'
back porch, Osborne felt a flush of guilt. Proximity to
death should never make someone happy, and yet he
couldn't help but be relieved with this turn of events. That
she needed the dental exams was a good sign. If he got
lucky, she might require more help.

He'd begun to think of their relationship as if it were a
river with stretches of smooth water, here and there a few
riffles and ripples caused by potential hazards, then a series of modest rapids—and always a deadhead or two. Ice
fishing was a deadhead: Lew hated it.

Fishing was the one good excuse he used to spend time
with her: fly fishing for trout and smallmouth bass in the
spring and the fall, bait fishing for muskie and walleye
when the streams grew too warm in midsummer. If fly
fishing was her first love, fly fishing with her was his. But
her hatred of ice fishing had made the winter ahead look
bleak. How quickly life changes.

Patrice Kobernot was waiting at the porch door. The couple was a study in opposites: She was petite, gifted with
an oblong butt turned horizontal and a mouth bookended
with a healthy set of jowls. Right now, following a polite
request from Lew, the jowls caught Osborne's eye as they
jiggled in tandem when she spoke.

"That is absolutely out of the question. You know perfectly well some stranger did this on our property. And I am so upset, I'm calling a patient of Dr. Kobernot's that I know you know—Senator Breske." Patrice was doing her best to imply that the planting and discovery of the body was a deliberate act of the Loon Lake Police Department.

"Before you pick up that phone—let me make two things clear, Mrs. Kobernot," said Lew. "First, it's not your property. You do not own the lake. Second, I head up the police department with jurisdiction over this area, and I insist that you and your sons take a look—now. The victim is young and could be a school friend of the boys." Patrice's jowls shook again, but Lew refused to let her comment.

"Out of respect for this poor person, if there is any chance that we can immediately identify the victim—and be able to inform a family that must be so very worried about their daughter. Mrs. Kobernot, if this were a member of your family, you would expect the same courtesy."

Patrice snorted. "You don't understand, my husband is the head of neurology over at St. Mary's—" Was the woman asserting that MDs and everyone connected with them never misbehaved? Osborne was enjoying this.

"*You* don't understand," said Lew, waving a finger at Patrice. "If you don't do what I've asked, I'll be happy to take your entire household into town, and we can continue our discussion at the police station. But I hardly think you want the appearance of your family members being suspects in the event that this is foul play. Now will you and the boys please follow me down to the dock and take a good look?"

Patrice stepped down from the dock first, hoisted herself over the snowbank, and studied the still form. "No, Mrs.—"

"Chief Ferris."

"No, Mrs. Chief, 1 have never seen this woman in my life." Patrice threw a look at Lew. She was damned if she would acknowledge Lew's authority over the situation.

Lew ignored her and motioned the two boys over.

"Your names, fellas?"

"Craig Junior," said the taller of the two boys. He looked like his father.

"Patrick," said the younger boy. He resembled his mother, though he had a friendlier face. Both boys looked so worried, Osborne wondered if they had ever seen the dead person before.

As the boys stepped forward together, their mother's eyes raked their faces. Boy oh boy, thought Osborne, she's more terrifying than what they see in the snow. If she was *his* mother and if he did know the dead girl, he'd be damned if he'd tell the truth.

Both boys shook their heads. "No," said one after the other.

"Okay, you folks are excused. Please do not use the rink or the entrance to the trail here—or your ATV—until we've completed our search of the area."

Once Patrice and her sons were out of hearing distance, Lew turned to Osborne. "Doc, it may take an hour or more for me to get everything under control here. Could we use your place as a command center for the next twenty-four hours? I doubt Dr. and Mrs. Kobernot—"

"Please, Lew, whatever you need—and I'll save you some pizza. I'm going to track down Ray and that fishing shack right now."

"Dammit," she said, looking around, "this site is right on the trail, isn't it."

"Is that a problem?" and Osborne, wondering why she sounded so frustrated.

"Yeah," said Lew, "it means any traces of vehicles or people have been wiped out with all the snowmobile traffic going by." As if to underscore her point, the beam from a single headlight swept across their faces, coming at them from across the lake.

six

My bones drank water; water fell through all my doors.

—Maxine Kumin, "Morning Swim"

"**They** removed the legs with a knife—quite carefully disarticulating the joints," said Bruce Peters, hands clasped as he leaned forward on his elbows over Osborne's kitchen table.

Eyes snapping with energy in spite of the fact he'd left Wausau early in the morning and it was now well past eight, Bruce was obviously pleased to be at work on his first serious cases since joining the Wausau crime lab. Either that or he had drunk way too much coffee.

"I'm the project manager assigned to the region, sir," he had said, introducing himself as he stepped through Osborne's back door thirty minutes earlier. He had then taken great care to knock the snow off his boots before setting them to the side in perfect alignment.

"You make this sound like road construction," said Osborne, helping Bruce out of his heavy jacket and giving it a shake before hanging it on the oak coat rack just inside the kitchen door.

"Well, we do construction, that's for sure," said the young man with a grin. "We just build backwards is all."

Tall, big-boned, and as square-headed as Osborne's black lab, Bruce Peters wore his dark hair short and trimmed carefully around his ears. An equally neat moustache hid his upper lip, and every few seconds the nose above it twitched while the fingers on his left hand drummed and the foot at the end of his right leg jiggled. Interested as he was in what the young man had to say, Osborne found himself mesmerized by the body action.

"What does that mean exactly—the *disarticulation* of the joints?" asked Lew, who was sitting across from Bruce, a paper plate with two generous slices of pizza in front of her.

"Disarticulation means they cut through the joints rather than the bone to take the entire femur," said Bruce. "They knew what they were doing, and they wanted to work fast. Amateurs would have used a chainsaw—or a hacksaw and cut through bone at the crotch. And, frankly, it's too bad they didn't. Much easier to trace."

"They?" asked Lew. "You're sure we're talking more than one?"

Bruce raised his hands as if admitting defeat. "Good call, Chief Ferris, I have no documentation yet to prove if it was one perpetrator or two. I'm *assuming* two or more because both victims are male, weigh at least 180 pounds each and were wearing heavy snowmobile suits and helmets—plus other gear like mitts and boots.

"Dismemberment is difficult under any circumstances, and that's a lot of weight to haul around. But I could be wrong. In grad school, I assisted on a case out of Little Scandinavia where a teenage boy chopped up his stepfather who weighed over 300 pounds, wrapped him in freezer paper, and stacked him in the family freezer—in six hours. Yeah, I suppose one person could do this." He looked around the table at Lew and Osborne as if they might know the answer.

"How long since you've been out of grad school?"

asked Osborne. He could not believe the kid was a day over twenty-five.

"Six months."

"A trapper could do it easy," said Lew, biting into her first piece of pizza, "and a lotta guys around here butcher their own deer. I'd sure keep the door open on that assumption. Umm, I think I was starving—good pizza, Doc. Thank you. Did you get enough?"

"Plenty. Bruce, help yourself to some pizza," Osborne said, shoving the box of pizza across the table.

Mark had arrived with three large pizzas, two of which Erin, Mallory, Mark, and the children had wolfed down within fifteen minutes. Then Mallory, aware Osborne was anxious to shelter his grandchildren from the activities down at the rink, insisted they all go rent a video to watch at Erin and Mark's.

"I'll be back by ten, Dad, okay?" she said.

"Fine," said Osborne. "If I'm not here, I'll be down at the Kobernots'."

Minutes later, as Osborne stood in the doorway watching them pile into their cars, Erin had run back for one of the kids' neck scarves. "Dad," she had said, speaking fast and keeping her voice low, "I'm worried about Mallory."

"Why? She looks okay to me."

"Yeah, well, you haven't spent any time with her since she got here, have you." The edge in Erin's voice pushed an old button of guilt.

Osborne had never been the father to Mallory that he should have. While he and Erin had always been close—she was the daughter he'd loved teaching to fish and hunt—Mallory was her mother's child. And the coldness that had grown between Osborne and his late wife had resonated, for reasons he didn't understand, between himself and his eldest daughter.

It wasn't until Erin stepped in, forcing Mallory to face the same family tradition that had nearly destroyed Osborne, that he realized how alike they were. Maybe that was the problem.

But with Mary Lee gone two years now, he had been trying to change that. Apparently he wasn't doing a very good job. Erin was right—how the hell could he know how Mallory was? He hadn't seen her in three months, and their only conversation of any length today had taken place over a dead body.

"She told me she got some unpleasant news this week—Steve has been dating Bridget Kelly, one of her best friends in Lake Forest."

"But, Erin, Mallory wanted the divorce. Why would Steve's seeing anyone upset her?"

"She found out from somebody that those two were seeing each other *before* the divorce. Dad, Bridget was a guest in their home so many times—it's one thing to be betrayed by your husband, but by a woman you trusted? A close friend? I just . . . I know she's feeling a little rocky, that's all."

"Oh . . ." He hated the sound of that. Mallory was just getting her life back on track. She was completing a graduate degree in business, she was seeing a psychiatrist she liked and, as far as he could tell, she was not drinking. He knew from his own experience that "rocky" was not good.

"Bruce, I'm sure you know that a human bite leaves a unique impression," said Osborne. "In a situation like this, is the same true of a knife?"

"Sure," said Bruce, "any cutting tool. Take hacksaws, which happen to be the tool of choice these days—easily available, easily disposed of, very efficient cutting edge. And every hacksaw leaves a definitive mark on bone that can be easily traced."

"Hacksaw*s*?" said Osborne, emphasizing the plural. "Are you trying to tell us dismembering bodies is all that common?"

"Dr. Osborne, the interstate highways between Milwaukee, Madison, and Chicago are *haunted* with drug deals gone bad. Hacksaws, chainsaws. When I was at the university, we called it Chain Saw Alley. But most of those cases involve cutting through bone—nowhere near the touch I saw today—and usually they cut up the whole body."

"Ah," said Lew, "that's what I've been wondering—why just the legs?"

"I have an idea," said Bruce. "I need to see more before I say anything. And check some files. I don't want to send us off in the wrong direction.

"But going back to what Dr. Osborne asked: Yes, the slash marks from a knife will leave distinctive markings. Once I get to work on those, we'll have something to go on. Granted it's not as good as if he had cut through bone—"

"So you're not looking for a woman?" said Osborne.

"How often do you see a female orthopedic surgeon? Bone work takes a great deal of physical strength."

"You two worry about slash marks; I want to find *where* those two were killed and *how*," said Lew.

"We'll likely know the cause of death sometime tomorrow, Chief Ferris. This deep freeze makes our job a whole lot easier."

Bruce's reference to the deep freeze reminded Osborne of the young woman lying so perfectly preserved beneath her coverlet of ice and snow. He was anxious to do his own exam. More than once he had used teeth and dental work to identify a victim. Even if he didn't know the individual, he might recognize the work of their dentist. Whether it be a crown, an amalgam filling, an implant or a denture—every dentist leaves a signature as unique as the teeth they treat.

And unlike Lew's law enforcement colleagues in adjoining towns and counties, dentists stay in touch. A past president of the Wisconsin Dental Society, Osborne had remained active with the local chapter of the organization in spite of his retirement. If that young woman had dental work done within a six-county radius, he was likely to know exactly where and by whom. And if he didn't know, he knew whom to call.

Tuning back into the conversation between Bruce and Lew, he heard Bruce say, "Bones are biohazards—if people aren't careful they can be infected with something like HIV. Same with teeth, right Dr. Osborne?"

"Oh, gosh, that reminds me," said Osborne jumping to his feet. He headed for the back porch. Reaching into the pocket of his hunting vest, he felt for the packet he had wrapped so carefully out in the woods. Back in the kitchen, he set it down on the table, turned up the rheostat on the antler chandelier suspended overhead, then carefully pulled away the wrapping.

"I found these in the woods when I was hunting today," he said. Osborne reached for his reading glasses, then leaned forward to examine his prize. Lew, having finished her pizza, shoved the paper plate to the side and looked over at him, mildly curious. She checked her watch.

"Those look like my great uncle's," said Bruce.

Osborne picked up the dental plates separately, turning each back and forth under the bright light. "Odd," he said after a few seconds. "I should see some ID engraved on these—a name or a Social Security number—but . . ." He turned the dentures over, peering closely. Finally, he set one on top of the other and leaned back in his chair.

"Now that is the strangest darn thing . . ."

"Expensive items to forget, huh, Doc?" said Lew. "What's a full set of dentures cost today? Five, six thousand bucks?"

"Something like that," said Osborne. "But not these— these were never meant to be worn. The teeth you see in dentures are artificial—these are real."

"Whoa, biohazards," said Bruce, scraping his chair back as he stood up to reach for his jacket. "Be careful, Dr. Osborne. Maybe you should have gloves on?"

"And each tooth is from a different person . . . the wear patterns on the biting surfaces don't match."

"You're the expert, Doc. You tell us," said Lew, standing up to put her paper plate and napkin in the trash.

"And none have been ground to fit," said Osborne. He looked over his glasses at Lew. "These are not dentures, they're models, sculptures. Someone assembled these with no intention of anyone ever wearing them. And to find all these teeth and fit them so well . . . someone spent *years* making these. Years finding teeth so closely matched in size and color. Now why would you do that?"

"Maybe they're very old and were used in a classroom once upon a time," said Bruce.

"That's a thought," said Osborne.

"Would they be worth money?" asked Lew.

"Well, they could have historic value—who knows? They could be a collector's item . . . they could be priceless."

"If you're into teeth," said Bruce.

Lew laughed.

Osborne reached into the kitchen drawer behind him for his needle-nosed pliers. Grasping one tooth, he gave a gentle twist. Off it came, exposing the gold pin that anchored it to the base. Osborne held the pin up to the light.

"This is expensive gold," he said. "You can't even buy gold like this today."

He looked up at Lew and Bruce. "I had planned to put these back right where I found them, but now I'm not so sure I should do that."

Lew shrugged. She could not be less interested. She was right, of course. Who cares about a bunch of used teeth when you've got four legs missing.

"Doc," said Lew, checking her watch again, "could we try Ray one more time?"

seven

Some men fish all their lives without knowing it is not really the fish they are after.

—Henry David Thoreau

"**Yo,** I smell pizza. Any left?"

A blast of cold air hit the trio in the kitchen. The door to the back porch swung open as something resembling a six-foot-five-inch uncooked bratwurst backed its way into the room. Tipping its head sideways towards the kitchen table, the face was half-hid by a hood rimmed with wolf fur. All you could see were miniature icicles frozen into the auburn curls of a full beard and the gleam in one eye. But it was a gleam in the eye of a very happy man.

"What's up, Ray?" asked Osborne, unable to resist a tone of irritation in his voice. His neighbor had a knack for commanding attention at just the wrong time.

Lew leaned back against the kitchen counter, crossing her arms as she rolled her eyes. She was not in the mood to be held hostage by any Ray Pradt shenanigans.

"Did you get my message?" asked Osborne.

"Ta da!" The figure, humongous in its gray-green parka, swung around and nearly decked Bruce with a set of fat frozen walleyes. Five luscious fish hung from the stringer that Ray held stretched tight, their bronze bodies glistening in the warm light.

"H-o-o-ly cow," said Bruce in awe.

Osborne gave a soft whistle. "Beauties . . . what—five, six pounds each?"

"Limit is three," said Lew. "What's the excuse this time, Ray?"

"I got two of Clyde's here. He needs me to clean 'em."

"Clyde? Clyde Schmyde," said Lew. "And if I buy that, what else will you sell me?" She sighed and shook her head. "But I'm not the game warden, and as long as you let me use that portable fishing shack of yours— you're off the hook this time."

"Chief, I'm serious. You know old Clyde—Clyde the Wolf Man? The one who made me this parka? Man *loves* to fish hard water, and does he know the Pelican. We drilled our holes along one edge of this sandbar, y'know? But you gotta know exactly *which* edge—"

"Ray, can you tell us about it later? I'd like you to meet Bruce Peters—he's new with the Wausau boys." Lew stepped back as Bruce waved two fingers. He couldn't shake Ray's hand, or the fish would fall on the floor.

"O-o-h," said Ray. eyes widening. "Problems, huh."

"Yep," said Lew, giving him a hasty rundown as the walleyes dripped onto Osborne's floor. ". . . That's why I need to borrow your fishing shanty—we've got a third victim down on the lake that we can't move 'till morning, and I've got Terry guarding the scene until Bruce here can work the site after daylight. Too dark to do a thing right now and way too cold."

"Sure, I got just what you need, Chief. Let me warm up a little, and we'll get everybody all set." Ray started to back out the door, then stopped to raise his stringer one more time. "Aren't they gorgeous?"

"Jeez Louise, Ray, shut the door," said Osborne. "The temperature in here has dropped forty degrees."

"Okay, okay—but pretty incredible, huh?" Ray looked

around the room as if expecting unending rounds of applause. The looks that greeted him were not happy.

Osborne resisted the urge to boost his neighbor along as he budged his way back out to the porch and through the back door to lay his prizes in the snowbank, arranging each with care. "What a night. Doc, what a night."

"You can say that again," said Osborne.

Back in the kitchen, Ray closed the kitchen door behind him, then pushed off his hood. An old leather aviator cap rested on his head, the furred flaps pulled down over his ears. Perched on top and somewhat crumpled from having been stuffed into the hood was a fourteen-inch stuffed brook trout. Draped across the breast of the fish was an old wood and metal lure—the metal sparkling like a Christmas ornament. In fact, it was a Christmas ornament. Ray had rigged up a tiny battery and thrust a miniature flashing light through the lure.

"In case you hadn't noticed," said Lew to Bruce without cracking a smile, "the man's an expert at making an entrance."

"And ice fishing!" Ray raised a grimy index finger, then lifted his trout hat with both hands, flicked off the battery and placed the hat carefully on the kitchen counter next to the coffeepot. Head down, he raked his fingers through the curls matted down over his forehead. Only then did he extricate himself from the heavy parka.

"How many years have you been wearing that thing?" asked Lew.

A whiff of wood smoke and sweat hit Osborne in the face as Ray plopped his coat in the corner behind Bruce. The interior was as grimy as the exterior.

The look on Bruce's face as he moved his chair away made it obvious he thought Ray might *live* in the garment.

"This?" Ray looked down at the parka, puzzling. "Well . . . Old Clyde sold it to me back in my early twenties. I guess maybe . . . fourteen years."

"Ever had it cleaned?" Lew was relentless.

"Now why would I do that?" The face that asked the question was ruddy with windburn, the eyes teasing. In his red and black plaid flannel shirt, black turtleneck, and heavy dark brown Filson wool pants, Ray looked the quintessential woodsman—hearty, happy, and healthy. Yep, thought Osborne, if ever a man had a heart that could warm a room—it was wild and crazy Ray.

Lew lifted an eyebrow towards the young forensic specialist who had an amused look on his face. "Never trust a man with a fish on his head, Bruce—or as we say in the department when we discuss friend Ray here: 'Misdemeanors today, felonies tomorrow.'"

Ray, pleased with all the attention, sat down to pull off a pair of ancient Sorel boots. He stretched out his long legs and wiggled his toes in their heavy socks. Everyone waited. Lew and Osborne knew from experience that the man could not be hurried, particularly not when he had something you needed.

"Spoil sport," he grinned at Lew as he bent forward to extend a hand to Bruce Peters. "Pleased to meet you." Ray flashed Bruce a generous grin. Too generous. Osborne did not like what he saw.

"C'mon, Ray, cut the razzbonya behavior." Lew looked away in disgust.

"Sorry, couldn't resist." Ray walked over to Osborne's sink, reached to pull a coffee cup from the rack by Osborne's old Mirro coffeepot and, leaning forward, spit half a dozen white worms into the cup.

Bruce was intrigued. "What's the deal? I see plenty worms in my line of work, but you got me on this one."

"Waxies," said Ray, shoving the cup at Bruce who backed away. "I keep 'em in my cheek so they don't freeze. Walleyes been hitting on these like crazy—you ice fish?"

"Nope," said Bruce.

"Good, I'll get you out there."

"No, you won't, Ray—the man's got a big job ahead.

The fishing will just have to wait, I'm afraid." Lew thrust her hands into the pockets of her unzipped parka. "As soon as you're warmed up there, let's get that shack of yours down to Terry."

eight

*Modern fishing is as complicated as flying a B-58 . . .
several years of preliminary library and desk work are
essential just to be able to buy equipment without hu-
miliation.*

—Russell Baker

"**Man,** that guy is hard to work with," said Terry Dono-
van, shaking his head as Lew, with Osborne and Bruce
close behind, hurried towards him across Kobernot's
dock.

"I told him to wait for me," said Lew.

"Well, he just drove off, Chief. And I had to force him
to shoot the site like you wanted, too. He took plenty of
photos of the victim, but try to get him to do any more
than that—I practically had to sit on the guy."

"But he got good body shots?"

"I think so. He brushed all the snow away. You should
take a look, Chief. That girl is well endowed. Very well
endowed. Pecore said it's all her, too."

"He would know," said Lew.

"Our coroner can be unique in his approach," said Osborne in answer to a quizzical look from Bruce.

" 'Inept' is the word, not 'unique'," said Lew.

"Ah," said Bruce, "I've heard about him from my colleagues—"

"Yeah? Well, you've got a few jabones down there, too," said Lew. Bruce's eyes widened, but he was smart enough to keep his mouth shut.

Pecore got no respect from Lewellyn Ferris. He was sloppy and lazy, and she despised him for it. More than once the chain of custody on a key piece of evidence was aborted, effectively destroying the department's case against a perpetrator, because of his poor record keeping. Worse than that was Pecore's habit of letting his two golden retrievers accompany him into the autopsy room. More than one Loon Lake resident whose dearly deceased required a postmortem exam made sure to accompany the body just to prevent any unwelcome canine interest.

But the position of coroner in Loon Lake was a political appointment—something about which Lew could do nothing except complain. Pecore had been coroner for twenty-seven years, and he had no intention of giving up until he qualified for his pension, and that was three long years away. Until then, Lew could grouse all she wanted: Pecore and his dogs were nonnegotiable.

Lew walked over to the flat white tent that cocooned the victim. She unzipped it and knelt down. Their interest piqued, Osborne and Bruce edged over. Terry was right. With the snow swept away to expose the entire length and breadth of the victim's nude body, the effect was startling.

"Still no sign of blood or a wound," said Lew.

"Her head is tucked down so tight, she looks like she fell asleep reading," said Osborne.

"Yeah, Pecore tried tipping the head back, but she's froze solid," said Terry. "He said he couldn't tell anything about cause of death until they thaw her out."

"Doc," said Lew, straightening up slowly, "you know what I'm thinking?"

"I know exactly what you're thinking. I'd have Ray take a look. He's familiar with that crowd."

The four of them huddled on the ice below Kobernot's dock to wait for Ray, their backs to the wind off the lake. Osborne brushed at his cheeks with his leather mitts. They were numb. Not even the glow of the full moon helped.

"This wind has to be blowing fifteen to twenty," he said to no one in particular as he hunched deeper into his parka, pulling the collar up to close the gap near the ear flaps on his racoon hat. "I'll bet the wind chill is twenty below right now."

"Feels like a hundred goddam below to me," said Terry, stomping and slapping at his upper arms with his gloved hands. "Chief, I hope you told Pradt to hurry."

Lew snorted. "We did our best. He'll be here in a minute with a setup that'll keep you warm, I promise."

"Let's hope he didn't get a phone call," said Osborne.

"O-o-h, Doc, don't say that," said Lew with a shiver.

"Speaking of phone calls, I called my wife, and she's bringing me some sheepskin mitts and a down comforter," said Terry. As he spoke, the wind gave a long howl through the tops of the pines guarding the shore, and Terry burrowed his chin deeper into the collar of his jacket. "I told her where I keep the will in case I freeze to death."

Lew gave him a sympathetic pat with her mitt. "Terry, it's a tough job, and you're low man on the totem pole. Sorry about that—but you're doing great."

Osborne looked around as they waited. The young deputy had been busy over the last hour. Lanterns were lit around the rink and five hundred feet out onto the lake, lighting the way so snowmobilers had plenty of time to stop before reaching the wooden barricades that closed the trail. A detour routed them around the site.

The tent covering the victim was anchored with spikes driven into the ice, and sand-filled pails rested on the spikes. Police tape cordoned off the entire area, including the dock and stairway up to the Kobernot home as well as around the utility shed where the ATV was parked.

"Pradt's got something in that old heap of his that's going to keep me warm?" Doubt crowded Terry's voice at the sight of Ray's battered blue pickup rocketing towards them across the ice. And rightly so. The only feature of recent vintage and in decent shape on the truck appeared to be the eighteen-inch walleye leaping off the hood, its rainbow hues flashing in the moonlight.

"Patience," said Osborne. "He's letting us borrow a prized possession, so be careful what you say."

Fifteen minutes later and just short a pair of flannel pj's, Ray had Terry all cozied up for the long winter's night. The portable ice shanty was a bastardized Alaskan Guide tent jerry-rigged into a vertical shape and sporting foldout walls that could expand to accommodate as many as four fishermen. The whole thing unfolded from an eight-by-four-foot locker that fit flat in the bed of his truck along with a portable generator and two metal boxes.

"Welcome to my chamber of delight, folks," said Ray, holding the entry flap aside. "As you enter, you will note the state-of-the-art oxford nylon walls featuring 1500 mm-rated polyurethane coating *and* . . ." he paused for dramatic effect, "an *extra*-thick floor." They all crowded in, and Ray zipped the flap shut.

"Now . . . over in this corner, boys and girls, we have a top-of-the-line Mr. Heater with two—not one but *two*, doncha know—propane gas cylinders guaranteed to keep you warmer than the arms of Patrice Kobernot."

"S-s-s-h! Voice down, Ray," said Lew.

"And . . . in that corner a small cook stove. Terry, note the coffee ready for brewing?" Two fold-up canvas chairs and an inflating air mattress completed the decor.

"Ready to party, man," said Terry, still a little uncertain.

"Now . . ." Ray raised both hands, index fingers pointing parallel, "the views . . . every angle has a view." He was right. Clear plastic windows ran along the walls, cut in and duct taped at a level that allowed anyone inside to see out easily no matter where they might be sitting. Terry could be warm and toasty near the Mr. Heater, yet able to view the entire cordoned-off area outside with only a minor adjustment of his chair.

"Ah, twelve windows," said Lew, acting innocent. "One for each tip-up?"

"Could be, though I'm a jiggerman myself, no tip-ups this winter," said Ray, dodging the trap. "Never more than what I am entitled to by law, Chief."

"Of course, any extras are for Clyde . . ."

Long the traditional way to ice fish, the tip-up is a wooden platform rigged with fishing line, a spring, and a red flag. The ice fisherman slips a live minnow on the hook, drops it into the water through a hole cut in the ice, then retires to a nearby fishing shack or a bonfire to wait and watch until the red flag pops up to signal a fresh-caught meal. Easy—but not what a jiggerman does.

A jiggerman fishes hard water the hard way, hovering over his hole, a short fishing rod in hand, which has been armed with an over-accessorized fishhook known as a "jig." Nominally, a jig is a fishhook with a lump of lead on it, but times have changed. Today's jig is likely to be artificially enhanced with colorful plastic "bodies," simulated fish eyes, or live wiggling worms.

And unlike the hook dangling at the end of the tip-up, the jig won't be static but constantly "jigged" by the attentive fisherman.

"How much does something like this cost?" asked Bruce, checking out the interior of Ray's ice shanty.

The star of the show grinned and twirled once around, arms open and the fish on his head just clearing a cross-hatch of aluminum poles overhead. "You're looking at 227 graves, my friend—with and without a backhoe."

Bruce looked confused.

"Ray supplements his income through the summer digging graves for Loon Lake's Catholic cemetery," said Osborne.

"Thirty-five bucks a grave," said Ray with pride.

"Oh . . . but not now, not when it's this cold," said Bruce.

"No-o-o, business slows down just as the lakes freeze, thank the Lord," said Ray.

"So what do you do then?"

"We keep 'em on ice—I help with the storage some."

"Enterprising sort, this guy," said Lew, shaking her head towards Ray. "Master of the easy buck." With Terry's situation under control, she had relaxed. "I'm ready to head out—Terry, you got any questions?"

"Didn't you want Ray to view the victim, Chief?"

"Oh right, I almost forgot. I think I'm tired. Ray, would you mind?" She glanced over at Terry, "Incidentally, what about Pecore—did he recognize her?"

Terry shook his head, "Not that he mentioned."

"If you need me to, I'll take a look," said Ray. He unzipped the entry flap and waited for Lew to lead the way out, his eyes serious.

Osborne and Bruce stood to the side as Lew unzipped the white plastic cover. The full moon threw shadows across its still and frozen occupant. As Ray knelt, he removed his hat.

Lew handed him her flashlight. The wind had died and the ancient white pines along the shore loomed somber and still. The ice took over, booming a dirge across the hard water.

Ray sat back on his heels. "I know this girl . . . she had a smile that could give you hope in February."

nine

Only dead fish swim with the streams.

—Anonymous

"I met her last August," said Ray. "She was tending bar on karaoke night at Thunder Bay. She's not a local, Chief. If I remember right, she's from a little town outside Oshkosh."

"She tended bar, huh. She didn't dance? With that body?" Lew was skeptical.

"I'm not saying she never danced. But she wasn't dancing when I was out there. What she told me was that she was trying to get out of a contract that she had signed with a club up near Hurley. I got the impression she'd been screwed over by the people she had been working for . . ." Ray paused. "Now that I think of it, she was quite careful not to name names. I'll tell you one thing—she was a very pleasant person."

"Ray, have you ever met a woman who wasn't?" Catching Osborne's eye, Lew gave a wry smile.

More than once, while mending their dry flies through riffles in a trout stream, they had chuckled together over Ray's wizardry with the opposite sex. Charm appeared to be his middle name, as few women—regardless of age, shape, or bank account—could resist. And whatever it was that made Ray so irresistible to the ladies, it eluded Osborne.

Eluded and disturbed. Once he had asked Lew if she knew Ray's secret, but she just shook her head, snorted and said, "If you don't know now, Doc, you never will." Then she had laughed and waded on up the stream, her back cast uncurling overhead as she set out to tease new and unsuspecting trout.

Osborne had hung back, working an overhang until he snagged his fly. The consequent angry yank was directed as much to the insulting branch as it was to his friend and neighbor. All that luck with the ladies was hitting a little too close to home as Osborne found himself more than a little unsettled by Mallory's ongoing interest in the guy. Good friend was one thing, son-in-law was quite another. The peripatetic lifestyle of a fishing guide was not what Osborne had in mind for his eldest daughter.

"Her name?" said Lew, quizzing Ray. "I'm sure you got that far."

"I knew her by Eileen. Just a first name, but that's not unusual at Thunder Bay."

"Excuse me," said Bruce, his right nostril twitching and his brow dark over his eyes, "mind if I ask what this place Thunder Bay is?" He stepped forward, elbowing Osborne out of the way.

Osborne moved off to the side. He liked the young man; he just hoped he didn't have the same bad habit as the rest of the Wausau boys: the urge to push Lew out of the way when the stakes in a case got high enough to further a career. Better men had tried and lost.

"A strip joint west of town," said Lew. "Lap dancers, that kind of thing. Changed hands recently after I fined the former owners ten thousand bucks for violations of Code 2116B. I wonder if she's been working for the new people?"

"I heard Karin Hikennen bought it," said Ray. "You know Karin, Chief?"

"What's that Code 21—?" asked Bruce, a question mark vivid in his eyes.

"Never met Karin. I knew the old lady, Karin's grandmother. She used to run the Kat House, one of Hurley's finest in the days when that town was wide open. I imagine Karin has inherited that joint . . ." Lew reached into her jacket for her cell phone. She asked the dispatcher to put her through to Thunder Bay.

"Thunder Bay is very popular with what we call 'da boys from da cities,'" said Osborne in a low voice to Bruce. "You know the crowd—up to hunt or fish with no wives in tow."

"And Ray hangs out there?" asked Bruce, his nose wrinkling like something nearby smelled bad.

"Five rounds of draft Leinenkugels, and our friend here is guaranteed at least one new client for guiding," said Osborne, answering loud enough for Ray to hear.

"Don't forget the bad jokes," said Lew as she waited for her call to go through.

"Yep, I stop by Thunder Bay a couple times a week in the summer," said Ray. "When it comes to R & D that's the place to be."

"R & *D*?" said Bruce. "Don't you mean R & *R*?"

"No, R & D—research and development—mining new clients. Bruce, I'm probably the only guy you'll ever meet who can deduct lap dancing from his taxes."

"Oh," said Bruce.

"Things are different in Loon Lake," said Osborne, shuffling his feet to keep the blood moving.

"I'm finding that out," said Bruce. "About that code—"

But before he could ask his question, Lew had snapped her phone shut.

"Thunder Bay's closed, dammit. One good thing about cell phones—they save time."

"Yep, closed Tuesdays and Thursdays," said Ray. "Open noon tomorrow though . . ."

Her eyes troubled, Lew mulled the tips of her boots. The three men waited in silence, turning their backs when a swirl of wind kicked snow across the rink. Osborne shivered. He never could stay warm standing still.

"Okay," said Lew, looking up, "here's what we'll do. Ray, I've got enough left in my budget through the end of the year to bring you and Doc on board to help out for a couple days. Do you have the time to track down some of the other girls working Thunder Bay? First thing in the morning? They may know more than Hikennen would ever tell us anyway. If Karin's anything like her grand-mother, she'll be mean, greedy, and close-mouthed. If you hit a brick wall—"

"I don't understand why he doesn't just go to the owner first," said Bruce. "They have to answer. What good is talking to a bunch of strippers—"

"If you don't have any luck with the girls, let me know and we'll see if Suzanne can help," said Lew, ignoring Bruce. "Incidentally, Ray, have *you* met Karin?"

"Nope, never set eyes on the woman."

"And who is this Suzanne?" An undisguised bossiness in Bruce's voice irritated Osborne. He turned and stared at him—second-guessing Lew was not the way to win friends at the moment.

"Bruce, you're here to help with trace evidence," said Lew, her voice level but her eyes hard. "I take care of the rest. Since you asked, Suzanne is my daughter, and she used to work at Thunder Bay. A few years back, right after her divorce, she danced and tended bar at Thunder Bay to pay her way through school. But that was six years ago— before I joined the force. Today she's a CPA in Milwau-kee, just opened her own firm. Remarried and I've got three grandchildren. Even so, she's kept in touch with several friends who have continued to work there—and they may know something."

"Not the most reliable sources," said Bruce. "Most strippers I've had contact with are into drugs or—" He stopped short.

Ray gave Osborne an amused look, but it was the expression on Lew's face that made Osborne feel a little sorry for the guy.

"Bruce . . ." Lew paused. "Just because a girl dances in a strip club does not mean she's a hooker or a drug addict. Yes, one or two may violate the code, but that's almost always under pressure from the boss, which is why I fine owners—not dancers. This is the northwoods, bud. It is not easy to make a buck—particularly if you are young, female, single, and a mother. And, frankly, I've known a few crooked cops in my day—"

"Chief—" said Ray, interrupting before Bruce could dig himself in any deeper, "look, I've got the time even if you *don't* have the money." He looked down at the white plastic covering the girl who once had a lovely smile. "She was a good kid—someone loved her."

"Doc, is that okay with you?" asked Lew. Before Osborne could say a word, she said, "Bruce, first thing tomorrow Doc will get us a dental ID on all three victims, including the two you worked with today—"

"Fine with me," said Bruce.

"Settled then," said Lew, nodding at Ray and Osborne. "I'll call Connie in the morning and let her know you two are on the payroll."

Turning to leave, she stepped up onto the dock, then paused, raising her hands to the moon in a gesture of frustration. Bruce almost bumped into her from behind. "You know, if it weren't for Pecore," said Lew, "if I didn't have to live with that jabone's seventy thousand a year salary— I could add another full-time deputy and not be forced to lean on people like Doc and Ray who have better things to do."

"I don't know about that," said Osborne under his breath as he hopped up onto the dock behind them.

"Now what the hell—? What is Ray doing out there?" asked Lew, peering over Osborne's shoulder.

The three of them looked out towards the fishing shanty, which glowed from inside. To its left, behind the frozen bier holding the young woman, all that could be seen of Ray was a dark shadow hunkered down near the snowbank.

His voice came to them muffled. "Did Pecore shoot this?"

"Dammit," Lew cursed as she jumped down off the dock and walked back towards Ray. "What now—I'm freezing."

Ray was staring at the snowbank behind the victim. "Did you move the body from where you found it?"

"No, she's exactly where she was found, so Bruce can work the site tomorrow morning."

"Well, I hope to hell Pecore shot *this*," said Ray.

"Shot what?" said Lew, moving closer to Ray. "I don't see anything."

"Right here—someone shoveled this snow. You got a plow pushing snow over there, but here it's been heaped. See how the pattern changes? It's slight but it's there."

"Whoa—you have a good eye," said Bruce shaking his head. "I didn't see any difference in how that snow was mounded. Tomorrow, in the light, I might, but in these shadows?" He whistled.

"Bruce," said Ray, "I do graves in the summer, snow removal all winter."

"He isn't kidding," said Lew. "We are in the company of a man with an intimate knowledge of plows and shovels."

"And an eye so good he can hit an aspirin with a BB gun," said Osborne.

Bruce knelt to examine the snowbank with his flashlight. Then he walked ten feet towards the rink and dropped to his knees again. "I see the difference now. This is good, this is very good. And you know what? I'll bet you anything that a shovel, like a knife, has to leave a distinctive mark." He looked up at Lew. "We've got to get photos before the weather changes. Can you get your coroner back here? Or find out if he took some already?"

"Sure," said Lew, "but from what Terry said, I doubt

Pecore took the time or made the effort—I certainly wouldn't count on it." She pulled off her glove and reached inside her parka for her cell phone. She punched in some numbers and waited. Then she tried another set of numbers. "No answer," she said. "That's interesting. He's not in his office and he's not answering at home. Where the hell can he be at this hour?"

"Chief, I've got some black and white film in my camera," said Ray. "It's right over there in the truck, under my seat. I was shooting a flock of migrating loons that landed on the lake before it froze over, and I haven't used it since. I'm sure I've got enough film—you want me to get a few photos?"

Lew threw up her hands. "What choice do I have?"

As she spoke, Bruce headed off across the rink, jogging and skidding in the direction of the boathouse where the ATV with the plow was parked. "I'll see if they got shovels in there," he said. "We don't want any of those disappearing."

"Up at the main house, too," said Lew. "I saw one on the porch."

Osborne never thought the warmth of his own home could feel so good. The house was dark except for a night-light over the kitchen stove.

"Dad? Is that you?"

"Find everything you need, hon?" The door to Mallory's bedroom was open. She looked sleepy and cozy, propped up against the pillows with a book in her hands. "We'll go find a tree right after I help Lew in the morning. Around ten or so? You sleep in, enjoy your coffee. . . ."

"Sounds great, Dad. I'll dress real warm, too, so we can take our time. You know me—I want just the right tree." She gave him a happy smile. "See you when you get back from town then. And, by the way, those dentures you left on the kitchen table? I put them up on the shelf near the cookbooks. Couldn't stand the idea of those greeting me first thing in the morning. Hope you don't mind."

Minutes later, after cracking the window very slightly, Osborne slipped under his quilt. He smiled at the thought of the busy morning ahead. And the relief he felt knowing Mallory was comfortable in the room next to his was palpable. That was all he ever wanted to do for his children and their children: keep them safe.

He woke with a start. The clock beside his bed read 3:43 a.m. Moonlight filled the room, making it easy to see that Mike still slept soundly on his bed in the corner. Osborne lay perfectly still wondering what it was that had awakened him. Then he heard it: the soft put-put of Ray's pickup moving up the rutted slope that served as his driveway.

What on earth could he be doing at this hour? Osborne waited, half-expecting a knock on the door. He got up to use the bathroom, then checked the other bedroom. Mallory was sleeping soundly on her side, curled up with her feet tucked under. Lifting an extra quilt from a chair in the corner, Osborne gave it a shake, flipped it up and over, and let it drift down onto his daughter as lightly as a dry fly onto a still pool.

His final thought as he drifted back into sleep was of Bruce. Wouldn't surprise him if that guy was still awake—searching computer files for the details of Code 2116B.

ten

Some of the best fishing is done not in water but in print.

—Sparse Grey Hackle

"Pecore is out," said Lew. Osborne reached for a kitchen chair and sat down. It was ten after six and he had been pouring his first cup of coffee when he grabbed for the phone on its first ring.

"Fired? It's less than ten hours since you last saw him, Lew. What on earth—" Osborne shook his head. How much trouble can a late middle-aged man get into after dark in a town of thirty-one hundred people? With an outside temperature of twenty-three below zero?

"He doesn't know it yet. I can't call Arne Steadman until after eight, and as mayor, Arne has to be the one to fire him—but I can't imagine he won't be out once I talk to Arne. So don't say anything if you run into him before then."

"Don't worry about that. But, Jeez Louise, Lew. What happened?"

"He showed up at Marty's Bar about eleven o'clock last night with eight-by-tens of that poor girl. Passed 'em around. I got a call from someone who was there."

"You can't be serious."

"I just hope her family, whoever they are, never hears about it. Unforgivable. And you and I both know it isn't the first time . . ."

She was right. More than once, Osborne's coffee crowd at McDonald's had heard rumors of Pecore misbehaving with photos taken of women under official circumstances. But only rumors; no one had ever caught him red-handed.

"The good news is Loon Lake will finally have a decent coroner. If I play my cards right with our city fathers, we may even get a professional."

"Careful, Lew. It's still a political appointment."

"You're right, Doc, but I'm thinking positive. Let me know if you have any thoughts on a good replacement. This catches me a little unprepared. And speaking of being prepared, I'm hoping the four of us—you, me, Bruce, and Ray—can go over a few things this morning before we all head off in different directions. Any chance you could make it to my office by seven?"

Before Osborne could answer, Lew said, "Oops, here's Ray now—"

"I'll be there in twenty minutes," said Osborne.

The door to Lew's office in the old courthouse was wide open when Osborne got there. In spite of the new jail with its fancy offices and conference rooms right next door, Lew had opted to keep this spacious room with its white walls, dark wood trim, and high, old-fashioned windows for her private space.

Just entering the bright, cheery room for an early cup of coffee always lifted Osborne's heart—especially when the reason for dropping by was to plan for a late afternoon's angling. Winter changed that. Though the room and its occupant still radiated warmth on his arrival, the visits were less frequent. A fact that kept him focused on finding a way to change her mind about ice fishing.

She, on the other hand, had been coaxing him towards

learning to tie trout flies—something he had no interest in whatsoever. Dead animal hair, fur, and feathers held little appeal for a man who loved the cool surfaces of porcelain, gold, and silver. As a boy, he'd been persuaded to turn his urge to sculpt towards dentistry, a significantly more lucrative career: While few people may have a driving desire for bronze figurines, most want to own a healthy set of teeth. Nope, he was not about to trade his love of line and form for something teensy, fuzzy, and furry. But he let her coax—the coaxing was fun.

As he had hoped, the coffeepot in the corner was still half full. The room was crowded, with Lew behind her desk and both chairs facing her occupied. Bruce sat in one, right leg crossed over his left, with the loose foot jiggling. Ray lounged in the other, right foot resting on his left knee as he leaned back, way back it seemed, and waved a coffee mug as he spoke. He looked wired.

"Morning, everyone." Osborne grabbed a straight-backed chair from the corner and plunked it down between the other two men. Then he unzipped his jacket, tossed it onto an empty chair near the windows, and poured himself a cup of coffee.

"Morning, Doc," said Lew, her dark eyes resting easily on his for a brief moment as he took his seat. She looked alert, rested, and happy. Even though the December sun shone only forty percent of the time these days, Lew's face maintained a warm and healthy glow. More attractive to Osborne than the makeup so carefully applied by the female friends of his late wife. He'd sneaked a peek once into Lew's medicine cabinet—the only makeup he could find was sunscreen.

"Ray was just telling us something I want you to hear. Start over from the beginning, Ray, would you please." She flipped her long narrow reporter's notebook to a new page.

"Doc," Ray dropped his foot onto the floor and leaned forward, elbows on his knees, "I was telling these two folks that as I was dozing off last night, I remembered something I saw . . . night before last . . . on my way in from ice fishing."

"On Loon Lake," said Lew, anxious to fill in gaps and hurry him along.

"What time was that again?" said Bruce. "I don't think I heard you right."

"Around two in the morning."

"I *did* hear you right. You fish at that hour of the morning?"

"I fish when the fish feed. And they were feeding after midnight so—"

"And then you get up early to plow snow and dig graves and—how do you that?"

"Well, we aren't digging any graves right now . . . but I catch a nap in the afternoon."

"We call it 'Ray time,'" said Lew, rocking back in her chair. "Rhymes with 'waste time.'"

"Thanks, Chief, nothing like appreciation."

Lew chuckled, "You're too easy a target." Then she raised her hands. "Just kidding. Please, Ray, you have the floor."

"Thank you. So there I was out in my truck on Loon Lake . . . the far side. I have four holes there, everyone knows they're mine—"

"Ray, please. Save the fishing details for later. I see Arne at eight, and we've got a lot to cover."

"I hear you, Chief. So I'm driving back over to my place, and just as I got near my dock, I happened . . . to look south, down the snowmobile trail . . . way down. And I see these blinking lights . . ."

"By Kobernot's?" asked Osborne.

"No, no, wa-a-y past their place. Down at the end where there's an incline, a couple seasonal cabins up on the ridge, nothing else—you know that real rocky bay area."

"Right," said Osborne. He knew exactly the spot. "Someone just cut a road in past those cabins. Big house going up next spring."

"So I see these lights blinking in a vertical line—one, two, three, four—like some kind of signal. I kinda thought about it, but it was two in the morning and I was pooped. I forgot all about those lights until . . . just as I was dozing off last night."

"So that's why I heard your truck so early this morning," said Osborne.

"Yep. Couldn't sleep thinking about 'em, checked the weather radio, and decided I better see what I could see before that storm moves in. So . . . I get over there in the deep dark of the morning . . . shine a flashlight around the general area where I think I might have seen those lights and . . ." Ray paused and looked at his companions, his eyes narrowed. Osborne often wondered if the man knew how moments like this tempted the best of his friends to shoot him.

"And?" Bruce made a winding motion with one hand.

"Wasn't a signal at all. Someone carrying a lantern tripped and fell down that hill. Someone in a hurry, because they left a few items behind . . . scattered all the way down to the lake . . ."

"Supposition. I'll determine what happened," said Bruce, now taking notes.

"I'm counting on you doing exactly that, Bruce," said Ray with a wink. Then he leaned sideways to zip open a large duffel that was sitting on the floor beside his chair. Pulling on a pair of rubber fish gloves, he said, "Just so you know, everyone, I haven't touched a thing without these on." He held his hands up, fingers spread.

Then he reached into the duffel and pulled out a minnow bucket, which he set on the desk. "Note, brand new." That was followed by a stainless steel ice scoop and a small electric lantern.

"You found these in the snow along with tracks from a vehicle," said Bruce.

"Yes, and I was careful to walk up and down one side, so you can tell my footsteps from the others. Plenty of footprints leading down to the lake and back up, and no doubt that someone slipped and fell. I threw two tarps over most of the area, too, in case it snows before you get there.

"Also . . ." Ray stood up and walked over to the wall near the window—"I found this." He held up a snow shovel that had been leaning there. "Brand new, too. Has its 'Ralph's Sporting Goods' sticker on it still. Last thing . . . I could see signs of a plastic sled having been pulled down to the snowmobile trail and back—but . . . no sled."

"Not unusual," said Lew to Bruce. "Most ice fisherman who don't have shanties will put all their gear in a big plastic sled and pull that out onto the ice. What's different in what Ray found is that shovel. No one uses a shovel ice fishing. No one I know, anyway. Do you, Doc?"

"Never."

"One other interesting thing, and you can check this out, Bruce," said Ray. "The footprints in the snow? One individual, very petite. Not a guy, unless he's got a hormone imbalance."

"A woman, you think?" asked Bruce.

"A woman or a boy. And that's a real nice ice scoop, too, doncha know. Cost twenty bucks or more. Which is why I think someone was in a hurry to leave. Why else would you leave all this good equipment behind?"

"So you think we can trace where they bought that stuff?" asked Bruce. "I'm sure we can get prints off it."

"I dunno about that. It's standard issue," said Ray. "Everyone who ice fishes uses the same type of lantern and minnow bucket . . . although . . . y'know, I just thought of something . . ." Ray bent down to pick up the bucket. He tipped it forward and back, pulled out the liner, and peered inside.

"The purpose of the bucket is to carry minnows, right? But this was empty. No minnows tossed out or spilled on the snow, none down by the trail—"

"Most people dump their minnows near where they're

fishing," said Osborne. "You don't haul them all the way back to your car."

"Most people I know don't dump any minnows," said Ray. "They're good for a long time. Even so, I don't see any trace of water in this bucket, not even a residue of water that might have frozen at the bottom. Look! There's a label stuck inside here—this hasn't even been used. Now why would anyone haul an empty minnow bucket out and back?"

No one said anything.

"If you ask me," said Ray, "I think it is quite likely the party in question may have pulled poor Eileen onto the ice in the sled, using the fishing gear as a front." He raised his palms as if to fend off an attack. "Just a theory, Bruce."

"I better get out on the lake," said Bruce, looking out the window as he got to his feet. "It's light, finally. All I get is eight hours and thirty minutes, too, so I better hustle."

"Less if the snow hits," said Lew.

"I'll take care of the situation at the Kobernots', then I'll check this other out."

"Before you go, Bruce, anything Doc needs to know as he heads over to do the dental exams?"

"Not that I can think of. Your man, Pecore, is the one to establish cause of death. You have two in the hospital morgue, Dr. Osborne, and if the coroner is on the spot when I get to the Kobernots', we should have the girl sent in shortly.

"Chief," said Bruce, "I was hoping Ray might have a chance to stop by the site where the snowmobilers were found. He knows these lakes so well, he might see something I missed." He pulled on his jacket, then reached down for his briefcase.

"Ray, still no sign of their sleds," said Lew. "Be nice to know which direction they were coming from before going through the ice."

"Happy to do it, Chief," said Ray. "That's not far from

Thunder Bay Bar, and I'll be starting there." Lew nodded.

"Other than that, the only significant finding I've got that's changed since last night is this." Bruce set his briefcase on the chair, clicked it open partway, and pulled out an object in a Ziploc bag, which he set on Lew's desk. "A Palm Pilot—we found it on one of the snowmobilers. It's double bagged because they had it in plastic, too."

Lew reached for the plastic bag, "I'll take this."

"No," Bruce put his hand on it, "I'm sending it down to Wausau, we've got a good tech guy—"

"Don't worry about it—I've got an excellent tech myself," said Lew, placing both hands on the package. She was not going to give it up.

"Okay, Chief, whatever you say. It's your case, I'm just here to help out," said Bruce, more than a little disgruntled.

"That's right, you are," said Lew.

After Bruce and Ray had left Lew's office, Osborne checked his watch and walked over to refill his coffee cup halfway. "Lew, I'm curious, who's this tech expert of yours?"

"I don't want Wausau getting their grimy hands on this."

"That's not what I asked you," said Osborne, chuckling. "Well?"

Lew pulled open a desk drawer and pulled out a small red leather address book. She flipped a few pages, then picked up the phone. "Marlene, get me Gina Palmer at this number, would you please?" She read the number from the address book over the phone.

"Gina? She's in Chicago," said Osborne."They're getting the brunt of the storm this morning."

"Then she'll be happy to leave, won't she? Especially when hears she better check out that property she bought on Loon Lake. We've had some burglaries in some of those seasonal cabins."

"It's Christmas, Lew. I'm sure she has plans."

"Last time I talked to her she was quite interested in the activities of a certain fishing guide we know," said Lew, giving Osborne a wink. "You want to put money on this?"

eleven

Fishermen are born honest, but they get over it.

—Ed Zern, *Field & Stream*

"Palmer!" barked the voice on the speakerphone.

"Gina, Lewellyn Ferris." Lew tipped back in her chair, grinning at the sound of Gina's voice.

Watching her prompted Osborne to remember the sight of the two women working side by side six months earlier, one with dark curls she constantly brushed back, the other with a sleek cap of black hair and never a strand that strayed. Where one was sturdy, strong, and of medium height, the other was small-boned, petite. One wore cop khaki, the other dressed in black. But they shared one unmistakable feature: grim determination. Only the foolish dared get in their way.

"O-o-h," Gina's voice slowed and relaxed. You could hear her smile. "Hey, Chief, what's up?"

"Little holiday action. I need some high-tech assistance up here in the hamlet. Got plans for the holidays?" Lew's eyes, alert with anticipation, caught and held Osborne's.

"Got a new job. First of the year, I start a fellowship with the IJNR—*Institute for Journalism and Natural Re-*

sources. Think I can get Ray to come clean that he's undercover for the DNR? Give me some good leads?"

Gina's speech pattern always ran at twice the speed of a normal person, which Osborne found amusing. Yep, the woman was an original—she might be tiny in stature, but she compensated with the eyes of a hawk and the voice of an auctioneer.

"If you can get Ray to come clean on anything, why don't you try getting him to stop hiding thirteen-inch walleyes under the liner of his minnow bucket," said Lew, winking at Osborne.

He had to hand it to her: Took less than twenty seconds for Ray's name to surface.

"What do you mean, Chief?" asked Gina.

"I mean that the legal length is fourteen inches—and the legal limit is three. How many do you think Ray slips past our hardworking rangers?"

"Some things never change, do they," Gina laughed. "You're giving me bad thoughts. I have a lot of cleanup to do down here."

"Yeah, but some problems you just gotta deal with in person, doncha know." Lew leaned forward, her face close to the speakerphone. "Had some trouble out near your property, Gina. Some jabones from somewhere are driving over the ice and breaking into seasonal cabins to steal antique hickory furniture. I'm worried about yours. That place you bought has some very nice pieces out on the porch . . ."

"Oh . . ." said Gina, radiating concern. Osborne knew she had overpaid for her cabin. Not only did she love the primitive little building and its prime lakefront location, but it had been put on the market fully furnished. While locals were ho-hum over the property, Gina was well aware of the value of the old furniture.

The former owner, who had died leaving no heirs, was the last of three elderly ladies who had held everyone living on Loon Lake Road, including Osborne and Ray, hostage to a telephone party line. Once she died, the phone company could no longer refuse to provide decent service, and so, following the old lady's funeral, Osborne and Ray got touch-tone phones—with private lines—and Gina got a hundred-year-old cottage packed with antiques. Everyone was happy.

Now it was Osborne's turn to wink at Lew. She had chosen the perfect lure: Gina could not bear the thought of a threat to her treasures. "Ray's got a key—would you ask him to check for me?"

"As soon as I have a spare minute, Gina. Right now I've got several criminal cases that are problematic." Lew gave Gina a quick rundown on the three victims, winding up with "... so I've got a Palm Pilot that was found on one of the bodies, and I have no idea what to do with it."

"You're kidding," said Gina, her voice taking on a new timbre. "My special projects reporters just teamed with the business desk to investigate an employee for a major manufacturer down here who was using his Palm to steal patent applications."

"See, I knew you'd know this stuff."

"At least you've got cell phones these days, right?"

"And high-speed Internet connections," said Lew. "Updated our computer system, too, since you were here last—it's the expertise I don't have.

"Hold on a minute," Lew motioned to Osborne to shut her door. Even with the door closed, she lowered her voice. "You know how I would hate to turn this case over to Wausau. The senior staff down there will put it on the back burner, and who knows when—or they'll solve it and land a nice budget increase, while we get nothing ..."

"Let me think about this," said Gina. "I know how you feel about those guys ..."

She was quiet on the other end, and Lew waited, saying nothing. "I promised my sister I'd spend Christmas with her and her husband in Evanston," said Gina. "They're having marital problems—fun, huh?"

"You've got that snowstorm down there, too," said Osborne. "Roads closed?"

"They're plowing," said Gina. "Can you guys find me a place to stay?"

Lew looked at Osborne, relief spreading across her face. "Motels are packed with skiers and snowmobilers," she said. "Might have to bunk you on Ray's sofa—or at my place."

"Oh, hey, if Ray's got room—"

"Gina, your meals and travel are on the department. How much time can you spare?"

"I start with IJNR on the fourth of January. And I do need a day or two to clean out this office. Mind if I ask you what makes you so sure you've got something on that Palm?"

"Wausau sent up a new guy, young, bright. Had to *pry* his fingers off it."

"That's a good sign. Look, I'll finish up here, pack, and check the roads. Look for me tomorrow around noon?"

"You betcha."

"Merry Christmas, Lewellyn Ferris," said Osborne as the speakerphone clicked off.

"Merry Christmas, yourself," said Lew, her eyes dancing. "This makes everyone's life a whole lot easier."

"I hope it means you'll go to the Dental Society's annual party with me on the twenty-sixth? Remember, I invited you last month."

"I'll try, Doc," said Lew, jumping up from her chair, "but no promises."

"I need to RSVP today . . ."

Lew paused in the doorway. "You know I'm not a fan of social gatherings."

"I want you to meet some old friends of mine."

"Not yet, Doc. I've got—" Lew waved her hands in frustration.

"It's okay, don't worry about it. I'll take Mallory." Darn, why did he always say the wrong thing. She'd been so happy and then . . . dammit.

twelve

Fish die belly-up and rise to the surface, it is their way of falling.

—Andre Gide

"You missed Dr. Pecore by about five minutes," said Carrie McBride as she handed the morgue register to Osborne for his signature. The young nurse was the daughter of a former patient of his from Sugar Camp. Very tall, tanned, and quite slim, she looked all of twelve years old, though he knew she had to be in her early twenties.

"You have three in there—they just delivered the woman. Dr. Pecore's paperwork is still on the counter. He's not done yet. He got a phone call and slammed out of here like he was mad at me or something."

"He's . . . not done?" said Osborne, catching himself. He wasn't sure when people would be informed of the firing.

"Sometimes I wonder," said the girl. "That man's so sloppy the way he leaves stuff around. Speaking of which," she pointed to a large cardboard box near the nurses' station, "you won't believe the clothes that came off those two men. One had a snowmobile suit that must have cost a thousand dollars."

"No. A thousand dollars?" said Osborne. "That's outrageous, Carrie. How can you spend that kind of money on a parka and snow pants?"

"Dr. Osborne, it's exactly what my boyfriend wants—rigged for cell phones and stuff like those portable CD players. Great for ice fishing. Dr. Pecore shoved it in a box and left it here. I don't know what he thinks I'm s'posed to do with it. You might want to check it out. You don't see stuff that expensive up here very often, y'know."

"I'll look it over and take it by the police department when I'm finished here," said Osborne, handing the register back to her. "Chief Ferris will want to see the clothing, and Pecore knows that. He must have other things on his mind. Thank you, Carrie, you've been a big help."

Carrie gave him a tight little smile, obviously happy to have undermined, even in a small way, the man who had treated her so rudely.

He hated the morgue. The smell. It wasn't a bad smell, just a smell that pierced his sinuses and stayed in his head too long. As always, the moment he entered he had the urge to leave. He set out to work as fast as possible.

The first victim, Peter Shebuski, was in his late twenties. His mouth was in good shape, teeth cleaned recently. Osborne guessed he was married with a wife who booked regular appointments with the dental hygienist. Eleven cavities filled and evidence of orthodontia. This was a man raised by parents who believed in good dental care. He would be mourned. Osborne paused, dropping his head for a moment, before continuing.

Victim number two, John Lobermeier, was interesting. He'd had his teeth whitened, causing them to look peculiar against the death pallor of the gums. Osborne guessed him to be about the same age as the first victim. Less careful with dental care of the kind not obvious to onlookers—this fellow would be needing some periodontal work for gum disease if he didn't start flossing. Osborne caught himself. Talk about a moot issue.

Ah, the young woman. He took a look at Pecore's paperwork. The cause of death was a puncture wound to the back. A Phillips screwdriver was Pecore's opinion. It had pierced the heart, likely causing death instantly. Little bleeding, all internal. That would explain why there was no blood in the snow. Otherwise, Pecore stated, the lividity of the blood in the corpse indicated the victim had been killed elsewhere and moved. That came as no surprise.

Osborne laid back the sheet to expose the victim's head. Her eyes were half open, cloudy as a winter sky. He drew down the chin. What had resisted when he had touched her out on the lake was now pliant. Her bite appeared natural and good. Ray was right—she would have had a very nice smile.

He tipped the head back gently, gloved fingers bracing the lower jaw as he peered into the mouth. What he saw didn't register at first. When it did, he stood up, took a deep breath, then adjusted the overhead spot for the best possible illumination.

The tongue had been neatly severed. A pristine cut. In all his years of practicing dentistry in Loon Lake, Osborne knew only two types of people who used knifes that worked so cleanly. One was a fisherman with a talent like Ray's for the perfect fillet, the other a surgeon. This was not the work of an amateur. He doubted if even Bruce or any of his cronies would find an identifiable mark from this blade.

The girl had exceptionally good teeth. One cavity from years ago. Two wisdom teeth in place, two extracted. One lateral incisor on the upper left slightly crooked. Regular cleanings and flossing. But no easily recognizable dental work. That was disappointing.

He charted the configuration of her teeth with lateral and anterior views, then sketched a diagram of the jaw and facial structure as meticulously as he could. He made a note to ask the new coroner for photos. At the very least he would pass those around at the society meetings next week. A full day of panels before the evening dinner party would give him a chance to run them by most of the attending dentists. With luck, someone might find her mouth familiar.

Once Osborne was satisfied with his exam, he gave Pecore's notes on the first two victims a quick scan. Curious. Pecore had noted that the woman's body appeared to have been wiped down with an antiseptic of some sort. He found no stray hairs, nothing—"unnaturally clean" were the words he used. Now that was a good catch on Pecore's part, thought Osborne. The man wasn't a total loss.

Osborne returned the paperwork to the counter where he'd found it. Lew would need to double-check those results with whomever the new coroner might be. Just as he was about to leave the room, he paused. He went back to the drawer holding the woman's body and pulled it out. He wanted a close look at the hands, those fingernails that had caught Mallory's eye.

Ah. Under the bright light, he could see why his daughter had called them holiday nails. Ten tiny Christmas trees glittered silver against the dark blue sky painted on the slender fingers.

Leaving the morgue, Osborne hurried down the hall. He was desperate for a breath of fresh air before he followed Carrie's suggestion to examine the clothes.

"I'll give you a hand," she said when he returned. Together they tugged at the garments, which were heavy under normal conditions and more so due to the fact they had only half-dried since the bodies were pulled from the water.

Pecore's notes had stated that he believed the clothing had been removed from the victims initially, then replaced with care. Whoever the killer was, he speculated, they had not planned for the victims to be found until sometime in the spring when nature would have roughened the edges of the cuts severing the legs.

Something he didn't write down but Osborne knew to be true: Enough snowmobilers would be trapped under ice until spring that Pecore, by his standards, would be too overworked to do detailed exams. When the ice goes out in the northwoods, every year an average of four or more missing people surface.

One set of clothing held no surprises—the first victim had worn a standard snowmobile parka and pants. But the other outfit was quite unlike anything that Osborne had seen before. Someone, probably Bruce, had tagged it with the name matching the victim whose teeth had been whitened.

"Jeff and I looked at one of these at Ralph's the other day," said Carrie, noting the confusion on Osborne's face. "Want me to tell you what I know about it?"

"Sure. I don't know where to begin with this thing," said Osborne, pulling at the arms of the parka as he tried straightening it out, "and I'd just as soon not ask Ralph."

He detested Ralph Kendall, the British-born owner of Ralph's Sporting Goods. The man was pretentious enough about fly fishing equipment without giving him this to lord over Osborne as well. Even though he was married, Ralph was always a little too obsequious around Lew. Add to that the fact that the word over morning coffee at McDonald's was that he'd been spotted more than once at a Friday fish fry in Boulder Junction with a woman who bore no resemblance to his wife. No, Osborne did not need to give that razzbonya any advantage.

"Jeff's a geek, see," said the young nurse as she shook out the snow pants. "He calls these 'mobile pants' because they have pockets for your cell phone here, a Blackberry or Palm there. See how they line the pockets and all the Velcro? Say you fall in the water—this keeps all your equipment nice and dry. Jeff dumped his snowmobile in Boom Lake last winter, y'know. Went in up to his neck," said Carrie, demonstrating, "so that's real important. And see on the parka . . ." she took the jacket out of Osborne's hands, "see how you can carry a minidisc player right here—then all you have to do is hit the 'back' button on your sleeve if you want to replay a song.

"And Dr. Osborne," she set the parka down to pick up the pants again, "you've got all these secret channels sewn in for the wires. Jeff wants to be able to carry his MP3 player and a digital camera just like this guy." Carrie set the pants down carefully. "Burton is the company that makes these, and Ralph will special order for you."

"You think this one came from Ralph's?"

"Oh no, this is from the cities," said Carrie. "I asked the family when they came in to ID the body." Osborne raised his eyebrows. "I asked *very carefully*," said Carrie. "With respect, Dr. Osborne." As she folded the high-tech suit back into the box, she paused. "I just wonder . . ."

Osborne waited. "Wonder what?"

"Well—where did all his stuff go? You don't wear this unless you're fully loaded, y'know."

"We have his Palm Pilot, Carrie."

"Yeah, there should have been more stuff, I think. Digital camera. At least a cell phone. A guy like this doesn't go anywhere without his cell phone."

thirteen

I know several hundred men. I prefer to angle with only four of them.

—Frederic F. Van de Water

The ID caught him by surprise.

He and Carrie had finished folding the snowmobile suits back into the box and taping it closed. Then, after pulling on his jacket, hat, and gloves, Osborne had picked up the box and was halfway down the hall when Carrie called out, "Dr. Osborne . . ."

He stopped and turned, thinking he had forgotten or dropped something. Carrie waved him back to the nurses' station. She looked around to be sure no one could overhear what she was about to say.

"I know her."

"Who?"

"That girl in there. The dead woman. I know her."

Osborne set the box back down on the floor. "You're telling me you know the victim in the morgue, Carrie?"

"Ye-e-ah." She dropped her eyes as if ashamed. "I wasn't sure about saying anything, but the more I thought about it . . . I felt bad. It's kinda embarrassing . . ." She lowered her voice another notch, even though there was no one around. "Jeff and I were snowmobiling last winter, see? And we stopped in at the Rabbit Den in Armstrong Creek for some hot toddies. You know that place?"

"Yes," said Osborne, knowing instantly why Carrie had been reluctant to say anything. The Rabbit Den was a strip joint that billed itself as a place "where good bunnies go bad." If a Thunder Bay dancer got caught violating Code 2116B, she could always get a job in the next county where the authorities were not quite as vigilant as Lew. No question, The Rabbit Den was not a place Carrie's parents would want her patronizing. Chances are she'd be the only woman there not working.

"That's where I first saw her—she was dancing. A couple months later I ran into her over in Rhinelander at Nicolet College. She was a year behind me in the nursing program. Eileen Walkowski's her name. We talked a couple times, and she told me she danced to pay for school."

"That makes sense." Osborne thought of Lew's daughter dancing her way towards a successful career as a CPA. Lew's description of why her daughter did what she did was succinct: "Sometimes being a survivor means taking an unconventional path. Doesn't mean you're bad, just means you're unafraid."

"About that time the Ranch people came up to recruit from the nursing classes and gave her a scholarship."

"You lost me. The Ranch people? You mean a nursing scholarship?"

Carrie was looking very embarrassed. "The Ranch is this place down near Oshkosh where they teach exotic dancing, but you have to be very . . . very—" Carrie used her hands, her face crimson.

"Well-endowed," said Osborne, nodding his head seriously. "And they recruit up here?" He wanted to kick himself for the incredulity he couldn't keep out of his voice, but Carrie didn't seem to hear.

"Yeah, well, most of their applicants have implants, but they say the best dancers are the ones that are natural. The last few years they've been hosting parties for the nursing students, and I guess they find a couple candidates that way. Not the male students, of course." Carrie rolled her eyes.

"Then what happens?"

"You go to the Ranch and train as a dancer for three months. They pay your room and board, and then they help you get a well-paying job like in Las Vegas. Girls go there from all over the United States. I've heard some of the dancers make a couple hundred thousand a year. Once you start earning, you pay them back. Kinda like those real estate schools, y'know."

Definitely real estate, thought Osborne. Too much like real estate.

"So that's what Eileen did. She dropped out of Nicolet and went to the Ranch."

"And that's the name of it? The Ranch?"

"No, there's more to it, like 'the Apple Ranch' or 'the Raspberry Ranch'—but I don't know exactly. Everyone just calls it the Ranch."

"Do you know anyone else who's there right now? Or went there?"

"No. I heard about it for the first time back when Eileen signed up. As far as I know the Ranch people haven't been back to Rhinelander recently. And I haven't seen her since she left—until they brought her body in this morning."

"Carrie," said Osborne, "I appreciate you being so forthcoming. This was the right thing to do. Just think how her poor parents must be wondering what on earth has happened."

Carrie nodded, relieved.

"I'm sure Chief Ferris will need more information from you," said Osborne.

"Okay." As if realizing what she had done was important, Carrie perked up. "I'll ask around, too, see if anyone else around here knows anything."

Before leaving he wrote down the phone numbers for Carrie at work, at her apartment, and her cell phone.

While Lew would be able to get the particulars on the victim and her family from the college, he had no doubt she would be very interested in the Ranch people.

"Carrie," said Osborne, picking up the box again, "if you should remember the full name of that place or think of anything else we should know about Eileen, please call me at home. I'll be sure we get the information to Chief Ferris right away."

"You won't mention this to my dad, right?"

"Of course not. You're an anonymous source. Don't worry about that."

For more reasons than her parent's ire, Osborne thought it wise to keep Carrie's name and her connection to the victim quiet.

Osborne pulled off a glove to knock on the door to Lew's office, balancing the oversize box in front of him. To his surprise, it swung open before he even touched it. Stumbling forward, he nearly knocked over Marlene, the switchboard operator, who doubled as Lew's assistant. A blowsy, cheery woman in her late fifties, Marlene had a habit of looking amused whenever Osborne walked in to visit Lew. Made him feel like a school kid with a crush on his teacher.

At the moment, however, she was no-nonsense. She stepped back to let him by, then gave him a hurried wave, "Chiefs not here, Doc—meeting with Pecore and the mayor." Marlene threw him a look; she knew what was up.

Osborne set down the box in the corner of Lew's office, then checked his watch. He found Marlene back at the switchboard, juggling incoming calls. He waited for a break, then spoke fast, asking her to tell Lew, when she called in, that one of the nurses had recognized the young woman. He took care not to mention Carrie's name, saying only that he had left a note in the top right-hand drawer of Lew's desk with details and phone numbers.

Marlene would know that meant the information was confidential.

Then he mentioned the box he had left and why. "Be sure that fellow from Wausau doesn't walk off with it until Lew has a chance to look it over, will you? She may want to hold on to that box so Gina Palmer can have a look."

"Okey-doke," said Marlene, "and Chief Ferris told me if I saw you to see if you could sit in on her second meeting with the mayor at four this afternoon. She said you were working on someone they might hire for you-know-what."

"I am. But, shoot, I still need to make a phone call on that," said Osborne, glancing at his watch again. Good. Four o'clock would give him plenty of time to make the call and find a Christmas tree with Mallory. "Tell Chief Ferris I'll be here."

Twenty minutes later he was in his own kitchen pouring a final cup of coffee. Mallory was in the living room happily pulling on her old snow pants, which she had just found in a box in the basement. That gave him time to make the call that he'd promised Lew. It was the number of an old college buddy who had retired to Manitowish Waters.

"Phil, Paul Osborne here. How are you?"

Phil Borceau had worked as a pathologist at one of the big hospitals in Madison before retiring. His wife had died recently of breast cancer, and Osborne knew the man was lonely. Lonely and at dangerously loose ends. When they had dinner together in October, Osborne had recognized the despair in his friend's eyes. He knew that valley; he'd been there.

Phil sounded pleased to hear Osborne's voice. "So it could be temporary," said Osborne moments later, winding up his description of what Lew needed in a coroner, "or it might be more time than you want to put in."

"Sure, sure," said Phil. "Sounds interesting, though.

The daily stuff is easy, but I haven't worked crime victims in years. Have to pull out my textbooks."

"I think you'll need some new ones, Phil," said Osborne with a laugh. "The science on some of this stuff has changed dramatically—certainly has in the field of forensic dentistry."

"You'll still be handling that, right?" said Phil.

"You better believe it—so long as Chief Ferris asks me. Phil, can you give me a brief rundown of your experience and your title at retirement? We're meeting on this later today."

"Why don't I fax it in? I have a résumé in my files that I used for a deposition I consulted on last summer. Would that work?"

"Better yet."

Osborne gave him Lew's extension and suggested he talk to Marlene. Osborne hung up feeling very good about Dr. Phil Borceau. He would be perfect for the position of Loon Lake coroner. Not only would it fill his empty days, but with Pecore and his bungling no longer a drag on the department, Phil could make Loon Lake Chief of Police Lewellyn Ferris look like a million bucks.

"Mallory—you ready?"

"All set." Mallory grinned at him as she walked into the kitchen fully rigged for winter weather. "You look happy, Dad. And kind of weird. Do you have to wear that hat?"

Osborne had pulled on his favorite winter headgear—a beaver hat lined with quilted silk. Attached so they could be folded up inside were woolen earflaps, double lined and cross-stitched. Very warm. When he pulled them down, they fit nice and close around his ears and the back of his neck.

"You're right about the hat—kinda makes me look like a Russian immigrant in the late 1800s, doesn't it?" He gave Mallory a sheepish grin. "But I'll tell you, that wind out there is stiff and it won't be any warmer when we get to McNaughton. So count your blessings, kiddo; at least your old man doesn't wear a stuffed trout on his head."

Heading across the yard towards his car, Osborne grabbed his oldest daughter around the shoulders to give her an impulsive, affectionate hug.

fourteen

. . . the good of having wisely invested so much time in wild country . . .

—Harry Middleton, *Rivers of Memory*

Osborne pulled into the exact same spot he had parked his car the day before. A light dusting of snow during the night had done nothing to obscure the tracks he'd left entering and leaving the forest.

"You really think we'll find a good tree in *here*?" Scanning the rust and bronze skeletons in front of her, Mallory looked around, her face clouded with doubt. Denuded by winter, the tamaracks facing them were hardly suitable for hanging with ornaments.

Her tone of voice reminded him of her mother—no tree was ever quite right, and his gifts to her always had to be returned: if not the wrong size, then the wrong color. Osborne made a quick, firm resolve that this tree search would in no way duplicate the unpleasant past. The ghost of Mary Lee would not be allowed to haunt this holiday.

"Trust me, Mallory. Back behind these tamaracks are some beauties. See over the tops?" Her eyes followed where he pointed. Ranks of dark green balsam spires pushed their way into the goose grey sky like guardians of the deeper woods.

"This is where I hunt grouse—they love to hide in those balsam. We'll top one off and have a perfect tree."

"Well . . . Erin said there's a tree farm out on Highway G . . ."

"I know what I'm doing, Mallory," said Osborne. He felt a little guilty not telling her the truth as to why he had picked this spot. Not only did he want to find a tree, but he was intent on retracing yesterday's mad dash. He wanted a better look at that spot where he'd found the teeth.

Handing Mallory the saw from the back of the car, he leaned farther in to uncase his shotgun. His daughter's eyes widened.

"Bird season is open 'til the thirty-first. And I told you about that wolf, didn't I?" He tried his best to sound cavalier when he was, in fact, beginning to have second thoughts about the wisdom of this venture.

"Whatever," said Mallory. "All I want is a Christmas tree, Dad, not a major northwoods experience. Guess you better lead the way, huh."

"Are you kidding me? *This* is where you found those teeth?" Hands on her hips, Mallory checked out the spot where Osborne had slipped the day before. "Someone's putting you on, Dad. This is Horsehead Hollow—don't tell me you never heard of it."

"That's this place? I thought Horsehead Hollow was up by the Flowage."

"Nope, this is it. You're thinking of *Big* Horsehead Lake. You take that path," Mallory pointed off behind a stand of balsam to the right. "and you'll end up at Little Horsehead. This is where we had all our beer parties when I was in high school. A pretty famous spot for anyone under the age of forty, I'd say."

"I don't see any beer cans."

"You would if you looked harder. See this tree?" Mallory laid a hand on the trunk of an unusually tall tama-rack. "This is the marker. We always came by boat from the public landing and found our way by this tree. I never knew you could get here from the highway like we just did."

"You have to know the logging roads," said Osborne. "It's not a straight shot. Boy oh boy," he added, tipping his head back for a better look at the tree towering over Mallory, "if that's a tamarack, it has to be a different variety."

The tree in question had shed its needles but kept a fringe of interwoven twigs that gave it the appearance of being cocooned in lace. Unlike the fingers of other tama-racks, twisting madly in all directions, these delicate spindles thrust their way towards the sky. And all through the spidery fretwork were nestled, like baby birds, millions of tiny pinecones.

"Dad, this tree is so stunning in the summertime," said Mallory. "Once when I was high, I wrote a poem about it. Think I still have it somewhere."

"Do you miss getting high?" Osborne brushed the snow off a nearby stump and sat down. He loved days like this when the winter sun was already moving into the west and snow clouds hung low. Snowy clusters on the branches of the young balsams surrounding them glittered in the sun's glow like diamonds on a ballerina's tutu.

The hollow under the big tree was so still and peaceful, he motioned to Mallory to find a spot, too. Moments like this were why he loved living here. An image of Lew's face, relaxed and content as she cast a fly line upstream, flashed through his mind. One thing he loved about that woman—they could spend hours together: not talking, listening. Somewhere a tree creaked. Mallory exhaled, watching her breath.

"Sure I miss getting high," said Mallory, her voice soft. "That's why I'll go to group tonight. I imagine I'll always miss that feeling . . . don't you?"

"Umm. Less so these days."

"Dad . . . I've been wondering lately . . . I know that you and Mom didn't have the closeness that some married people have."

Osborne glanced over at his daughter. "Mallory, could we not talk about this right now?"

"That's not my point, Dad. I don't want to talk about Mom. What I wonder is why . . . when you were finally on your own and could do things the way you wanted . . . Why is that when you started drinking? Why not before?"

It was a fair question. And one he'd asked himself often. He had an answer—not sure it was the right one, of course.

"You know what I've found is that you spend a lot of time thinking how much you give to another person, or give up of yourself to accommodate that person—until they're gone. Only when they aren't there anymore do you realize what they gave you. Let me rephrase that, Mallory: *what you took from them.*

"In your mother's case, she gave my life structure—from sunrise to sunset, she had a plan. When she was gone, the structure was gone. Without her bossing me this way and that, I didn't know where to begin . . . or when to stop."

Mallory looked satisfied with his answer. "I feel that way about Steve. He's gone, I'm glad he's gone—but, Dad, it is hard work filling that space." She gave a slight smile, then leaning to look past his shoulder, she pointed. "Hey, there's a tree. It's full, it's straight. Think that'll fit in the living room okay?"

He turned to look at where she was pointing. Before he could say a word the dull bark of a shotgun echoed through the snowy silence. A gentle rain hit the back of his head, cushioned by the heavy fur of the hat.

Osborne remained perfectly still for a long moment. He kept his head turned away. Birdshot on the back of the head was one thing, in the face, quite another.

"Don't move, Mallory. Don't look back."

Too late, she was already on her feet.

"Dad, what the hell? Is someone shooting at us?"

"Who's there?" Osborne shouted. Staying low, he scrambled for cover. The hunter had to be a good hundred yards away and aiming high. "Get down!"

"Why are they doing this?" asked Mallory, crawling towards him on her forearms and knees.

"Some goddam bird hunter with bad eyesight . . ."

Another blast hit a stand of trees off to their right. Again, the aim was high. He motioned for Mallory to stay low behind him, then raised his twenty gauge and released the safety.

"It's either an accident or a warning . . ." Holding their breath, they could hear the crunch of boots in snow heading their way.

fifteen

You can't say enough about fishing. Though the sport of kings, it's just what the deadbeat ordered.

—Thomas McGuane, *Silent Seasons*

"**Damn** kid better have a good excuse," muttered Osborne. The slender figure heading their way climbed with ease over the dead limbs and stumps of forest slash, then bounced like a young deer over snow-covered humps, only to stop short about a hundred feet away.

Screened by a clump of aspens that had toppled into each other's arms, the boy raised his shotgun. Though his face was shadowed, Osborne could make out the brim of a shapeless felt hat, the kind once favored by local moonshiners. The kid was small, maybe five foot six at the most, and very thin. In spite of the cold, all he wore over a long-sleeved flannel shirt was a tattered hunting vest, pocked with stains.

"What the hell you think you're doin' back here?" asked the boy, his voice gruff. Too gruff. The voice didn't match the body. Osborne's chest tightened.

When his daughters were teenagers, he warned them about going down back roads with boyfriends. "You never know who's living back there," he would say. "They don't

want to meet you, and you don't want to meet them
Don't giggle—I'm not kidding."

And he wasn't. "Them" were people you rarely saw in
town. "Them" were people who lived in shacks at the end
of lanes without fire numbers, who never showed up on
IRS rolls, who blasted a shotgun *before* calling 911
"Them" were the ones referred to by the McDonald's coffee crowd as "those who eat their young."

Something about the man heading their way—the hat
the gun, the voice.

Osborne stood up but tightened his grip on his own
gun.

A ray of late sun hit the man's face. Mallory gasped
The body that had moved with the grace and ease of
youth lied. It belonged to a face more crumpled than the
hat on its head—the face of a very old man.

"Clyde?" said Osborne, hesitating, but sure. He'd met
the man only once, but that was a face you never forgot
The band across his chest loosened.

At the sound of his name, the old man lowered his shotgun a notch.

"Clyde, you know me." Osborne stepped into the fading sunlight, anxious to be seen. "I'm a friend of Ray
Pradt's. Ray and I are neighbors. You . . . we met a while
back."

Osborne wondered if the old man could possibly remember meeting him. Had to be four years ago at least,
standing in the rutted lane that passed for Ray's driveway,
and they couldn't have exchanged more than a few words.
Ray was the one who had the knack for socializing with
old recluses like Clyde, not Osborne.

He never knew quite what to say—or how to say it. The
few times he'd had one of the old codgers in the dental
chair, he would try to break the ice with a little humor,
maybe a comment on the weather—but all he ever got in
return was a flat look and silence. Maybe a grunt.

"Ray Pradt, huh." The gun dropped slightly. "Who'd
you say you are? Speak up."

"Paul Osborne—Ray's neighbor." Osborne raised his voice to an unnatural level. "Say, you and Ray been catching some nice fish lately. He showed me a couple beauties you caught just the other night." Osborne winced. False ocularity was not his bailiwick.

"Oh, yeah—you know Ray, huh." Clyde's gun was pointing down at the snow.

Osborne took a deep breath. Another tentative step towards the old man. He was less than fifty feet away now. Close enough Osborne could see a stag-handled Bowie knife hanging in a holster from his belt.

"Dad . . . ?" Mallory wasn't so sure that was a good idea. The old man was ambling their way.

"Nice gun you got there," said Osborne when they were about twenty feet apart. "But, jeez, Clyde, you almost nailed yourself a retired dentist—not a partridge."

"Oh, I wasn't shootin' at no birds," said the old man making a whistling, sucking sound as he spoke—the sound of ill-fitting dentures. "I thought you was someone else."

Osborne tried not to stare, but the difference between the youth in the old man's movement and the age in his face confounded him. He knew from Ray that Clyde lived somewhere in the backwoods near McNaughton and made his living trapping beaver. Was it working outdoors that kept him so spritely? Or was it the lack of having to deal with human razzbonyas?

"Yeah, I been havin' trouble with a coupla dumyaks driving back in here on their snowmobiles and wrecking my traps," said Clyde. "But you two," he looked at Osborne's shotgun, then the saw in Mallory's hand, "what the hell *you* doin' back here?"

"Looking for a Christmas tree," said Osborne.

"With a shotgun?"

"Few days left in bird season—thought we might chase a few out from under the snow cover. I hunt back here pretty often—but I keep to state land, Clyde."

"Yep, that's your right. Birds, huh. If I was you, I'd

keep an eye out for wolves. Got a pack of four moved into the region—wiped out my rabbits."

"My dad and I, umm, we found a nice tree right here," said Mallory, edging her way out from behind Osborne and pointing. "All ready to cut down. We'll be out of your way in a few minutes . . . if that's okay." She gave Osborne an anxious look.

"Don't bother me none. It's those damn kids I don't like. You see 'em, you tell 'em keep those goddam machines of theirs on the trail—I'll shoot 'em if they come back here again. I will."

"You mean to tell me they're riding off trail—right through the woods here?" Osborne looked around. He didn't see any snowmobile tracks. The old man must be losing it.

"Not through the woods, up and down my streambeds I got traps laid around the beaver dams back in here—and I don't need them messed up. This is my living. You just ask Ray, he'll tell ya.

"Hell, last week, I caught two of 'em back in here. Some young fella and his girlfriend. They got stuck, see. Coupla nincompoops. Didn't know that the ice over the springs back in here don't freeze solid. Wouldn't ya think they'd know that? Anyone who lives up here knows that.

"So middle of the night I hear all this hullabaloo. I go traipsing on over and come to see one of their machines is frozen halfway into the ice, doncha know. Prob'ly goin' deeper without my help. So I go get my pickup with the winch and chains I use when I break a beaver dam and pulled 'em out." Clyde paused, giving his teeth a good suck.

"That was nice of you," said Osborne.

"Not fast enough for the little lady—pretty nasty that one. Not one word of thanks. You'd a'thought they'd give me five bucks . . . something. Wouldn't you?" Clyde's voice cracked with anger.

"They sure shoulda," said Osborne. He wanted to humor the old guy, get the tree and get out of there. Ray might think Clyde was a wizard when it came to fishing hard water but Osborne had limited tolerance for backwoods hermits. They tended to have bad teeth, bad breath, and conspiracy theories that begged logic.

"You wouldn't believe it," said Clyde, punching at the air with the stock of his gun. "I get that gal unstuck and next thing she's accusing me of poking holes in the ice to make it happen. It was a *beaver* hole for chrissake. Tried to tell her that but, man, she yelled at me."

Clyde shook his head. "The mouth on her—worse'n an old girlfriend of mine." The craggy old face made a strange move, which Osborne recognized belatedly as a wink.

Oh, no, he prayed silently, please dear God—don't let this be a story longer than one of Ray's.

Encouraged by Osborne's blank look, Clyde chewed and sucked, then said, "That old girlfriend—she was a hooker come up from Chicago and wanted me to marry 'er. When I said, 'no sirree, gal,' you shoulda heard *her*. But that lady the other night—she was something else, I tell ya. You ask Ray. I gave him a rundown of the language that gal used. But—" Clyde gestured towards Mallory, "not when the young lady's around. Men only for that kinda talk.

"I let her know I don't intend to see her and that goofy boyfriend of hers back here no way, no time. If I do, so help me Jesus—boom! Won't use no shotgun neither— might try my deer rifle on those two." Clyde cradled his shotgun as he rocked back on his heels, content now that he had a plan.

"Oh, I doubt they'll be back," said Osborne. He couldn't imagine anyone being that stupid. Clyde was scary enough *without* a gun.

"So you know my buddy Ray, huh," Clyde stepped closer, and Mallory moved back. "Now there's a boy knows fish. Did he tell ya we got a mess of walleyes other night? Got an even dozen, smallest one three pounds."

"Yep, he sure did, Clyde. Showed me some real beauties—n-i-ice fish."

"You betcha they're nice, more'n our limit, too," the old man made a hooting sound that was supposed to pass as a laugh. "I have a good time with that boy." Clyde hooted and sucked. The stench of stale tobacco was overwhelming.

"Where's your place?" Osborne looked around, hoping a change of subject might ease Clyde on his way. "I don't think I've ever seen a road into a home back here."

"I'm in 'bout a third of a mile that direction," Clyde pointed. "You access my place from the other side of the lake."

"So you must be on Little Horsehead."

"Nah, sold that land a couple years ago. I'm just south—back in near a couple ponds that feed into the lake. Been there nearly sixty years now. I made a deal with the highway department way back when to trap beaver. Been a good enough living. I own forty acres crisscrossed with some decent streams and two real nice spring ponds. But this here is state land, so you and the young lady are not trespassing. Sorry about that buckshot, Doc, just tryin' to scare those other fellas."

"Don't worry about it." Osborne motioned to Mallory to hand him the saw. Then he paused. "Say, Clyde, one last thing. I was hunting birds out here the other day, and I came across a set of dentures that someone left in a stump over there for some reason. Those wouldn't happen to belong to you? I need to return them if—"

"Hell, no. Got my own. Been wearing 'em for years. You find anything strange back here, it's those damn kids use this hollow for beer drinkin'. I spend half the summer picking up their trash. Ought to try a little buckshot on them one of these days."

Clyde gave a wide grin. In the dimming light, Osborne could barely make out his upper plate for the black tobacco stain.

"Dad," said Mallory, climbing into the car after they had tied down the tree, "give up on those dentures. I'll bet you anything that some kid stole those from a high school science lab. Just a prank. Thank goodness they don't belong to that old man. Yuck." She shivered.

"You could be right." Osborne turned to watch over his shoulder as he backed up. "So you don't think you'd like to go ice fishing with Ray and ol' Clyde?"

"Da-a-d, hardly." She gave him a dim eye.

"That's what I love about Ray," said Osborne, shifting into gear. "His door is always open—whether it's an oldtimer like Clyde or a beautiful woman."

Mallory said nothing, but a dark look settled across her brow. Osborne kept his eyes on the road, forcing himself not to grin. Fond as he was of his daughters, each had inherited some of their mother's more irritating traits. Erin would run around, insisting on doing too much in too little time, while Mallory would always be a bit of a snob.

Maybe, when it came to Ray Pradt, that was okay. Much as he loved the guy, Ray was just not son-in-law material. He had peculiar friends, kept odd hours, and you never knew what the hell he was going to do next.

Yep, sucking and hooting, old Clyde had just done Osborne a big favor.

They drove back towards town in silence. Just as the lights of Loon Lake came into view, Mallory stirred. She sat up straight.

"What?" said Osborne. "You look like you just made your mind up about something."

"I did. You have to hand it to Ray, Dad. At least he's never boring. Some people I know, they're so boring you get tired of them even when they're not around."

Osborne looked over at her. Maybe he was wrong.

sixteen

We have other fish to fry.

—Rabelais, *Works*

Arne Steadman, a boulder of a man, was blocking the doorway to Lew's conference room. That didn't surprise Osborne. When it came to blocking anything, the man was more talented than a tight end for the Green Bay Packers.

As chairman of the county board for twenty years, Arne had specialized in blocking every DNR effort to encourage natural shorelines and reduce the number of homes being built too close to the water. He insisted his resistance was coincident to the fact that the proposed regulations might apply to land owned by parties related to him by blood or by marriage.

After a mild heart attack, Arne had appointed himself to the lesser role of mayor of Loon Lake. All he had to do now was block local efforts to improve the signage on Main Street shops, keep snowmobiles off cross-country ski trails, or reduce the number of Steadmans on the county and town payrolls. His cousin was the postmaster, his wife's brother the town clerk, his son the tax assessor. And so it had been in Loon Lake since the days of Arne's grandfather.

"Excuse me, Arne . . . Arne? Excuse me . . ." Osborne gave up. The man's hearing must be going. He tapped the massive right shoulder and waited for Arne to wedge his body sideways so Osborne could squeeze past. Once he was safely in the conference room, Osborne sat down at the empty table. He knew he was a few minutes early.

The mayor, on hold for a call on his cell phone, swayed back and forth in the doorway, the phone barely visible between his hand and his balding head. It was a remarkable head that had always impressed Osborne as most closely resembling a box eight inches square, including the distance between his ears.

Arne wore his usual meeting attire: a bright red Polartec pullover that did nothing to diminish the impact of his rotund torso, the latter supported by pudgy legs encased in well-worn Levis. Stark white tennis shoes attempted to balance the ensemble.

Winter or summer, Arne wore those damn tennis shoes. They looked so funny, so inadequate for the weight they had to carry, that behind his back the McDonald's coffee crowd referred to Arne as "Mr. Potato Head." *Whispered* behind his back, that is; no one wanted to be on the bad side of the mayor.

Osborne peeled off his parka and leaned back in his chair to wait patiently. He had left the house in a rush only to find he was running a good half hour ahead of schedule. Now, with everything under control, he could relax. He left the tree leaning against the house, ready for his return, and Mallory had instructions on where to find the tree stand, the lights, and two boxes of ornaments. She planned on calling Erin to see if the kids would like to help decorate.

Driving into town, Osborne couldn't remember when he'd felt so happy and busy and efficient. Not the early darkness, not even the minus-twenty wind chill could quell his spirits. When he found he had time to make a quick stop at Ralph's Sporting Goods and pick up the gift he had ordered for Lew, he felt even better.

"I had to go on eBay to find these," Ralph had said, half-admiring, half-grousing as Osborne wrote the check. "Cost as much as an engagement ring, Doc. These a gift or for your own collection?" Osborne just smiled and tucked the little box in his pocket. The holiday was looking better by the moment.

As he walked down the street to where he had parked his car, Osborne mulled over the Dental Society dinner. Maybe he could approach Lew from another angle. Why not? He never gave up on a big fish.

Arne slapped the cell phone shut and stepped back to let Lew enter the conference room. "After you, Chief Ferris."

"Hey, Doc," said Lew, pulling out the chair across from Osborne, "got the fax from your friend." With a pleased lift of her right eyebrow, Lew scooted two pages across the table to Osborne.

Arne shook Osborne's hand, then took the chair at the head of the table.

"Mayor Steadman, I appreciate your support this morning in the matter concerning Dr. Pecore," said Lew, once they were all settled. "After our meeting, I asked Dr. Osborne to scout some possible candidates for the coroner position because, as you know, I have a critical situation at hand. Given his experience as a health professional in our community and as a forensic dentist, I thought he might be able to assist me in finding someone who could help us out."

Lew beamed at Osborne. "And he did. Dr. Osborne, please . . ." Lew gave Osborne a nod.

"Dr. Philip Borceau from Manitowish Waters has indicated to me that he is willing to step in temporarily," said Osborne. "I let him know the budget might mean another change down the road, but this will buy Chief Ferris and you folks on the town committee some time."

As Osborne spoke, Lew slid a copy of the résumé along

the table to Arne, then leaned forward on her elbows to wait while he looked it over. Arne glanced down at the two pages, then pushed them aside.

"I've got the man for you."

"But—" Lew looked puzzled.

"No 'buts,' Lewellyn," said Arne, raising his right hand as if giving a "down" command to a dog. "Wave at Marlene, will you? Tell her to send young Bud on down. He's waiting up front"

Lew threw Osborne a quizzical look, then pushed back her chair.

"Hey, Gramps, how's it goin'," said the young man who ambled in through the doorway, leaned forward to give Arne a high five, then shuffled down to take a chair at the end of the table, opposite his grandfather. Osborne's first impression was that the kid bought his Levi's at the same store as his grandfather but wore them significantly lower.

A burly twenty-something, Bud showed signs of inheriting the family physique with the exception that his square head was not bald. Quite the opposite. Osborne could make out every hair on that head, each one moussed to stand straight up from the scalp. And every hair on the head matched an equally stiff bristle hiding the line of the jaw and the chin. If Bud spent any time outside, you would never know it. His skin was milky white, almost translucent. Lavender-tinted granny glasses rested halfway down his nose.

"My grandson, Bud Michalski," said Arne. "He moved back from Appleton a couple months ago. Was working there as a phlebotomist, but he's been studying part time to be an undertaker." Arne relaxed back into his chair and thrust his legs out in front of him. "His uncle runs the funeral parlor over in Armstrong Creek—plan is for Bud to take over when the old man retires."

"Yep. I've completed two courses online and an internship with a funeral director in Rice Lake last summer," said Bud, his face open and cheerful. He pushed at his glasses. "Before I left Appleton, I was working for a company that collects plasma. They send it to Germany, do things to it and when that stuff is shipped back here it's worth millions. *Millions*." Bud looked around as if he expected the people around the table to believe that he personally executed every step of the process, vial by vial, tube by tube.

"Ah," said Lew, arms crossed, eyes moving from Bud to Arne and back again. "Where are you from, Bud?"

"Milwaukee. That's where I grew up and—"

"Bud's got ideas," said Arne, interrupting. "He's gonna go far in this business. And the price is right." Arne pursed his lips, then spoke clearly, deliberately. "I told him we expect him on call full time, and I told him thirty thousand plus bennies—less than half what we were paying Pecore."

"No offense to you, Bud," said Lew, acknowledging the young man with a slight nod before turning to his grandfather, "Arne, I need someone with forensic experience. We could certainly use Bud part time, but at this moment I have three dead bodies in that morgue and a half-written report. We'll be fined by the state if things are not done properly, and this young man is neither a pathologist nor a licensed medical examiner. It's not fair to Bud—or to me and my department."

"C'mon, young lady," said Arne, his tone supercilious. "You need expertise—call Wausau. Why the hell you think we pay them a retainer? Bud, here, can handle the rest. Hell, he knows blood. Pecore said he hasn't been doing more'n two autopsies a year for St. Mary's anyway. He told me there's no money in forensic pathology these days— you never saw a man so happy to take early retirement. All we need's a coroner who can take pictures, draw blood, and keep the records straight."

"Chief Ferris," said Bud. "Gramps is right. You have no need to worry. I'll contract with some local docs and funeral directors to make this a top-notch operation. I know a lot of the science from my work last summer. I was telling Gramps, with what I know we might be able to make some serious money for the town, too."

"How's that?" asked Lew, her voice flat. Sitting up

straight with her forearms on the table, she held her hands clasped stiffly in front of her. The expression on her face was too alert, too serious, the dark eyes just this side of challenging. When she was bullied, Lew's usual offense was a gentle toughness. This wasn't looking so gentle. Osborne tensed.

"Well, anytime we have an unidentified or unclaimed body, we can harvest many of the natural elements of the deceased—this includes organs, of course, but skin, ligaments, even bone. Fact of the matter is, on the open market for allograft tissue—the human body is worth $272,000."

With an eagerness that reminded Osborne of the ecstasy displayed by his black lab on retrieving a downed grouse, Bud made eye contact with each of the three people sitting at the table. Neither Lew nor Osborne said a word, but that did nothing to dim Bud's enthusiasm.

"I'll put it all on paper, flush it out for you. Timing is key, y'know—you have to harvest early. Early and fast."

"Around here, it can be days before we have a confirmed identification on a body," said Lew. "A hunter has a heart attack out in the woods, a snowmobiler goes through the ice and isn't retrieved until spring. We're a destination spot for tourists; I don't see how—"

"Yeah, we got issues to skirttail," said Bud with a hearty grin. "But we can do it. Like I told Gramps—you have just two animous deceased donors a year and the town budget has a surplus."

"You mean 'anonymous?'" said Lew. She had relaxed her shoulders. A good sign.

"That's what I said—'two animous donors a year,' and Loon Lake is in the black."

"Bud's the man," said Arne.

Lew threw up her hands. "No argument here." She pushed her chair back, "But in that case, I need to talk to Wausau right away, so if you'll excuse me." She stood up and reached across the table to shake Bud's hand. "Why don't you and I sit down tomorrow morning, Bud. You can flush out a few things for me then."

"Done deal," said Bud. "I forgot my résumé in the car. You want it?"

"Please. Just drop it on my desk."

"Well, then we're all agreed." Arne heaved himself to his feet. "Merry Christmas, everyone."

"Cool Yule," said Bud, jumping up to follow his grandfather out the door.

Lew hung back, waiting until Arne and Bud were at the far end of the hall, then closed the door very quietly.

"Sit down, Doc. I need to 'skirttail' a few things—like will you give my apologies to Dr. Borceau, please."

Osborne studied her face. The lines around her eyes had tightened, but she looked less disappointed than determined. "Of course. He'll understand. Too bad, though. This is going to cost you so much time—"

"Time? My time is nothing compared to the tab this town will get from every subcontractor I will have to hire in order to cover Fuzzhead's ass." A sly smile crept across Lew's face. "What Arne doesn't know is I got a new billing schedule from the Wausau Crime Lab for next year. Whopping increases. Whopping, Doc."

"So this doesn't upset you."

"What good would that do?" asked Lew. "Arne thinks he can come in here and beat me up—it's important for me to keep him believing that."

She didn't say another word, but the look in her eye was the look she got whenever she caught a glimpse of a brown trout, a lunker who was under the mistaken impression he was well hidden by an overhang. She had a way of teasing big guys into trouble—and she knew it.

A knock on the door startled both of them.

"Come in," said Lew.

Marlene poked her head through the doorway. "Couple messages for you, Chief. Your daughter called. It's snowing so bad down south, she and her husband don't want to make the drive up until after Christmas."

"O-o-h, that's too bad," said Lew, disappointment sweeping her face.

"And I hate to give you this next one . . ."

"Don't tell me Gina Palmer called to say she's not coming either." Lew's voice held an edge of alarm.

"No, no. Tomahawk called. They've got a snowmobiler who's been missing six days now. Point last seen was singing karaoke at Thunder Bay."

"Oh great, so they're dumping that on *my* desk, are they?"

"They're pretty worried, Chief. They checked all their trails and the family of the missing rider hired two off-duty officers to canvass our trails—no sign of him anywhere."

"O-o-kay," Lew sighed, "Good thing Suzanne and the kids aren't coming—looks like I'll be working the holiday."

"Lew," said Osborne, pulling on his parka after Marlene left, "why not spend Christmas Eve at my place? Stay over. Surely you can take *some* time off."

"Doc, you're sweet." She leaned up to kiss him lightly on the lips. Never had she ever said she loved him, a fact he was acutely aware of at moments like this. "The answer is no, but thank you. And don't worry about me, I'll have Gina to keep me company."

"That's not the same . . ."

She pushed him towards the door.

"Okay, okay—but come by later if you're not too tired. Mallory is making a big pot of chili. Erin will be there with the kids to help us decorate the tree . . . popcorn . . . hot chocolate . . ." The bustle of Erin and her children always brought a smile to Lew's face.

"Can I call you? It all depends on how long it takes me to reach Bruce and see if he can help me snag someone from the Wausau crew to complete the preliminary reports on those victims. I cannot keep those families waiting any longer."

Hunching his shoulders against the icy wind blowing across the parking lot, Osborne fumbled for his keys. He could not get in the car fast enough, it was so cold.

Phooey, he thought as he felt for the ignition, what happened to that good feeling I had less than an hour ago? He knew the answer: The increased burden on Lew put a crimp in his plans as well. When would he find the right moment to deliver his surprise?

As the engine warmed up, he mulled over Lew's dilemma. He should have seen it coming. If all these years in Loon Lake had taught him anything, it was this: Outsiders are not welcome. By Loon Lake standards it was Bud, not Phil, who had the right credentials: family, family, and family.

Pulling out onto the snowpacked street, Osborne shivered. Count your blessings, old man, he told himself. At least you aren't some poor idiot on a snowmobile trying to find your way through the woods on a night like this.

The idea of another missing rider, coupled with the two bodies he'd examined earlier, nagged at him as he drove home. Something didn't fit. But it wasn't until he pulled into his own driveway, relieved to see all the windows lit from inside and Erin's car parked in the drive, that he knew what it was.

It had to do with the type of snowmobile accidents, too many fatal, that he had assisted with over the thirty years since the sport had transformed the northwoods. It had to do with all the teeth that had been lost, the dental surgery required in the dead of night. Snowmobiles were hard on heads—young, old, male, and female. He would never forget the twenty-year-old girl who thought she could fly her machine off an icy rise, only to land face first, breaking both jaws, knocking out her front teeth and damaging all the rest.

Something about those accidents . . . but he couldn't be sure. He was glad Gina Palmer was on her way. If he was right, she would know how to prove it.

seventeen

You take the lake. I look and look at it.
I see it's a fair, pretty sheet of water.

—Robert Frost

Blond, round-faced, three-year-old Cody was jumping up and down, fists clenched, as he watched his mother, standing a little too high on the stepladder, as she tried to maneuver the Christmas angel onto the top of the tree. Twice it fell, and twice the youngster whirled in place, overcome with worry and excitement.

"Cody, careful. Now stand back and stand still or you'll knock me over," said Erin. But with the bouncy notes of "Rudolph the Red-Nosed Reindeer" reverberating through the room and four mugs of caffeine-laced hot chocolate mainlining his arteries, no way was that child able to stand still. Watching from the easy chair across the room, Osborne braced his elbows on his knees, ready to catch either Erin or the tree, depending on which toppled first.

"Hey little guy, you come over here by your grandpa," said Osborne. Doing his best to keep a lid on his whirling dervish of a grandson, he reached in vain for an arm as it flashed by.

Osborne was amazed as always that Cody with his

pumpkin cheeks, sturdy but petite build and cap of straight, white blond hair was related to him. Nowhere in that child's face or bone structure was there a hint of Osborne, much less the child's great-great-grandmother.

A stranger would have a tough time believing that the two were blood relatives sharing a Métis heritage. Take Osborne with his high cheekbones, open forehead, wavy black hair, brown black eyes, and skin so quick to darken with sun. Add to that his lanky frame and 6' 2" of height—and no one would guess that he was an ancestor of the blond fireplug bouncing off the walls in the living room.

Except for the smile. For his birthday that year, Erin had surprised her father with a framed photo of Grandpa and Cody celebrating the landing of Cody's first bluegill. For all the contrast between the two, their smiles were identical: wide, easy, and infectious.

Every time he looked at that picture, hanging on the kitchen wall, Osborne felt good.

Erin started down the ladder, confident the angel was secure. Just as her foot touched the floor, a blast of cold air swept the room.

"Howdy, howdy, howdy," boomed a voice from the kitchen. "Who stole my kushka?"

"Ray! Ray's here, Mom!" With a squeal of delight, Cody ran for the kitchen, followed by his sister, who had been helping Mallory unwrap ornaments.

Ray, bundled in his parka and sporting this time, not his trout hat, but a huge head of wolf fur, looked less the fisherman than a huge bear. "Who wants to go fishing?"

"I do! I do!" Cody levitated.

"Me, too," Mason joined in. "If Cody goes, I get to go. Don't I, Mom?"

"Ray, we're trying to get the tree trimmed," said Osborne, getting up from his chair.

"Not when you've got company like this you don't—" Ray stepped to one side and beckoned towards the door from the porch. Another whoosh of air and a smiling face, cozy under Ray's trout hat—the ear flaps down and tied under his chin—stepped through the doorway. Only one person other than its owner was ever allowed to wear that hat.

"Nick!" said Osborne. "I didn't know you were coming for Christmas."

The previous summer, Nick, the son of Ray's high school sweetheart, had met Ray. They had survived getting to know one another and kept in touch.

Osborne suspected it was because Nick found his mother's less than appropriate ex-beau a good escape from normal life. Though he attended a boarding school outside New York City and his permanent residence was an expensive Manhattan duplex, he was able, on occasion, to persuade his mother to let him spend a few vacation days in the trailer and on the water with Ray.

And Ray, who alleged he was still smitten with his high school heartthrob, even as she was on her third—and richest—husband, loved having the boy around. Nick, oddly enough, was as tall, gangly, and loose-limbed as Ray had been at that age. Except for Nick's fairer complexion, you could mistake them for father and son.

"I didn't expect to be here myself," said Nick. "I'm supposed to be at my grandmother's, but she's stuck in Minneapolis. I guess she drove over to do some shopping two days ago, and the roads have been too bad to drive back. Mom's spending Christmas in St. Bart's with my stepdad. So when my plane landed this afternoon and no one was at the airport to meet me, I called Ray. He picked us up about an hour ago.

"This is my friend Lauren. She's stuck, too."

As Nick spoke, a tall, slim girl, her eyes shy and her shoulders hunched into a fleece jacket, tiptoed into the room. She did her best to hide behind Nick. Meanwhile, all the commotion had brought Mallory and Erin into the kitchen to see what was happening.

"Lauren goes to school with me," said Nick. He grabbed her sleeve and pulled her forward. "Don't be so

shy; these are my friends," he said, but the girl hung back.
"She thinks she's imposing. I tried to tell her *not* . . . but,
well, okay." Nick gave up with a shrug.

"We were on the same flights, and her dad was supposed to drive down from Three Lakes, but he didn't
show up and no one answers their phone. We're pretty
sure he might have got stuck trying to drive down. Ray
said if we have to, we can sleep on his living room floor
tonight."

"Yeah." Lauren gave a faint giggle. Apparently, from
what Osborne could see, when it came to the prospect of a
night with Nick, the girl didn't look at all unhappy.

"Does your dad have a cell phone?" asked Mallory
from across the room.

"Yeah, but it just rings and rings, too. And he hasn't
called me on mine."

"If he's a mile out of town, that's all you're gonna get,"
said Osborne. "Cell service up here is random to say the
least. But you should hear something soon. In the mean-
time, Lauren, I'd like you to meet my daughters, Mallory
and Erin, and these are two of my grandchildren." He introduced her around the room.

"Fish are waiting," said Ray, getting antsy. Osborne
suspected he wanted to get the kids on the lake before any
incoming calls could ruin his plans.

"Young lady," said Osborne, "you do not look dressed
for ice fishing."

"No-o-o," Lauren shivered, "I'm not." Her eyes, a pale
brown that matched her hair, darted shyly from face to
face.

Having raised two daughters of his own, Osborne knew
exactly what she must be thinking as she pulled her jacket
close and hunkered down. Given her lightly pimpled face
under a mess of 'hat hair,' Lauren probably felt life at this
moment could not be more embarrassing.

"I'm sure someone here can find you something warmer
than that fleece," said Osborne.

"Now, Ray," said Mallory, teasing, "if Cody and Mason

get to go fishing that means I can go, too—right?" From the look on the face framed in wolf fur, that had been the plan from the beginning.

Osborne caught Erin's eye. She knew the score as well as he did. Unless they were into breaking the hearts of children—one of which was Mallory's—there would be no decorating any tree until after the fishing expedition.

"You are as welcome as the flowers—everyone," said Ray with a sweep of his arm. "But we have to hurry, folks. Conditions are ideal at this moment: A front is moving in, the sky has clouded over and the fish are biting. No better time to go play, doncha know."

Ray packed everyone into the bed of his pickup, seating his passengers on white buckets left over from some construction project and making sure each had something to hold on to during the short drive onto the ice. Excitement combined with warm clothing and the thrill of the cold night air made everyone a little giddy, including Osborne.

"Doc, Mallory, you ride up front with me," said Ray. "Everyone else—hold on tight."

Mallory wedged her parka between Ray, her father, and the gearshift. "Did Dad tell you we ran into your friend Clyde today?" she said as the little truck rolled out of the driveway.

Ray checked through his back window to make sure he didn't lose anyone as the pickup bumped from the driveway down onto the road. "Old Clyde, huh. Did he tell the secret to the beer batter he uses on his perch?"

"No. He told us he was going to shoot some people on snowmobiles, though."

Ray laughed. "He will, too. He hates those machines. One of these days he'll throw enough lead around, some jabone will run into it. Old Clyde can be a little explosive, y'know. That's why he's never been able to hold a job."

"Say, Mallory," Ray glanced over at her as he edged the front tires onto the snowmobile trail that would take them across the lake. "Do you like chicken?"

Osborne looked out the window and sighed. This had to be the tenth time he'd heard this one.

"I *love* chicken."

"Wanna neck?"

"Oh Ray, darn you." Mallory punched him in the arm. "That is so bad. You never change, do you."

Ray chortled.

Osborne continued to look out the window, which was down and had been down for seven years. Fortunately the wind was not from the north, so the cold air was invigorating. Too bad Lew couldn't be along, thought Osborne. This was fun.

Ray slowed the truck. He wiped at the windshield as if he couldn't see clearly. "What the—"

"What's wrong?" said Mallory.

"See that shanty and all those tip-ups?" Ray pointed through the windshield. "That's my spot. What do those razzbonyas think they're doing?"

"Plenty of fish in the lake, Ray. Let's move down a few yards," said Osborne.

"Not my fish. My fish are right here." Ray parked ten feet from the shanty.

"Aren't we a little too close?" asked Mallory.

Ray said nothing. He got out of the truck and pulled down the back gate, letting the five occupants tumble down onto the ice. Then, grabbing a hand auger, he walked over to a spot within five feet of the shanty and started to drill. The occupants, whose tip-ups were within fifteen feet, opened their door.

"Hey you," said a gruff voice, "this is a big lake."

"Yep," said Ray, drawing himself up to his full height in the dark. Clouds covering the moon threw shadows that made him look even more intimidating. "Plenty deep, too."

As the door closed, Osborne heard a muffled obscenity.

Ray continued to work his auger, though he didn't move any closer to the shanty. Eight-year-old Mason, familiar with the drill from previous expeditions with

Grandpa's neighbor, followed with the ice scoop. Meanwhile, Erin, Nick, and Lauren unloaded some firewood and kindling. With Osborne's help, they got a bonfire going.

After drilling three holes, Ray walked over to where Nick and Lauren were watching the fire build. "So, Nick—where does a six-foot-five fisherman fish?"

"I dunno, Ray, where?"

"*Wherever* he wants."

eighteen

While the child is catching fish
fishing will catch the child.

——From an ad by Eagle Claw/Wright and McGill Co.

Cody squealed with rapture as Ray plucked a wax worm from inside his cheek, impaled it on a hook, and handed the child a well-used jigging rod. From where he sat on his upended bucket, Cody leaned forward to keep his eyes riveted to the spot where his line entered the water. He did not move. Ray rigged another rod for Mason.

"Keep your eyes glued, you two. Remember what I said—jig those rods e-e-ver so gently. You want to tease that old crappie into biting. When you see your line quiver, lift quick and gentle to set the hook. Not *too* hard, or you'll lose him."

"Hey, Mason and Cody!" Erin called to her children from where she knelt beside Osborne, both of them feeding more kindling into the fire. "I want to hear you say 'thank you, Ray.'"

Osborne could make out only the shapes of his grandchildren. A sudden scrim of fat, heavy snowflakes had turned them into shadows, but their voices came through high-pitched and happy as they followed orders.

"Ah, moonshine of snow," said Ray, lifting his face to the sky as he walked back from the truck with more rods and a small tackle box. "Lauren," he said as he headed for the second hole, "you're next. Nick, you come over here, too, so I don't have to go through this twice."

"You betcha," said Nick, grinning and poking Lauren with his elbow.

"Taking lessons, Dad?" Erin kept her voice low. "New flirting technique: right elbow to left rib." Osborne chuckled.

The teenagers hurried over to where Ray had set down his equipment. Both were better dressed for the cold now. Mallory had unearthed an old parka of Erin's buried in the guest bedroom closet that fit Lauren fine. Nick wore Osborne's downhill skiing jacket—with the trout hat. Ray had extra mitts, and Mallory loaned Lauren a fleece neck warmer with a stocking cap to match. The cap and neck warmer happened to be an odd shade of cerise, but Lauren didn't complain. Everyone was muffled, comfortable, and happy.

"Okay, Lauren, you sit on that pail right there." Ray handed the girl a rod slightly longer and heavier than a twig. A tiny reel was attached to one end.

"I'm going to teach you what it means to be a jiggerman," he said, turning over another pail to sit beside her. "I don't use tip-ups like those jabones over in that shanty. I like a jigging rod—much easier to fish any depth.

"Now watch . . . I've rigged this with a two-pound test line, and I'm going to add . . ." Ray's fingers shuffled through his tackle box. "A special jig . . . ah, here it is!" He held a lure out for her to see. "Lauren, this jig is very special. It's my own design, patent pending."

Listening from where she was warming her hands over the bonfire, Erin snorted. "Lauren, everything that man does, says, or wears is 'patent pending.' "

Mallory and Osborne, sitting nearby on upended pails, chortled in agreement.

"You're right about that," said Nick. "When he met us

at the airport wearing this goofy fish hat, I told Lauren not to worry—that's just Ray—a re-e-al original."

"That's not all you said," said Lauren, teasing.

"Lauren . . ." warned Nick.

"You laugh," said Ray. "You can all laugh, but one of these days . . ." He paused to look closely at the lure he was about to tie on to the jigging rod. "Oops, this hook is dull." Ray reached into the deep cargo pocket of his parka and pulled out a small file. Holding the hook against his knee, he gave it a couple swipes, examined it closely, and was satisfied.

"How can you do that with bare hands in this cold?" asked Lauren.

"I'm acclimated," said Ray. "I do this every night. In fact," he added as he yanked off his wolf hat and unzipped his parka, "at the moment, I'm sweating."

"Br-r-r, not me." The girl shivered.

"What's your last name, Lauren?" asked Ray.

Osborne winked at Erin. A non sequitur from Ray was likely to mean a bad joke was on its way. A lengthy bad joke, the kind that tried the patience of dedicated clients and drove good friends from the room.

"Theurian," said Lauren.

"Haven't heard that name before," said Ray.

"My dad just got remarried and moved to Three Lakes from Kansas. He's kinda retired."

"Well, Miss Theurian, you are one of the privileged few chosen to fish with . . ." Ray dangled the lure, "Ray Pradt's new and unique . . . Hot . . . *Mama*."

Erin caught her dad's eye. All that was missing was a roll of drums. "Jeez, Ray," she said, hollering over towards Ray and the teenagers, "sounds like you're introducing a stripper."

"I am kinda, thank you—my all-new X-rated walleye jig." Everyone sitting around the fire shook their heads. It might not be a bad joke, but it was bound to be close.

"And now," said Ray, pausing for dramatic effect, "I will explain the extraordinary advantages of this flat-out fantastic lure. But first, Lauren, tell me—what did I say was the name of this unique new product?" He leaned towards Nick. "Checking to see if my product nomenclature, so to speak, has staying power." Ray raised a cautionary index finger. "Branding is key, doncha know."

"I think it's memorable," said Nick. The two men waited for Lauren.

"The Ray Pradt Hot Mama?"

"Close. I've been calling it just the Hot Mama—but . . . maybe I *should* call it the *Ray Pradt* Hot Mama. I like the sound of that. What do you think, Nick?"

Before Nick could answer, Osborne interrupted, "Ray, could we get on with the fishing, please? Some of us don't want to be here all night."

"Okay, okay—ready, Lauren?"

"All ears, sir."

She wasn't the only one. Osborne was very interested. He could see that Erin and Mallory were concentrating on every word as well. The design and marketing of new fishing lures was big business in the northwoods. More than one mom-and-pop operation had hit the big time. Why not Ray? He knew more about ice fishing than most people.

"See the little skirt on her? Couple reasons for that. One, we're fishing water that's stained dark by tannins and humates produced by trees and swamp vegetation, so you need something light and fluffy to generate movement in the water—get the attention of the fish.

"Two, we're fishing a hump under this ice, a sandbar that's quite weedy. This skirt will keep the jig from getting caught on the weeds. Now . . . the secret to my Hot Mama is . . . when you jig it this way . . . and *just* this much no more," said Ray as he demonstrated, "you set off a sexy little wiggle. *Fish love it.*"

"Sexy wiggle?" said Nick. "I know someone who does that." He rocked sideways to nudge Lauren with his shoulder. She giggled.

"Is that what Clyde was using the other night?" asked Osborne.

"Nah, he swears by a Swedish Pimple with a chunk of minnow, but I've been catching a lot more fish with this."

"And the skirt—what's that made from? Silicon?" asked Osborne, curious as to why Ray had been so close-mouthed about this new contraption. "This is quite an interesting lure, Ray. Why haven't you said anything about it?"

"Perfecting the details, Doc. Perfecting the details."

Osborne nodded. That made sense. Of course, with Nick here, guess who couldn't help showing off.

"But to answer your question on silicon, Doc, no sir-r-e-e. No Thunder Bay influence on my little gal—not an *ounce* of silicon in *my* Hot Mama."

"Ray, if you're serious and you think you got something, you do need to apply for a patent," said Erin. "Talk to my husband. He's got a friend from law school who's a patent lawyer in Chicago." She walked over to get a better look at the lure. "You need special tools for that?"

"Yep, a shovel," said Ray.

Erin gave him a dim eye. "I'm only trying to help."

"And I'm not kidding," said Ray. "The reason I don't use silicon for the skirt is because I found a road kill albino squirrel that has enough tail to make a million of these. Hence . . . the unique motion in water." Seeing the confusion on Lauren's and Nick's faces, he added, "I used a shovel to scrape the dead squirrel off the road."

Ray looked up at Erin. "Are you happy now—forcing me to give away trade secrets?"

"Yeah, right," she said, walking back to the fire. "Check it out, Dad. It actually looks pretty cool." Osborne swung around on his pail for a better view.

"OK, Miss Theurian . . ." Ray knelt beside the hole, the Hot Mama still in his hand. "Ready to jig? Better pull your pail a little closer to the edge."

"Sounds like a dance," said Lauren, scooting forwards.

"Much more gentle than a dance. One last thing . . ."

Ray reached into the small tackle box by his knee. "Now . . . you can't see it in this light, but I got a split shot here, a tiny piece of lead that we'll clamp on to keep her down. And I put a teensy dot of red marker on that, too."

"What's that for?" asked Nick, leaning closer for a good look. "Do the fish see that?"

"I dunno," said Ray. "Haven't been under the ice myself lately, so I'm not sure what they see. All I know is something about this entire con-fig-ur-ation . . . catches fish. Could be what they smell on that fur skirt she's wearing. I really don't know." With that, Ray reached into his cheek for a wax worm, which he set carefully to one side.

"What is *that*?" asked Lauren, leaning back so fast she almost fell off her pail.

"A waxie. Sometimes I use mousies," said Ray.

"Baby mice?"

"Maggots."

"Oh, yuck!" Lauren was so appalled she forgot to be self-conscious.

"And the piece de re-sis-tance—" Ray pulled a small plastic container from the vest pocket of his parka. With thumb and forefinger, he plucked something tiny that he squeezed onto the hook before adding the waxie. He dangled the bait for Lauren and Nick to see. "Perch eye."

The teenagers looked on, dead serious. "Now, what you're going to do is lower the jig into the water like this, almost to the bottom."

"Okay . . . how do I know it's at the bottom?" asked Lauren.

"Because I said so. I fish here all the time, so just take my word for it. And now . . . you ever so gently . . . jig . . . like this." Ray held her arm and elbow until she had the movement correct.

"That's it, Lauren. You want to start at the bottom, then work your way up re-e-al slow . . . yeah, that's right. Keep a close eye on the line and pay attention to the *feel* of the rod because when a fish inhales that jig—the tug is very, very subtle. All you'll see is a quiver in the line, or it might move from one side to the other. When that happens, you set the hook like this," he gave a quick, gentle tug, "then let the line run and set it again. Set twice, run twice—that's the rule."

"You really think I'll catch a fish?"

"I *know* you'll catch a fish." Ray dropped his voice. "We are sitting on a ten-by-ten-foot hole full of walleye. Those jabones in that shanty over there? They think they're on it, but they missed by a couple feet. Whenever I know someone's watching me catch fish, likely planning to steal my spot, I drill a couple holes to fool the idiots.

"So, yes, you will catch a fish. The only question is how soon. Okay, Nick—you're next."

Ray was helping Nick get set up on the third hole when a loud squeal from Mason signaled the landing of a good-sized crappie. Another shout, and Cody was swinging his rod through the air. Erin ran over to keep him from hitting his sister in the face with a flapping fish.

"Ray, Ray, what do you call this?" yelled Cody, jumping up and down.

"Hey, bud, I call that something for nothing. A little piece of heaven for no money at all."

"Also known as a northern pike," said Erin, helping her son unhook his fish.

As Lauren laughed at the kids' excitement, Osborne could see her hunched shoulders relax. Concentrating with an intensity to match Cody's, she kept her eyes glued to where the line entered the water, not even darting a glance towards Nick and Ray.

Ray was slipping a perch eye and wax worm onto Nick's Hot Mama, when Lauren jumped to her feet. "I got one! I got one!"

"Okay—don't let the line go slack," said Ray, running over. "Drop that rod tip into the water—you don't want your line to catch an edge of ice and break."

Lauren tried to hand him her rod. "No, you keep it, you're doing great. Set that hook once more, good, now let it run."

Everyone from the fire gathered around to watch. "All right," said Ray, "let's coax her on in." Lauren's eyes were shining as she swung her prize up through the ice.

"You got yourself a small walleye, young lady. A little too small to keep but good work." Lauren was beaming even as Ray eased the fish back into the hole.

"That's the first fish I ever caught," said Lauren. "1 love this!"

"Bummer, Ray," Nick called from where he was perched on his pail, "I think I'm hooked on a weed. I can't move this thing."

"You probably got a stump—be right there," said Ray, helping Lauren drop a newly baited jig into the water.

"Hey, youse razzbonyas," said Ray to no one in particular as he ambled over to the frustrated Nick. "Who's not havin' fun? Mallory, would you mind pouring me some hot coffee from that thermos I got on the floor of the truck, while I help young Nick here get unhooked . . ."

"Sure thing." Mallory jumped up from her pail. Ray circled behind where Nick was sitting, yanking his line from side to side in a vain attempt to loosen the hook.

"Here, son, let me give it try." But just as Ray reached for the jigging rod, the line moved.

"Hold on, Nick . . . okay, give it a tug." Again, the line moved.

"That's no stump." Ray's voice turned serious.

Osborne never knew how *he* got over to the hole, but intuition born of fifty years of fishing had him there in an instant—just in time to see what Ray and Nick saw. The back of a creature surfaced, catching light from the fire. Black, brown, and glistening, it was a back so massive that as it moved past the hole in the ice—it *filled* the hole. Another instant and it was gone—disappearing into a swirl of dark water.

Erin and Mallory crowded in.

"Lauren, put your rod down and get over here," said Ray, keeping his voice low.

Everyone was quiet, watching as the line moved slowly from one side to the other then back again. "Okay . . . coax it . . . coax it . . . you're undergunned with that two-pound test," said Ray, "but she's yielding . . ." The eight humans stood, reverent and waiting. Another swirl and a roll of the magnificent back . . . then the hook pulled and the fish was gone.

Ray whistled. "Man, that is the *largest* muskie I have seen in my . . . *lifetime*."

"You're shaking," said Nick.

"You bet I'm shaking. That . . . that fish was fifty inches—maybe larger. Holy cow." Ray sat down onto Nick's pail with a thud. Mallory handed him a mug of coffee. "Holy cow."

"I think he ate your Hot Mama," said Nick.

"It's a she. We're lucky she didn't eat the rod. Look at me, I'm still shaking. I tell ya, Nick, if you had landed that fish? You'd have had to quit school and take a full time job just to pay the taxidermist."

"That big? Whoa! Wait till I tell the kids at school. Darn, I wish I didn't have to go to my grandmother's. That fish will be here tomorrow, right?"

"That fish will be here next summer, Nick," said Osborne. "I'll bet you anything you hooked my 'shark of the north.' I've been hunting that girl for over thirty years."

"C'mon, Doc," said Ray, "if you've been fishing her thirty years—that fish would have to be fifty, sixty years old."

"Prime of life, my boy," said Osborne. "Prime of life. Takes that long for a muskie to grow that big. You know that."

Nick looked at the two of them. "How do you know it's the same fish?"

"When you've fished as many years as I have," said Osborne. "You just know."

Twenty minutes later, as Cody and Mason began to complain about the cold, the adults decided to call it a night. This time Osborne and Mallory rode in the bed of the pickup with Lauren and Erin, letting the youngsters and Nick enjoy the blast of Ray's heaters in the front seat.

"So, Lauren," said Mallory, "what was it Nick said about Ray that he didn't want you to repeat?"

"Yeah," said Erin. "What *did* Nick say?"

"Actually, he told me this while we were waiting to board in O'Hare," said Lauren. "We were talking about our families, like how many times our parents have been married and stuff. Nick said he wished his mom had married Ray. He keeps hoping she will someday."

"That's a long shot," said Mallory.

"Why? Nick said Loon Lake feels like home. I like Ray's trailer," Lauren grinned. "It's so happy."

nineteen

The best chum I ever had in fishing was a girl, and she tramped just as hard and fished quite as patiently as any man I ever knew.

—Theodore Gordon

Osborne tiptoed through the house, making sure all the lights were off. Plunging through the cold snow along with all the excitement of catching fish had put Mason and Cody in the mood for bedtime. Tree trimmed or not, when their mother said it was time to go home, they didn't argue.

After they left, Mallory hung some of the more delicate bulbs on the upper branches. Then she, too, was ready to crawl under warm blankets. Osborne was pretty tired himself. And a little disappointed that Lew hadn't come by. He decided the tree could wait.

Spotting one last box of ornaments on the floor, he set it up on the mantel over the fireplace, where Mike wouldn't be tempted. Ever since the dog had eaten the remote control for the TV, Osborne had known better than to leave anything small, shiny, and electronic within chomping distance.

"Right, fella?" Osborne reached down to scratch behind

Mike's ears. The dog had been padding softly behind him, making sure to hoover every crumb dropped by Cody and Mason. "At least *you* love me, doncha, guy." Mike lifted soulful eyes. Oops. Osborne headed for the back door. Someone had scored too many chocolate Santas.

Just as he opened the door to let the dog out, headlights swept across the driveway. Mike bounded out barking. A few seconds later, Osborne heard the soft slam of a car door and the crunch of boots on the snow.

"Doc? What are you doing up?" Lew let herself in through the gate. "1 was sure you'd be asleep. I was planning to leave this on the back porch." As she walked towards him, she held up the shopping bag she was carrying in her right hand.

"Heavens, no, Lew, I was just reading. I've been hoping you'd stop by. Why don't you turn the car off and come on in. Have you had anything to eat?"

"Bruce and 1 grabbed a burger at the Pub. But Doc, it's so late. Golly," she checked her watch, "it's almost eleven. Really, I should get going."

"Can't you come in for a few minutes?"

"Okay." He knew right then she wanted to.

"Hot chocolate? I can microwave it—takes two minutes."

"I would love a cup, thank you."

Lew pulled off her parka and draped it over the kitchen chair. She reached into the shopping bag to pull out a small, flat box. "These are for your tree. The way things are going, I didn't think I would have time to drop by tomorrow."

Then she pulled out another box. It was long, narrow, and wrapped in silver and gold striped paper, with a big silver bow anchored to the top. "This goes *under* the tree for Christmas morning—but this little one I want you to open now."

"Marshmallows?"

"You betcha." While Lew walked into the darkened living room to slip the wrapped package under the tree, Osborne stirred the cocoa mix into the hot water. Was this the moment to deliver his own surprise? No. It wasn't even wrapped yet—and he would much prefer to have a time when they wouldn't be rushed. On the other hand, he did want her to have it for Christmas. Still . . . he decided to wait.

Osborne set the two mugs on the kitchen table. Lew sat down, then handed over the small box. Inside were four handmade wooden ornaments, each a little different version of Santa Claus.

"You made these, of course."

"Yes," she said. "These are my new designs. Just four, but I'm pretty pleased with how they turned out. I burned out on angels. I like these better." She gave him a warm smile.

He knew she loved woodworking. Winter evenings she spent in her workshop, carving walking sticks from aspen and pins from walnut in the shapes of eagles, grouse, and trout. Her work was sold in one gift shop up in Boulder Junction, and the money stashed in a savings account to be spent on fishing equipment for her grandchildren.

At Osborne's urging, she had recently begun to make miniatures of herons and beaver and cattails, securing them to pieces of driftwood. If he was lucky, the long box might hold one of her dioramas.

"Lewellyn, you look tired."

"Tired? I'm beat."

She collapsed back into the kitchen chair. "But we got a lot accomplished tonight. Bruce was able to get one of the lab pathologists up here by six, and the two of them finished up a little while ago. So I don't have that hanging over my head. Interesting results, too." She took a sip of her hot chocolate.

"Arne hiring Bud may be a mistake, but I sure am glad Pecore's out. He would have delayed this investigation seven ways from Sunday. At least now I've got an expert autopsy right out of the gate."

"So what's the story?"

Osborne sipped from his own mug, enjoying the sparkle in the eyes of the woman across from him. Why was it with Lew it always felt so good to talk shop? He had never discussed work with his late wife—and if he had, Mary Lee would have been bored to death.

"For starters, the preliminary results indicate that both male victims had significant levels of flunitrazepam, which is a drug I've never heard of—"

"It's a tranquilizer."

"You're right. Doc, similar to valium but more potent. Bruce said they've been seeing a lot of it in Milwaukee and Chicago. The street name is "roofie," and it's been a popular date rape drug for the last year or so. The pathologist spotted it right away since he's seen so much of it recently. I won't have a final toxicology report for a couple weeks but he's certain he's right. What's odd is they don't usually find it in men. And both had some water in their lungs."

"So they drowned"

"We-e-ll, they're not so sure about that. Bruce has arranged for detailed testing down in Wausau. Cause of death for one of the two, maybe both, appears to be a heart attack. Both victims showed evidence of laryngospasm."

"Heart attacks? Those are young men, Lew."

"Right. And in good physical condition. Bruce thinks they were drugged, then submerged in very cold water, which could cause the larynx to close and restrict the amount of water reaching the lungs. Then severe hypothermia, followed by irregular heartbeat and cardiac arrest. No one survives thirty minutes in water temperatures of thirty-five degrees and that's what we have around here."

"So he thinks they were dropped into a lake or a river?"

"Yes."

"And what about the mutilations?" asked Osborne, hesitant to know more. This case was taking the glow off the holiday.

"The pathologist is convinced the limbs were severed after death—*soon* after. Additional testing will confirm that. Bruce is of the opinion that the bodies were then put back in their clothing and shoved under the ice with the idea being that they would stay down until spring."

"By which time it would be assumed they had gone through by accident." Osborne was quiet, thinking. "And because everyone would assume an accident, there would be no autopsies."

"Highly unlikely. We talked about that tonight. The cost of an autopsy is prohibitive these days—over three thousand dollars. Loon Lake is not going to spend that kind of money unless we have good reason to suspect foul play. Same for the families. If you remember, Doc, I had three riders go through the ice last year. No autopsies. We assumed that any damage to those bodies was caused by natural predators. Why should this be any different?"

"Did you tell Bruce about Bud?"

"I did. He was pretty taken aback. He said if he had known, he would have applied for the job."

"Really," said Osborne, surprised.

"And I mentioned Bud's little revenue scheme, too. Bruce found that idea pret-ty darn ridiculous. He said Bud's been watching too much TV."

"I have to say I agree with him on that. But what's his take on why those bodies were mutilated?"

"Oh, Bruce is adamant on that. He said it's a calling card and he's seen it before. The legs were severed as a signal that someone has trespassed—whether that's literally or figuratively, who knows. As far as the young woman and the fact that her tongue was cut out? According to Bruce it's very simple: She said the wrong thing to the wrong people."

"Does he think the girl's murder is related?"

"No, he doesn't, but he didn't rule it out either."

"Drugs?"

"Could be, but I haven't had any reports of major drug traffic in the region since we shut down those couriers last summer. The only contraband that's been coming across the Canadian border in recent months has been five-gallon toilets." She gave a soft laugh. "I'm not too worried about that. If I had a new house and one of those new low-flush—"

Lew set her mug down quickly. "Y'know, I just thought of something. All this antique furniture that's been disappearing from the seasonal cabins and that big resort up in Eagle River? Whoever is breaking in is entering the properties from the lakeside, over the ice. And they certainly know antiques, which means someone is fairly well-educated."

"Not only that, Lew. The antique trade is sophisticated," said Osborne, "middle to upper middle-class, and you would need to be trusted in those circles to move your merchandise. You've got two victims who are certainly middle-class individuals, judging from the quality of their dental care and the fact they were in good physical condition and expensively dressed. Could be a connection. I'm curious—any estimate how much money is involved?"

"A lot. The appraisal from the resort that was robbed came in over a hundred thousand dollars. And the appraisers said that if the antiques made it to the east coast, they would be worth two to three times that much."

"So the money is there."

"Yeah," said Lew. "But going back to the victims for a minute. Whoever killed those men must have flunked physics."

"Because the bodies surfaced so soon."

"Right. Whoever dropped them should have known enough to leave the clothes off. Those snowmobile suits are terrific insulators. Not only are they resistant to wind and water, but they float."

"And they dropped them too close to shore," said Osborne. "Worse yet—too close to a spring near the shore. Everyone knows underwater springs make for a very thin ice cover. So whoever did it got the exact opposite of what they wanted: They wanted anchors, they got human bobbers."

Lew swallowed the last of her hot chocolate. "Which

knocks out our locals. I don't know an ice fisherman around who isn't aware of the potential for open water or thin ice, especially along shorelines."

"On the other hand, the same is true for snowmobilers like your victims. Too many take foolish chances."

"And," Lew said as she walked over to set her mug in the sink, "the ones who get into trouble are from the cities."

A distant drone from the lake caused both of them to turn their heads towards the windows in Osborne's living room. "That's a short list," said Lew with a snort, "like every driver out on the lakes at this moment—a few hundred at least.

"Enough of this, Doc, it's late," she said, pulling on her parka. "Did I tell you Bruce is interested in learning how to fly fish?"

"Really. And how did that subject come up?" asked Osborne, trying not to sound disgruntled. It was beginning to sound like Bruce was moving in.

"I was explaining to Bruce about underwater springs and how they affect the ice. He wanted to know how I know so much about it. That got me on the subject of spring ponds and brook trout and fly fishing. You know me, Doc. One thing led to another, and he asked me if I'd take him fishing some time.

"Hey, you, don't pout." She punched him lightly with her gloved hand. "You can come, too, of course. You've never fished a spring pond with me."

"I suppose Bruce is in your office tomorrow?"

"No, he's off until after Christmas. I promised to call him if Gina finds anything on the Palm Pilot.

"You know, " said Lew, "Bruce is very professional, but he's squirrelly. He had Marlene pull that Palm Pilot for him when I was gone. After I specifically told him that I was handling that end of the investigation. Said he had to test it for fingerprints."

"That makes sense, Lew."

"I know, I just don't like how he takes control when I'm not in the office."

That made Osborne feel a little better. He walked her out onto the back porch. "Any news from Gina?"

"Shoot!" Lew slapped her hand against her forehead. "That's what I forgot—I was supposed to check with Ray and see if she could stay at his place. And I need to know if he was able to get any information on that young woman from the girls out at Thunder Bay."

"I don't think he had a chance," said Osborne, giving her a quick rundown on Nick and Lauren's unexpected arrival. "At least he didn't say anything to me about it."

"Come along, Mike," said Osborne as he headed for the bedroom, his heart light with the memory of Lew's goodnight kiss.

Mike hesitated in front of his own bed, a round plump pad covered with fake sheepskin that Osborne had put through the washing machine that morning. Before curling up, the dog gave a good long back roll, anxious to spread his scent and reclaim his territory.

Clyde stood on the porch of an old wooden house. Beaver pelts hung from the rafters. The old man's eyes burned with anger. As if they were six shooters, he held a knife in each hand, blades pointing at Osborne, "What did I say? If they come this way again, I'll shoot 'em. This is *my* territory."

Osborne humored the old man. "C'mon, Clyde, let's go fishing."

The old man let the blades drop. His face cracked a wicked wink. "Hell with fishing, let's go to Thunder Bay."

Osborne woke with a start. The dream had seemed so real he needed to make sure he was home in his own bed. He was and the dog was. Mike was snoring.

twenty

See how he throws his baited lines about,
And plays his man as anglers play their trout.

—O. W. Holmes, "The Banker's Secret"

Osborne didn't show up at Lew's office until after one. The morning had started earlier than he expected with a six a.m. phone call from Ray.

"Yo, Doc, ready for breakfast?"

Osborne raised himself up on one elbow. He could have slept another half an hour. That plus the thought of everything he wanted to accomplish that day made him cranky.

"What do you need?"

"Not a thing. Just thought you'd enjoy some blueberry pancakes with me and the kids."

"Ray, I've got a busy day—this is Christmas Eve." Osborne waited.

Four years living next door to the house trailer with the neon green musky painted across the front had taught him to decode Ray's offers. Sautéed bluegills were payback for something borrowed without asking, while an offer of pancakes was a precursor to a request for a favor, a big favor.

"Now that you mention it, I was hoping I could borrow

your car this morning. Nick and I thought we'd drive Lauren up to her dad's place in Three Lakes, then I'll drop Nick off at his grandmother's and get the car right back to you. That open window on my truck will be hard on the kids the way the wind is blowing this morning."

"Yeah, well, you can fix that window, y'know." Osborne exacted some pleasure in not making it too easy. "A little duct tape and plastic . . ."

"I know, I know. But, Doc, I can't drive up to a multi-millionaire's house in a truck taped shut with duct tape. How would that look? Think how embarrassing that would be for poor Nick."

Poor Nick, baloney. Ray was cooking up a scheme of some kind. Much as he loved his battered old truck with its missing window and the walleye leaping off the hood, what he relished most were the looks he got when he drove up. For Ray, making an entrance was a work of art—carefully planned with precision timing. Thus, any change in costume and choreography was meaningful.

Osborne had a hunch that if he could peek through the trailer window at this moment, he would see a Ray Pradt freshly showered, closely shaven, and with his beard neatly trimmed: a man in need of a nice car. No doubt about it, he was up to something.

"Why doesn't Lauren's father come down here and pick her up? Wasn't that the plan anyway?"

"Well, ah . . ." While Ray sputtered, Osborne ran down his agenda for the morning. He had to finish trimming the Christmas tree, he didn't mind passing on coffee at McDonald's, as holiday chores meant that very few of his buddies were likely to show up, and Mallory's car was available if they did need a trip into town.

"Okay, okay, take the car. But I need it back by noon. No later."

"Love ya, man."

As Osborne rinsed and loaded the coffeepot, he mused over his neighbor's motives. Of course Ray wanted to drive up to Three Lakes. He was dying to meet a man rich enough to send his daughter to a prep school out east. Guys like that were prime client material. Not only did they book fishing guides on a full-day basis, but they often asked the guide to hold one day a week all summer long—and paid whether they used it or not. Yep, landing a client like Lauren's old man could make Ray Pradt's summer.

Maybe he was wise to play down his eccentricities until he got to know the client better. Especially in the winter when he didn't have his boat and all his fishing equipment hitched to the back of the truck. Summertime, Ray could count on his professional accoutrements to counter the wacky personal appearance.

But there was one problem with this technique for scouting new business over the winter: He needed someone else's car to do it. "I'm paying your overhead," Osborne would complain, then hand over the keys.

He did owe the man. How many nights might he have skipped the meeting behind the door with the coffeepot on the front, if Ray hadn't insisted on driving together, in his truck, window or no window. Without Ray and the AA meetings, there would be no Lew, no trout stream, no merry Christmas.

Nor was that all that he owed Ray. It was nearly three years ago now, that Osborne had called down to the little trailer desperate for help.

Nearly two feet of snow was blocking the Osbornes' driveway the night that Mary Lee's simmering bronchitis turned deadly. St. Mary's emergency room was their only hope, but a raging blizzard put it an impossible six miles away.

Forget that the woman had done her best through constant haranguing to get Ray's trailer home moved from the sight lines of her living room windows. Forget that she had called the county inspector on at least five occasions to report that his septic "technique" was highly illegal (which it was, but the inspector was a fishing buddy of

Ray's who owed him big time for the forty-seven-inch muskie mounted over his fireplace).

The intensity of Mary Lee's animosity towards Ray had escalated to a point where Osborne finally had had enough and for only the second time in their thirty years of marriage, he told his wife to "put a lid on it." Whereupon she stomped off and refused to talk to him for three days. To his surprise, they were not the worst three days of his life.

But all that was set aside the moment Osborne called. Ray did not hesitate to go out into the driving snow, bolt on his plow, and drive them into Loon Lake. He waited with Osborne the long two hours that ended in sorrow, then drove him in silence to his daughter's home. When it came to tragedy and grief, Ray Pradt did not fool around.

Osborne poured a cup of coffee and walked back through the living room to look out at the lake. A gray landscape greeted him, soft with promise that the sun was lurking somewhere. At the moment, refracted through a smother of clouds, its only influence were brushstrokes of lavender and mauve crisscrossing the icy dunes. He could feel a snowstorm hovering overhead, holding back for its own reasons.

He sipped from the hot mug. Maybe he should rethink this son-in-law thing—at least that way he could write off Ray's miles as a business expense.

The door to Lew's office stood open, and he could hear voices from the far end of the room, opposite her desk. Osborne peered in. The armchairs she used for informal meetings had been shoved back against the wall. In their place stood an oblong metal folding table and a wooden stool. A laptop computer lay open on the table.

In front of the computer was perched a slim woman in a bright red turtleneck and black pants. Two thick catalogs on the seat of her chair boosted her high enough to bring her arms level with the keyboard. One person stood looking over her shoulder. Neither she nor Lew had heard him enter, so intent were they on the computer screen.

He recognized the visitor by her cap of sleek black hair. He enjoyed the contrast between the two women: one petite and small-boned with porcelain skin that set off the black of her hair and eyes; the other much taller with a sturdy, athletic frame. Standing beside Gina Palmer, Lew's shoulders looked wider, her breasts fuller, her skin darker.

But Osborne knew that when they looked his way their eyes would share the same alert intelligence. And though the women could not be more different in their background and experience, Lew had once offered up her theory on why they worked so well together: "We're on the same wavelength. That's all. She's 'take no prisoners,' and I like that."

Osborne rapped lightly on the open door, and the two women turned. Delight spread across Gina's face as she hopped down to head his way, dark eyes snapping.

"Doc-tor Os-borne!" she said, her voice booming as she stood on her toes and reached up to give him a big hug. He'd forgotten how loud she spoke—and how fast.

"Where have you been—I got here at eleven—and where's that Ray guy? I need to give him my stuff before all my makeup freezes in my car, dammit." As quickly as she had crossed the room to greet him, she hurried back to the stool. The woman had the patience of a dragonfly.

Lew leaned back against the table, arms crossed. "I told Gina she's welcome to stay with me. I didn't know if Nick would still be at Ray's—"

"No, he borrowed my car to drop Nick and Lauren off this morning. Gina, you can stay at my place, too," said Osborne. "My daughter is visiting, but I have plenty of room—"

"Thanks, you two, but no thanks." Gina hoisted herself back up on the catalogs. "I love staying at Ray's. I can walk from his place along the lake to my own property, which I plan to do every morning while I'm up here. Take some coffee in my thermos, sit on the bank, and reflect on my good fortune."

"Oh, sure," said Lew. "Stay with Ray so you can check out your property, huh. And if I believe that, what else can you sell me?" The two women laughed.

"Hey, I'm a big girl. My honor is my business." Gina winked. "So that's settled. Now, listen, I love you guys, and I've arranged to stay till New Year's. If I can finish this up today," she pointed at a small black unit on the table next to the computer, "I'll have almost a week for fun and games in the snow."

"Chief," her voice dropped a decibel, "Does Doc know what we have here? You said he's helping with the case." Gina threw Osborne a quick glance. "I could not believe what Chief Ferris told me about this new coroner. I'll do a search later today—I know I can find documentation on how towns and municipalities the size of Loon Lake require that the coroner position be filled by a licensed medical examiner—not a political appointee. I mean—this is absurd—you could have a bartender as your coroner."

"We did—before Pecore," said Osborne. "Gina, I'm sure Lew's told you that documentation does not stand up to connections in a town like Loon Lake. I wouldn't waste the time."

"Doc, come over here and take a look," said Lew, pointing to the computer screen. "Gina's only been here since eleven, and she's already got more detail on one of the victims than I was able to get out of talking to his wife and parents."

"I downloaded his Blackberry—"

"Yeah, Bruce was wrong by the way," said Lew. "He told me this was a Palm Pilot but it's not."

"O-o-h, Mr. Answer Man was incorrect? How could that be?" asked Osborne, borrowing Ray's nickname for a type of client, always male, and always the expert on everything.

"I'm sure he meant to say it was a '*palmtop*,'" said

Gina. "This model looks a lot like one of the newer Palms."

"You're being kind," said Lew. She gave Osborne a look: She was ready for Bruce to make a mistake.

"We're lucky the poor guy was smart enough to know he had to keep his battery at a decent temperature—he had that thing wrapped so tight to keep it from freezing that it prevented any water damage. It's working great.

"And it's a recent model, the 6710, with a neat feature: It lists all his communications, phone calls, e-mails, and so on—in the same box. Here's what it's told us so far . . . the guy was a sales rep for a paper products company, and he's on the road quite a bit."

"Which I know from talking to his family," said Lew. "But not much more than that. Marlene is checking recent phone calls."

Gina's fingers moved over the keys. "We've got his appointments for sales calls, client phone numbers, personal numbers, memos on his sales calls, but the big news is the last e-mail in his inbox. Take a look, Doc."

Gina sat back so Osborne could see what she had on the screen. "It's a copy of an e-mail he received from a friend—who happens to be the other victim."

She scrolled the text slowly for Osborne to read. "So they had plans to meet up at the Thunder Bay Bar . . . and . . . is that date the day they disappeared?" asked Osborne.

"Looks like it," said Lew. "Keep reading."

"These are directions from Thunder Bay—but to where?" asked Osborne. He tried visualizing the path of the written directions, but it wasn't making sense. "Got an atlas, Lew? Let's check this route on the map."

"We think from the tone of the e-mail they were going to a party" said Gina. "The other victim was single, and he sounds excited about a plan to meet some women at a location they're going to by snowmobile."

"I understand that," said Osborne. "These are the trail signs to watch for. But what is odd is here where they are supposed to turn at a landmark and travel down to another trail sign."

"What's odd about that?" asked Gina.

"Why not turn at another trail sign?" said Osborne. "Turning at this boulder and a fork in the trail. I don't know. Maybe it makes sense when you see it."

"Something else," said Gina. "That may be the last entry, but it is not the last time someone accessed it. Someone looked at this yesterday. Your man Bruce?"

"I'm sure," said Lew. "I told him to leave it alone. Takes orders, huh."

"He just wants to know everything you know, Lew," said Osborne, secretly pleased. The way things were going, nosey-rosy Bruce was nosing his way right out of a fly fishing lesson.

"Question," said Gina, raising a forefinger. "Where's the other guy's palmtop? It's likely he had one to send this, and I'm guessing he copied those directions from another e-mail. Be nice to find out who e-mailed him."

"Nothing like that on the other victim," said Lew. "We looked through everything in the cabin he rented over on Lake Tomahawk, too. No sign of anything like this."

"Oh, so they weren't staying together?" asked Gina.

"No, the owner of this Blackberry was staying with other friends outside Rhinelander—and got in late from sales calls in Wausau, which is why they made plans to meet at Thunder Bay."

"Gina, is there a way to find out how many snowmobile riders have accidents *on* the trail versus *off*?" asked Osborne.

"Do you need an exact figure, or are you looking for a percentage? Because if a percentage is all you need, I know a quick way to do that. I'll do a random check of the accident reports of small, medium, and large papers in the state. I'll see what we get."

"We have seventeen snowmobile fatalities this year—statewide," said Lew. While they were talking, she had walked over to her desk and placed a phone call. "Is that what you're asking?"

Before Osborne could answer, she covered the mouthpiece. "Doc, do you have the time to check out those directions with me? I can have Roger deliver our department snowmobiles to a trailhead out there."

"As long as I'm home by five," said Osborne. "And, don't forget. Lewelleyn—you're expected for Christmas Eve dinner. You, too, Gina. Ray knows. He's bringing his famous pickled northern."

Lew hung up and walked around her desk. "Forget it. With this cloud cover, by the time Roger gets those snowmobiles out there, it'll be pitch black. How about first thing in the morning?"

"Christmas?!" said Osborne. "Lew, aren't you taking *any* time off?"

"Well . . . what are *you* doing?"

"Opening presents with Mallory and Erin's family at Erin's. She's planning Christmas brunch. I guess I'm free after that."

"Great, Doc. You have breakfast with your family, then meet me here. We'll be on the trails by noon when the sun is high."

"On one condition, Lewellyn—you have to show up tonight."

"I will, I will—I promise."

"I used to be Snow White but I drifted," said a deep voice from the doorway.

"Ray Pradt, you old thief you!" Gina spun on her stool, nearly knocking Osborne over. "That's a Mae West line."

"No-o-o . . . how do you know that?" asked Ray, a hurt look on his face as he lumbered into the room.

"Everybody knows that, you jerk," said Gina.

"It may be a Mae West line, but when it comes to Ray, it's accurate," said Lew. "He has indeed drifted. Care to see the file?"

twenty-one

There is no substitute for fishing sense, and if a man doesn't have it, verily, he may cast like an angel and still use his creel largely to transport sandwiches and beer.

—Robert Traver, *Trout Madness*

"You look amazingly civilized this morning," said Lew as Ray pulled one of the armchairs away from the wall, unzipped his jacket, and, like an accordion closing, folded his way down into the chair. "What's wrong?"

"Not an iota," said Ray, sliding back in the chair, extending his legs and crossing his ankles. "Life is lovely."

Ray was lovely. Osborne hadn't seen his neighbor look so spiffy in months. Was it the anticipation of meeting Lauren's father or Gina's arrival that booted him out of the smelly parka and into the trim charcoal gray Gore-Tex jacket?

"Lew's right—you look downright sartorial today," said Osborne. Under the jacket, Ray wore gray tweed Filson pants and a matching wool sweater. The rolled collar of a cream turtleneck completed the effect. "New boots, beard trimmed, hair tamed—jeez, Ray, if I didn't know better, I could mistake you for somebody with a full-time job."

"Or a funeral director," snorted Lew.

"Stop the torture, you guys. He's just trying to impress me," said Gina, beaming at Ray from her perch on the stool. "Hey, so I get to stay at your place, right?"

"You are more welcome than the flowers."

"Ray, when you finish with the charm, we need to talk," said Lew, walking over to close the door to her office. She jerked her head towards the chair in front of her desk, next to the one where Osborne was sitting. "Have you been out to Thunder Bay?"

"Just now, Chief. That's why I came in."

Ray finished smiling at Gina, then pulled all six feet five inches up and over to the chair near Lew. "I was able to talk to two of the women who work there, Laura Donaghue and Michelle Roderick. Laura tends bar, Michelle dances. Neither one knew much. Apparently Eileen was pleasant enough but kept to herself. She lived up in Ironwood and would drive down Wednesdays with this young Japanese-American fellow who runs their karaoke night.

"The two would stay overnight at the Comfort Inn, and the next morning Eileen would collect the week's receipts, take care of some ordering, then leave."

"So she was around only those two days," said Lew.

"Correct. But Laura told me something interesting. She said that over the last six months, she's had about four different patrons complain that their credit card numbers had been stolen—and they accused her of having something to do with it.

"She said it was pretty upsetting and she thought she was going to be arrested—so she confronted Eileen."

"Wait, wait, Thunder Bay—that's the strip joint, isn't it?" said Gina from the other end of the room. "Why on earth would you use a credit card out there?"

"They serve pizza and burgers," said Ray. "A group of guys come in after hunting or fishing and, with beers, they can run up a good-sized bill. I've had clients in there a number of occasions and a lot of those guys don't carry cash, everything they do is on a card. Something to do with frequent flier miles."

"So she brought this up with Eileen and—" Lew urged him along.

"Eileen was surprised. She told Laura not to worry—that she would check it out."

"How long ago was this?"

"Last time she was down—two weeks ago. Oh, and I asked Laura if Eileen had ever danced there. She kind of laughed when I asked that. She said Eileen was furious with the owners and made no bones she was looking for another job. She thought she had a handshake deal to dance for fifteen hundred a week plus tips, only to have Karin renege and tell her five hundred with tips going to the house."

"That's nasty," said Lew. "What about Karin—I take it she wasn't there?"

"She's never there. Neither Laura nor Michelle has ever even seen her."

"What did Michelle have to say?"

"She's new, only been dancing there a month, and she was hired by phone, so she's never met Karin. All she could add was that she had noticed Eileen but never talked to her."

"And the manager?"

"The manager quit right after Karin took over, and no one has been hired to replace him. Whoever tends bar has been keeping time sheets and getting marching orders from Eileen. Up until last week, Eileen would call every night to see who hadn't shown up. This is not a ritzy operation—two bartenders and one dancer weekdays, two dancers on the weekends."

"What about skimming?" asked Lew. "How does our absentee owner deal with that problem?"

"Excellent point," said Ray, raising an index finger. "I wondered the same thing. A little difficult to believe they would pick the receipts up just once a week like that.

Turns out there's a bouncer who keeps a very close eye on the cash drawer and the bartenders—"

A sudden knock on the door interrupted Ray mid-sentence. Osborne turned to a chubby face wearing lavender glasses.

"Chief, finally found that résumé. Here 'tis," said Bud, striding across the room with a jovial look on his face. He held a sheet of paper in one hand. Osborne thought of Phil's extensive curriculum vitae. What a travesty this was. He shook his head.

"Did you ask Marlene to let me know you were here?" asked Lew, her voice sharp.

"Hell, no, she had a call on the switchboard—I just came on back."

"Well . . . *Bud*," Lew stressed his name as she stood up to take the piece of paper from his hand, "when that door is closed, it means I'm in a meeting. Next time, please ask Marlene to page me and see if I can be interrupted."

"Oh? Gee, sorry if I threw you for a curve. Say, ah, Gramps asked me to pick up the reports on those two dead guys." Bud nudged his lavender glasses up the bridge of his nose, waiting.

Lew stared at him. "Arne wants those reports?"

"Yeah . . . that's what he said." Bud sounded a little uncertain.

"We won't have those for weeks, Bud," said Lew. "The toxicology tests will take two weeks at the very least."

"But we thought that—"

"Tell your grandfather that since you are not a pathologist, the official autopsy is being handled by Wausau. Quite a few of those folks are on holiday break, so the reports may be a little late.

"Just to flush it out for you, Bud," Lew's voice stayed even, "a licensed medical examiner has to sign off on the autopsy results—it's the law. By the way, I'm expecting you can be reached if we have any accidents over the holiday. You're responsible for any photos I may need. And I'm assuming you plan to be here the day after Christmas so we can go over a few things—get you set up in Pecore's old office."

"Sure thing. Gramps suggested I volunteer to help out with some of your police work, too. Maybe help cut down on the money you spend on deputies, he said."

"I hear you," said Lew. "We'll talk about that. Okay, all set?" She folded her arms and gave him a tight smile. Bud backed out of the room, closing the door behind him. Lew hurried over to be sure it was closed.

Turning around, she leaned against the door, her arms behind her, and said, "In the two years that he's been mayor, Arne has never asked to see a report of any kind . . . never."

As Lew walked back to her desk, Gina piped up, "What's all this *flushing* business?"

"It's a long story," said Lew, rubbing her forehead as if she were trying to erase a migraine. "Hardly worth getting into. I really don't expect that kid to last a month. When Arne gets the bill from the Wausau boys . . ."

"Can I see that résumé of his?" It was a rhetorical question—Gina was already at the desk, grabbing Bud's résumé. She gave it a quick scan as she walked back to her perch at the table. "I'm a whiz at background checks. Let's see if I can't put another nail in the old coffin."

"Be my guest," said Lew. She turned to Ray and Osborne. "Now where were we?"

"Let's show Ray that e-mail with the directions," said Osborne. "See if he knows the trails they're talking about."

Ray studied the printout. "Yeah, I know this area. This is right close to Clyde's place, Doc. Isn't that where you said you got your tree yesterday?"

"Yes, and I've been bird hunting in there, too. But I've never gotten far enough in to hit one of the trails."

"I know the area somewhat," said Lew. "There's a spring pond back in there where I used to fish brookies. Haven't fished it in years though."

"Here's what puzzles me, Ray," said Osborne. "Most of

that land is swamp. I can't imagine two young guys going to a party back in there. No cabins. And see where they mention a fork in the trail with a boulder as a landmark? Why turn there, why not at a trail sign?"

"Well, there's a trail marker farther down from the turn, according to this." Ray looked up. "These directions don't give you distance. Since I haven't been back in there on a snowmobile in a couple years, I can't tell you what's where without eyeballing it. You know, Doc, the clubs mark the trails, not the county or the forestry service. Some areas are just poorly marked."

"I checked the plat book in the county clerk's office this morning—no new fire numbers," said Lew.

"Yeah, well, think about it," said Ray. "Clyde's been living back in there for how many years, and he's never had a fire number."

"That's a fact," said Lew. "Absence of evidence is not evidence of absence. Well, that takes care of that. I have to check this out from the trail. Doc and I are going in tomorrow."

"Well—" Ray looked over at Gina, "let's do it together. I'll bring Gina on the back of my machine. Maybe stop over at Clyde's. If anyone knows that land back there, it's the old man."

"Suits me," said Lew. "By the way, " she added as she held a photo out towards Ray, "this is the snowmobiler who's reported missing by my Tomahawk colleagues. Since he was last seen at Thunder Bay—stayed to have one more after his buddies left—I'm supposed to find him.

"Roger said he covered all the trails under our jurisdiction yesterday and found nothing. No stalled-out machines, no signs of bad ice, nothing. Ray, does that face look familiar to you?"

"Nope. He can't be a local, or I think I'd know him."

"From Milwaukee—has a cottage on Lake Nokomis."

"So no connection to the other two victims?"

"None whatsoever. This man's friends have never heard of the victims."

"Chief," said Gina, from where she was sitting on her stool studying the page from Bud. "Interesting little item here—your new coroner did his internship at a funeral home in Rice Lake where they had a double murder last spring. The owner and his son were shot and killed by an intruder."

"How do you know that?" asked Lew.

"I saw it on the Associated Press newswire down in Chicago," said Gina. "While you were talking, I went online to be sure my memory serves me right. It's the same place.

"Our paper was doing an investigative series on the funeral industry. My special projects team worked on some of the stories. We covered Illinois and Wisconsin because there was a spike in consumer complaints on both sides of the state line. The reason I remember this name and location is because the murders occurred just before one of our reporters was due to interview the owner.

"I can pull the series sometime in the next day or two— should be able to find that particular story. Oh, and I see he lists his uncle as a reference . . . and the *uncle* runs a funeral home?"

"In Armstrong Creek," said Lew.

"May as well check that out, too," said Gina. "You won't believe the abuses we found when we did the series. Too much money to be made and very little oversight, especially when it comes to harvesting allograft tissue. And you have some major players here in Wisconsin."

Lew sat back in her chair, a thoughtful look on her face. "That's exactly what Bud talked about in the meeting yesterday—allograft tissue."

"It's the hottest thing going in the funeral business," said Gina. "Wait until you see our series. You'll know more than you ever wanted to know about commercial cadavers and stripping body parts.

"In fact—" Gina hopped off the stool and headed for the door, "I'm going to call down to the paper right now before they're all gone on holiday. See if someone can't e-mail that story to me here. At the very least, you'll have a better idea of what your Bud guy is talking about."

"So, Ray," said Lew while they waited for Gina to return, "what's your opinion of Bud?"

"Don't know him. Never saw him before today. Who is he, and where's he from, anyway?"

"Arne's grandson. Originally from Milwaukee."

"That fits," said Ray. "with that spiky hair and those purple glasses. Another jabone from the city—just what we need."

"Speaking of city boys, how was Lauren's father?" asked Osborne.

Ray's face fell. "Never met the guy. Nobody was home. Big place though. Bi-i-i-g place. Brand new. Six . . . car . . . garage. Lauren said her old man just bought a Hummer. Man, I can't wait to see that! And back behind the house he's built a huge new warehouse for his business. Whole place had to cost a damn fortune. Sorta hated to leave that poor kid there all by herself . . ."

"Ray, you hated to leave without meeting a guy with that kind of dough."

"That, too—but I felt bad leaving Lauren there all by herself. I didn't know until after we dropped her off— Nick told me that she lost her mother right about this time last year. Suicide."

"Ohhh," said Osborne, remembering the lost, shy look in Lauren's eyes. "That's hard."

Just then Gina bounded back into the room. "Okay, okay, Marlene is going to watch for the e-mail and print it out for you, Chief. Time for my reward."

"What's that?" asked Lew.

"I get to go home—I mean, go to Ray's. Take a bit of a nap and get a good hot shower in time for dinner."

"Which is at my place," said Osborne, standing up.

"Everyone here is expected at six. And, Lewellyn, that in-cludes you, y'know. I'll pick you up around five- thirty."

"Doc, no. I'll get there on my own."

"Promise? You won't back out?"

"Promise," she laughed. "I need a break."

"And I will arrive with pickled northern and Ms. Palmer in tow," said Ray.

"You're sure I'm not intruding," said Gina.

"Of course not," said Osborne. "I'll just have Mallory set one more plate." That's when Lew's eyes caught his: Oops.

twenty-two

The congeniality and tact and patience demanded by matrimony are great, but you need still more of each on a fishing trip.

—Frederic F. Van de Water

Mallory took the news of an additional guest okay—until she heard who it was. Then silence and that certain set to her jaw so like her mother that Osborne couldn't help but think: What price will I pay for this?

But the table was set with the extra place, two potatoes added to the boiling water, and the living room festive from the lights studding the tree and the flames in the fireplace. As they waited for their first arrivals, Osborne poured himself a Diet Coke from the bar he had set up on the porch. Mallory emerged from the bedroom, elegant in a black suede skirt and a black sweater.

"Well, don't you look nice," said Osborne, struck by the beauty of this child of his: her black brown hair sleeked back and tied with a red ribbon, miniature Christmas ornaments dangling from her ears, her cheekbones and eyes highlighted and glowing. "I never could get your mother to wear black, and it suited her just like it does you."

Mallory gave him a dim eye, then brushed him aside to pour herself a Coke. He got the message.

"It's not my fault," said Osborne, striving for a jovial tone. "You're the one who invited the guy. How many times have I told you—you never know who's likely to show up when you invite Ray. I've had him walk in with a couple jabones fresh out of the hoosegow. We're lucky he's bringing someone civilized." Still that set to the jaw.

"Mallory," he said, resting a hand on her shoulder, "Ray is the caretaker for Gina's property, and he has guided her muskie fishing a number of times. They have a *business relationship*. It just so happened that Lew needed her help unexpectedly, all the motels were filled, and Ray offered to do Chief Ferris a favor. Gina's a sport—she's making the best of it." That was stretching the truth, but it sounded good.

"Merry Christmas, Dad," said Mallory with a brisk clink of her glass against his before she walked quickly back to check the kitchen. She didn't believe a word of what he said.

As he watched her tie on an apron, he could hear car doors slamming and boots crunching in snow. Within seconds, Mason and Cody spilled through the kitchen door, followed by their parents. Just as that crew finished pulling off their boots, Ray and Gina arrived. The noise level escalated as Osborne carried coats, hats, mittens, and scarves to the bedroom, prepared a gin martini for Gina, Shirley Temples for his grandchildren, and opened Leinenkugel's Original Lagers for Erin and Mark.

Lew arrived, "right on time," as she pointed out, stomping her feet at the back door. He took her coat, and she followed him through the kitchen and into the bedroom. Making sure no one was standing close enough to hear, she cut her eyes towards the outer room as she said, "I caught that pout on Mallory's face. Bit of a toxic combo, those two? Mallory and Gina?"

"All parties are behaving so far," said Osborne, heaving a sigh. "But I have to say, this reminds me of that old rule: Never pet a friend's dog when your dog is watching."

"Why don't you suggest to Ray that he give Mallory a hand in the kitchen," said Lew. "He's always bragging about his mashed potatoes."

"You think that'll level the playing field?"

Lew chuckled and brushed his cheek with a kiss. "I'm just trying to get us through the evening."

A little over an hour later, the adults began to gather in the living room, each finding a comfortable spot not too far from the fire. Dinner was over, the coffee cups half full, and Osborne had turned down the lights so that the flames in the fireplace and the lights on the tree were the only illumination. Everyone seemed relaxed and content.

Mason and Cody, too excited to sit still, were banished to the porch to watch a Christmas video.

Lew was sitting on the floor near the fireplace, legs extended, her back against the stone mantel. She was dressed in dark brown corduroys and a black jacket embroidered with dark green and gold acorns. A lemon yellow turtleneck peeking through the collar of her jacket enhanced the glow of her winter tan. Or maybe it was the flames in the fireplace. Whatever it was, Osborne thought she had never looked so good. Mike agreed. The lab had snuggled in next to Lew, his head in her lap.

"So you won a Pulitzer Prize for that series? You didn't tell me *that*," said Lew, looking over at Gina who sat side saddle on the arm of Osborne's leather easy chair, the chair being occupied by Ray, immersed in a recent issue of *American Rifleman*.

"You read it already?" Gina was surprised.

"Marlene handed me the printouts as I was leaving the office," said Lew. "I had a little time to browse through before driving over tonight. Need to go back and read it more closely, but I can tell you right now it sure puts a whole new spin on this new coroner I have to work with." She paused as Osborne held out the dessert tray to select a Christmas cookie. "Thank you, Doc."

"We won several prizes," said Gina, "including the Pulitzer, all of which were awarded to the paper, not me personally. Just so you know," she laughed. "Thirty reporters and editors worked nine long months to put those stories together. My special projects team handled several."

"I couldn't help but notice it was a Milwaukee firm that seemed to be one of the major culprits," said Lew. "Are they still in business?"

"Oh yes—but they got their hands slapped," said Gina. "The irony is that almost all the managers working there have since moved on to more lucrative positions elsewhere. I'm not sure we didn't help them get those jobs. But I expect the paper will revisit the issue—check out the next boondoggle, and the same names will show up. Too much money in the tissue trade. And it is *not* going away." Gina brushed some crumbs from her lap.

"That Milwaukee company is the reason we did the series in the first place. Two college kids in Chicago, both good athletes and in excellent physical condition, died from infections that set in after simple knee surgeries. And the infected tissue came from that firm, which is a tissue processor."

"We lost a boy in La Crosse, similar situation," said Mark, who had walked into the room and leaned against the wall, listening. "Infection set in after he had ACL surgery. A good friend of a buddy of mine from law school has the case and they expect to settle for a substantial sum. I don't know who the company is that's at risk on that one."

"Oh, so you know something about this," said Gina.

"Not much," said Mark. "I understand that there's a federal law governing organ transplants but not other tissues. Correct?"

As he spoke, Mallory turned off the lights in the kitchen, where she and Erin had just finished loading the dishwasher. Entering the living room together, they found spots on the floor a comfortable distance from the fireplace. Osborne was relieved to see that Mallory was looking happier.

"Yes and no," said Gina in response to Mark's question. "The National Organ Transplant Act governs the donations and transplanting of major organs, such as the heart, kidneys, lungs, and liver. But while it bans making money off those organs, that is not the case when it comes to less glamorous stuff like bones and ligaments and skin.

"The problem is . . ." Gina took a final sip from her cup, then placed it on the saucer and set it off to the side. "The language of the law is very fuzzy. Not just fuzzy but unfortunate. It has a loophole that allows for the charging, and I quote, of *reasonable fees*—for the collection and processing of human tissue such as bone and ligaments.

"So now you have one company *collecting* tissue for a fee; another *processing* the tissue for fee. And what do you need to build your business? Tissue. *Lots* of tissue if you want to make *lots* of money." Gina folded her arms and grinned over at Mark. "You want a business model with room for abuse? You got it."

Osborne stepped carefully around the room, coffeepot readied to refill cups, but all eyes were on Gina.

"If I read your first article correctly," said Lew, "anyone can collect tissue. There's no license required, no special training—"

"The only license required is license to *steal*," said Gina. "I'm sorry, I didn't mean to interrupt, but I'm pretty passionate on this subject, Chief. Even after editing reams of copy, I can tell you I am still appalled at what we found."

Raising an index finger to emphasize her point, she said, "We tracked over five hundred funeral homes, morgues, nursing homes, *and* hospices—in addition to hundreds of medical examiners and coroners throughout

Wisconsin, Minnesota, and Illinois. You would not believe what is going on—"

"Give us an idea of the kind of money you're talking about," said Erin. "Couple thousand dollars, a hundred thousand? I'm trying to figure out why people would do this. I mean, you're talking about removing tissue from dead bodies, right?"

Gina winced. "Exactly. You sure you want to hear all this . . . on Christmas Eve?" Rapt silence greeted her question.

"O-o-kay, you asked for it. To answer your question, Erin, keep in mind I'm working from memory here. if you need accuracy, you'll have read the articles—or I can get you an update." Gina crossed her arms again.

"We did a sidebar breaking out the figures. An Achilles tendon costs a thousand, skin goes for fifteen hundred to two thousand *per square foot*, and a single heart valve can sell for as much as ten thousand dollars. When I say *cost* I mean that is what hospitals pay—that doesn't get *close* to what the patients or their health insurers pay.

"Now, on the front end, say for a heart valve, the person who harvests the tissue—the collector—makes a thousand dollars or about a tenth of what it will sell for after processing and shipping. Think about it. A thousand dollars for a heart valve? A hundred bucks for a tendon? That's a lot of money for a small funeral home or some country coroner."

"Did I hear you say bone is something they take, too?" asked Ray, *American Rifleman* lying ignored in his lap.

"O-o-h yes! Bone is a *bonanza*," said Gina with a wink. "Fortunes are being made because medical science has determined it is better to use bone than metal for hip replacements, plastic surgery, fractures of all kinds. Because it's biologically more compatible than metal, orthopedic surgeons prefer using screws, dowels, pins, even paste made from human bone. As far as the money to be made? One teaspoon of bone putty costs a thousand dollars. *One teaspoon*."

"Okay, okay," said Mark, "so let's say I'm killed in a motorcycle accident and one of my legs is severed. What's that worth?"

"Five thousand bucks minimum," said Gina. "A processor can turn a single femur, depending on condition, into ten machine-tooled allografts for spinal fusion, fifteen to twenty vials of powdered bone, and several bags of bone chips."

"What do you mean by 'condition'?" asked Lew.

"Oddly enough, when it comes to bone—the older the better. Take Dr. Osborne here. He may be worth more dead than alive."

"That's a happy thought," said Doc.

"I don't think so," said Lew. She winked at Osborne, who beamed, embarrassed, but pleased. He saw Erin and Mallory exchange grins and felt even better.

"But it is a reason I'm gonna argue with that guy from the Wausau crime lab on why he thinks those snowmobilers were cut the way they were," said Gina. "He sees one thing; I see something very different—"

"Like what?" asked Osborne, relieved to hear he wasn't the only one questioning Bruce's theory.

"I think it's just been a matter of time until we started to see crimes like this. In my opinion, those bodies were mutilated for the same reason banks are robbed, corporations inflate their earnings, and people cheat on their tax returns: greed."

The room was very quiet. The only sound was the flames crackling in the fireplace. "I can't imagine anyone up here doing something like that," said Ray. "Truly, I don't know anyone capable of such an act." He arched his eyebrows to lighten the mood. "Poaching fish is one thing—but poaching people?" No one laughed.

Lew caught Osborne's eye and held it. He gave a slight nod. He, too, agreed with Gina.

"Look, everyone," said Gina, raising her hands as if to quiet a crowd, "you may think I'm exaggerating the scope of this but hospitals are desperate. We have institutions in Chicago where the annual budgets for allograft issue, which is what we call tissue harvested after death, have grown, just within the last five years, to well over a million dollars.

"Think about it. Patients today get to choose if they want a surgeon to use tissue from their own bodies or from a cadaver. The greater percentage are likely to go for less surgical trauma to themselves and opt for allograft tissue instead. What would you do?"

Everyone nodded. Osborne wondered what *he* would do? He thought of the teeth sitting on the shelf in his kitchen. Could the same ever be true in the world of dentistry? He could not imagine such a thing—but it did make him wonder anew why someone had gone to all the effort to assemble those upper and lower plates.

"Gina," said Lew, "this harvesting, collecting, whatever you call it, is exactly what our Bud Michalski is suggesting we do here," said Lew. "Until the meeting yesterday, I had never heard that word *allograft* before. Now you're telling us this is big business?"

"Indeed it is," said Gina. "A billion dollar industry. That Milwaukee firm we talked about earlier has annual revenues of a hundred million dollars, and it is publicly traded. The problem is, these companies have way too much money to throw at lobbyists, so even though there is a drastic need for regulation, it'll be difficult to come by. You wait and see.

"The bottom line is that the tissue has to come from somewhere. I predict that until that law is changed more people will die from infected tissue because of sloppy harvesting—and more than a few families will find their loved ones' bodies stripped without permission."

"Jeez Louise," said Erin shaking her head. She glanced over at her husband. "Mark, let's make sure the kids don't hear any of this. Talk about nightmares . . ."

Everyone laughed a little nervously, then waited for Gina to say more. Looking around his living room, Osborne didn't see a room full of young adults: He saw kids at a campfire bewitched by ghost stories. All except Lew. Her features, so soft and relaxed earlier, had tightened, gaining the flintiness that had a way of intimidating men twice her size.

"This new coroner who has been *appointed* to work with me," she said, making it clear he was not her choice, "this guy said that the human body, deceased, can be worth as much as $272,000. He wants Loon Lake to approve his collecting—and selling—allograft tissue from any unclaimed or unidentified bodies. Since his grandfather runs the town, chances are good that may happen."

"Whoa, hold on a minute," said Ray. "Think about this . . . the holidays," he waved his right index finger, "are *the* busiest time of the year for the cemetery. Bless their hearts, people hang on through Christmas, then . . . check out just in time to avoid the traffic jam on New Year's." Everyone groaned. "I'm not kidding. More people die over the holidays than any other time of the year.

"And . . ." again the finger waved, "it so happens Jeff Cornell left me a message yesterday that he needs at least five graves dug as soon as this cold weather eases up. Meanwhile, they've got that nice little mausoleum where the caskets . . . with our dearly departed . . . are stored until we can get the ground ready. Now . . . at five times $272,000, are you telling me that Duff has the equivalent of 1.4 million dollars stacked in that brick cooler of his?"

Gina shrugged. "You can look at it that way."

"Then forget the grave gig—I should be a security guard!"

"Actually—aside from your mastery of bad taste, Ray," said Gina, "you're not that far off the mark."

"Gina," said Lew, "what's your take on Bud's proposal? I find it unsettling."

"I am not surprised," said Gina. "That funeral home he lists on his résumé—the one where he did his internship? They were players in the business—they were making serious money harvesting allograft tissue. He certainly got his training in the right place."

"But it *is* legal," said Osborne. "You said that. You said that federal law allows this."

"Yes, but what the law allows and what actually happens are two different things," said Gina. "And that's where it gets interesting.

"For one thing, the window for healthy harvesting is brief—preferably within an hour or two of death. However, collectors are allowed twenty-four hours for recovery, packaging, and shipping to processors. But there is no monitoring of the time spent, no way to be sure the recovery didn't occur eighteen hours after death, twenty-three hours. No way to be sure the tissue is handled safely after the recovery either.

"Nor are there any mandated controls over who can collect allograft tissue. It could be temporary help making less than minimum wage. Could be a funeral director's kid, could be a nursing home aide, could be a country coroner, whose day job is auto repair.

"Here's an example of what can happen. Our investigations turned up six cases of life-threatening bacterial infections in knee surgeries after patients were given donor knee tissue from a cadaver. Three of those people died, and each of those three had received their donor tissue *from the same donor.*

"What went wrong? That tissue was harvested at a funeral home by a part-time worker for the owners. He collected it late, way later than two hours after death, and he did not handle the tissue in a way that would keep it germ-free.

"It goes without saying that this was also a person who was in no position to know if the deceased might have had an undiagnosed condition, such as cancer, TB, or some fungal or bacterial infection that might have infected that tissue.

"By the time we went to press with the last articles in our series, we had *fifty-four* reports of bacterial contamination leading to infections—and all from allograft tissue. And all from our region." Gina leaned forward to emphasize what she was about to say. "Think about the rest of the country."

"I don't understand," said Mark. "Isn't there a consent form that must be signed by family members before any organs are donated? Or have the people you're talking about found some loophole there, too?"

"Mark, to say those consent forms are obfuscatory is hardly an exaggeration. Families are grieving, they are not reading small print. When they see that consent form, they think *donation*. They see donating as a way to turn the loss of their loved one into something positive, a way of keeping their memory alive. Yet rarely are they told how much will be harvested and to what extent the donated tissue will be commercialized."

"*Commercialized*," said Lew. "Now there's a word our new coroner didn't use—not that I could recognize anyway."

"Commercialized is what it's all about," said Gina. "Families sign off on donating skin, thinking that it will be used for burn victims, right? But it's much more profitable to sell skin for cosmetic surgery. And what did our reporters discover are the most popular uses for donor skin in today's market? Lip jobs and penis enlargements."

Again the room groaned. Gina threw her hands out, saying, "I kid you not. The demand for skin is so high that we found one coroner who would get the consent form signed by the family, then rush to the phone and hold a bidding war between his two major processors."

"Jeesh," said Mark, shaking his head.

"Oh—and they hide behind the loveliest names, these processors," said Gina. "The Ministry Tissue Bank, Central Wisconsin Tissue Center, Heart of America Tissue Bank. Don't they sound like nonprofits? So you can see how families are fooled."

"As I said, this is a billion-dollar industry. In less than two years, the number of companies collecting and processing allograft tissue went from 118 to over 400. And the number of people angling for jobs as coroners and medical examiners these days has skyrocketed."

"Hence I get handed the beautiful Bud Michalski," said Lew. "I should have known Arne would have an interest beyond sentiment."

"Keep an eye on those two," said Gina. "Kickbacks are rife in this business. Kickbacks, secret arrangements between hospital employees and tissue collectors—"

Mallory, who had been silent while Gina held center stage, spoke up from where she was sitting on the floor. "Has it occurred to you that your paper may have won the Pulitzer partly because this is such morbid and sensational material? She said. "Great for marketing, right?"

Osborne didn't like her tone.

"We certainly had people upset that we reported some very gruesome stuff in a family newspaper," said Gina, her voice even, but her eyes sparking.

"I think it verges on a kind of pornography," said Mallory.

Gina gazed over Mallory's head for a second. Then she said, "I'd like to say we won the highest award in journalism because we were willing to show—and we needed those details you find so morbid in order to make the point—that right now is the time to demand changes in the National Organ Transplant Act. Someone has to act *in order to save lives.*"

"But this is all about harvesting from the dead," said Mallory.

"Sure," said Gina, "but what happens when orders are up and you don't have enough cadavers from which to fill those orders?"

Osborne's phone rang. He reached for the handset on the lamp table in the corner. "Don't worry, he's right here—I'll let you talk to him."

Osborne handed the phone to Ray. "It's Nick. He sounds upset."

Ray listened, then sat up straight in the chair. "I'll be there in five. Now settle down, I'm sure we'll find her.

And Nick—dress warm." He handed the phone back to Osborne.

"Nick just had a frantic call from Lauren's father. She's been missing since noon."

twenty-three

She was now not merely an angler, but a "record" angler of the most virulent type. Wherever they went, she wanted, and she got, the pick of water.

—Henry Van Dyke

"Where do I turn?" asked Osborne. He glanced towards the backseat, where Nick sat crammed between Ray and Mallory. Even with Ray's reassuring arm around his shoulders and Mallory patting his knee as if he was six instead of sixteen, the boy appeared close to tears.

Gina had insisted they drop her off at Ray's first. She was exhausted. Erin and Mark had been more than happy to hustle the kids home and off to bed, especially with Santa under pressure to assemble a new bicycle before dawn. Osborne had tried to persuade Lew to go home as well. "Call in Roger or Terry to help us search," he'd said. "You need a good night's sleep."

"Terry has today and tomorrow off, and I can't call Roger out tonight," said Lew. "He worked until two this morning—a bar fight. Plus, it'll cost me overtime. I'm salaried, I'll go."

At the look on Osborne's face, she said, "Doc, I'm not

as tired as you think, so don't argue with me. I'm down to the wire on the budget for this fiscal year, and any overruns now will just give Arne ammunition. The last thing I need is Bud assigned to the department."

With Lew giving Osborne the go-ahead to do seventy down the county road, they were able to reach the driveway to Nick's grandmother's home in less than ten minutes. He was waiting on the curb.

"Take Chicken in the Basket Road up to XX, and your first right on Y," said Ray.

"Man, is this forsaken territory," said Mallory, peering out the car window into the dark. "I don't know that I've ever been back in here."

"Lots of big houses going up on these lakes," said Osborne, keeping his voice matter-of-fact in an attempt to soothe Nick's nerves.

"Tell you what I don't understand," said Lew. "If this girl has been missing since noon—why didn't her parents report it earlier?"

The car swung onto a snowpacked Chicken in the Basket Road, and Osborne slowed. Nights like this with a dusting of new snow on the slick surface made the curves treacherous. He had noticed during the thirty-minute drive north that it was snowing more heavily now. At last the weatherman was accurate.

"Her dad said he just assumed she drove down to see me," said Nick. "When she wasn't home by seven thirty, they got worried. He said they're having a big party tonight, so he and her stepmom were running around all day. When she wasn't in her room, he checked to see what car she took—but all the cars were there."

"That's one heck of a big house," said Ray. "I'll bet you anything she's tucked away in a corner somewhere reading a book."

"Or on the Net. She loves games and eBay," said Nick, hope brightening his face. "You could be right. She could be gaming and just lost track of time."

"What's eBay?" asked Lew.

"This big Internet auction site," said Nick. "Lauren thinks that Ray should sell his Hot Mama on eBay. Could be she's checking out the sites selling fishing lures . . ." His voice trailed off. Mallory patted his knee again.

The road twisted back past silhouettes of pine and hemlock so towering that Osborne knew this had to be an area of first-growth timber, one of those rare parcels of land to survive the logging boom of the late 1800s. Some lumber baron must have saved it for use as his private forest preserve, then passed it down to future generations.

If all this belonged to Lauren's family, speculated Osborne, it would be extremely valuable property—and devoid of neighbors. He did not like the idea of a girl with limited outdoor skills wandering through a forest this deep and unpopulated.

"Does Lauren know how to use a compass?" he asked Nick.

"I have no idea. I doubt it."

"Slow down, Doc," said Ray, "I think the road to the house is right around the corner. Yep."

Osborne turned onto a recently plowed lane. "Where the heck are we, Ray?"

"Firefly Lake. Private water. Remember Glen Schraufnagel? He used to fish bass up here. I snuck in a couple times to fish it with old Glen, got some good-sized crappies. I heard they got monster walleye, too. I'll have to give it a try one of these days."

Osborne was relieved to hear Ray was somewhat familiar with the area. Lew might complain, and the wardens might cite, but there were times when Ray's penchant for poaching came in handy.

A soft glow in the distance morphed into strands of diamonds sparkling under pillows of snow, the strands lacing their way along a low wooden fence towards a portico outlined with millions more of the tiny jewels. Parked cars crowded both sides of the drive.

"How absolutely lovely," said Mallory, her voice soft

with amazement. "Now who would ever expect to find this stuck out in the boondocks?"

"Mr. Theurian said we should go around to the back," said Nick as they neared the blazing lights. "He's waiting for us."

Osborne's car pulled around to the back of the contemporary brick and glass structure and into a paved, circular area between the main house and a six-car garage. A slight figure in gray slacks and a black sweater stepped out onto a wide, well-lit deck. The man waved the car forward, then hurried towards them as everyone got out.

"You're fine—just leave the car there," he said.

Lauren's father was fair-haired and balding with serious, slightly bulbous eyes set into a head as square as that of a purebred Labrador retriever. A pale brush of a moustache hid his upper lip. In coloring and stature, he bore no resemblance to his tall, lanky daughter.

Extending a hand as they hurried through introductions, he said, "Dave Theurian. Thank you so much for coming. My wife and I are worried sick."

But if he seemed relieved at first, his eyes widened when Lew introduced herself as chief of the Loon Lake Police Department, and Osborne got the distinct impression he was suddenly less grateful than alarmed. Osborne shrugged it off. The seriousness of the situation had to be just dawning on the guy.

"Chief Ferris and Ray know—" said Nick.

Before he could continue, the door to the deck banged open and a diminutive figure whirled towards them, feet flying down the stairs. At first glance, she reminded Osborne of the Christmas angel. She wore a full-sleeved ivory blouse over a long, wine red skirt of some crinkly, rich-looking fabric. A gold buckle on a wide black belt cinched the small waist, and Osborne half expected to see a jeweled tiara nestled in the froth of white gold curls. He didn't need Mallory to tell him those were diamonds in the chandeliers dangling from the woman's ears.

She was a Scandinavian beauty: her features fair and

fine-boned. But the face under the blond fluff was flushed at the moment, so ruddy it matched the burgundy of her skirt. And her eyes belied any delicacy in demeanor: They were large, dark, and demanding.

"I don't need this right now," she said, as if Lauren's absence was their collective fault. "I've got sixty-two guests to entertain, and I know that . . . that . . ." she struggled to restrain herself, "I know my stepdaughter did this on purpose. She's not lost, goddammit, she's hiding.

"I'm sorry you came all this way, but it is absolutely not necessary. She'll show up just fine once she's sure she's ruined the evening. Dave's overreacting."

Her voice was low-pitched and throaty, as sensuous as her face. No matter that the emotion driving her was anger, she was a stunning-looking woman. Though the anger did prompt Osborne to refine his first impression: Forget the Christmas angel, this was the Queen of Spades.

Lew stepped forward. "Mrs. Theurian, just to be sure, we'll take a look around. With this cold weather, we will all feel better once we know your stepdaughter is safe and warm. As the head of law enforcement for this region, I do need to follow procedure. My deputies and I cannot leave until we know the situation is under control."

"The police?" The woman whirled on her husband. "You called *the police*?"

Theurian raised both hands in a gesture of helplessness. "I called Lauren's friend Nick. I thought maybe—"

"Look, folks, it's late, it's Christmas Eve, and we all have places we would rather be," said Lew, her voice loud and firm. "We'll double-check the interior of the house and canvass the perimeter—"

"No need. I already checked every goddam room. She is *not* in the house," said the woman, spitting out her words.

"Mitten, will you please calm down," said Theurian. "Look, if I can locate Lauren, the party will be much more enjoyable for all of us. So please, go back to our guests and let me handle this."

"I told you I checked everywhere, and I don't want strangers in my home."

"Mitten . . ."

As quickly as she had arrived, the woman spun around and dashed back up the stairs. Theurian watched until she had slammed the door behind her.

He turned back to face them, his voice calm, almost gentle, as he spoke. "I disagree with my wife. Lauren's not a spiteful kid. She's just wandered off somewhere in this big place of ours and doesn't realize we've been counting on her to help us entertain our friends."

"And who are these people?" asked Lew, indicating the cars parked up and down the drive.

"Our church group—we're hoping to go caroling at midnight. I was just made a deacon, so we're celebrating with friends and the church choir. No one Lauren knows—at least not yet."

"Well, we *should* check the house," said Lew. "You have no idea how many missing people we find working in the basement or asleep in front of the TV—after the family insists they're not home."

"Then let's do it," said Theurian, leading them up the stairs. "You'll find this house to be a little different. My late father-in-law was a bit of an eccentric. He designed it as a series of linked pavilions—each one is a suite with its own bath and sitting rooms. And each pavilion has its own interior and exterior entries, which we try to keep locked. I'll get the master key to save time."

He paused. "Do you think we might avoid the center hall and the main lodge where the party is?"

Poor guy, thought Osborne, what he really means is: "Can we avoid my wife?"

"I see no problem with that," said Lew, letting him off the hook.

Once inside the back foyer, a utility room outfitted from floor to ceiling with handsome cherry cabinets, Theurian pulled a ring of keys from his pocket and used one to open the top drawer of a counter running along one wall. The drawer held a white plastic box divided into squares, each containing a key.

"Jeez," said Ray, "that's one heck of a lot of keys. Your father-in-law must have been paranoid."

"He was detail oriented," said Theurian, "and we do use these, but it's a pain. We're installing a computerized security system that will make life easier, but it requires some major rewiring. Until that's up and running, we have to make do with these."

He selected a key, then pointed to the door at the far end of the foyer. "We have five pavilions opening off that center hall. Two are bedroom suites, one for my wife and me, the other for Lauren. We use the other two for offices—my wife has her own business—and the fifth is our media room."

"Basement?" asked Lew.

"Main basement is under the lodge. The others have insulated crawl spaces for heating and air-conditioning units. The suites are locked this evening. With so many people here, we thought that was a good idea. We can't risk someone toying with the computers." He looked chagrined, as if that might not have been his idea.

"Are you saying that Lauren is locked out of her room?" asked Lew.

"She should have a key."

"And the outer buildings," said Ray. "We'll need keys for those?"

"I know she's not in the warehouse," said Theurian. "That's been locked since yesterday. You'll want to check the garage, of course."

"What about your dock and the waterfront?" asked Lew. "Do you have a boathouse? Any cabins near the water?"

"No," Theurian said, shaking his head. "Only my ice house—and I can't imagine why she would go out there." He reached into the drawer for two more keys, which he handed to Lew. "This opens the garage—and this is for the ice house."

Lew handed them both to Ray. "You and Doc check the outer buildings, please—take Nick with you. Mallory and I will do the house. Mr. Theurian, do you mind coming with us?"

The man looked relieved to be included. "Not at all, but if you'll excuse me one minute, I'll let the caterer know where I am if someone needs me." He walked through the door to the center hall, leaving it ajar behind him.

Ray opened the door to the outside. "First thing we need to do is check for any tracks leading away from the house—before this new snow makes it difficult."

twenty-four

God never did make a more calm, quiet, innocent recreation than fishing.

—Isaak Walton

Pristine snow greeted the three as they trudged the perimeter of the Theurian property. The only footprints leading in and out of the forest belonged to deer, squirrels, rabbits, a fox, and other assorted wood rodents. If Lauren left the house on foot, she had to have used the road or headed across the lake.

They tackled the buildings next. Even though Theurian had said the warehouse was locked, Ray went straight to the building with the "Theurian Resource Systems" sign across the front. "The minute you tell a kid 'don't go there,' that's exactly where they want to be," he said.

"No one knows that better than you," said Osborne. But Theurian was right. Both the front double doors and a side entry were locked, as was a rear loading dock. Ray banged on each, but they heard no response from inside.

The vast, L-shaped garage was unlocked and silent. Not empty. Two red Hummers, a spotless Honda Pilot SUV, and four gleaming 700cc Yamaha SRXs were squeezed into the six stalls. The wall alongside the snowmobiles was outfitted with hooks holding snowmobile suits and shelves with helmets, gloves, and goggles.

"Lauren didn't tell me that her dad owned *these*," said Nick, hovering over the snowmobiles and sounding like he had just found a good reason to visit more often.

"Those machines go from zero to sixty in less than three seconds," said Ray, his eyes as big as the teenager's. "I've seen 'em do it. They're quiet, too. No fumes. Four-stroke engines do make a difference. Too bad they cost so much."

Back up on the deck, Osborne tried each of the dozen light switches on a panel just inside the back door. The last one worked, throwing light down the path to the lake, along the entire length of the dock, and pooling out towards the snowmobile trails. From the dock, it was easy to see the wooden structure Theurian called his ice house.

Ray got there first. He tried the doorknob, then looked back at Nick and Osborne. "Unlocked," he said. He pushed the door open.

"Hel-l-o . . ." said Ray, stepping inside. Nick and Osborne crowded through behind him. Silence. The room was pitch black. Osborne fumbled along the wall to his right, more out of instinct than logic. His gloved fingers found a switch, and the room exploded with light.

A narrow table holding wildlife carvings blocked their way. Just beyond that was the back of a sofa, which faced a circular glass coffee table. Along one wall was a bar with stools and a small TV suspended overhead. Measuring about ten by fourteen feet and surprisingly warm— they were standing in a miniature version of any suburban family room.

As Osborne's eyes adjusted to the bright light, a head of matted dark hair rose slowly from the sofa. Pushing her bangs back from her eyes, Lauren blinked sleepily, then stared.

"Omigod, Nick, what are *you* doing here?" She scrambled to her feet, her eyes searching their faces.

"We've been looking for you," said Nick. "Your dad

called me thinking you were at my place. When I said you weren't, your mom and dad thought you were lost."

As Nick talked, Ray stepped outside to shout the news up to the main house.

"*Who* called you? Had to be my dad, right?"

"Yeah—I called Ray to help out, and Dr. Osborne came along, too."

"Lauren, your family has been worried sick," said Osborne.

"Gee," said Lauren, "I didn't mean to upset everyone."

"So what's the deal with this place," said Nick, looking around the room. "What the heck are you doing out here?"

"Hiding from my dysfunctional family," said Lauren with a thrust of her chin. Osborne thought he saw a sly grin appear and vanish. "You would, too, if you were stuck out here."

Pointing at Ray who had just walked back into the room, she said, "It's all his fault. Right, Ray? Didn't you say when the world gets you down, go fishing."

"Guilty as charged," said Ray. "But this isn't exactly what I had in mind. You have to tell people where you're going, y'know."

Just then Theurian appeared in the doorway. He rushed around the sofa to grab his daughter by the shoulders. "Lauren! Honey! Where the heck have you been all this time?"

She twisted away in embarrassment. "D-a-a-d, I told you I was going fishing. I guess I fell asleep."

She bent over the coffee table and lifted it up to expose a neat circle of open water. What had appeared to be glass was a plastic cap-like unit, flat on top and designed to cover the fishing hole cut into the ice beneath the house. Lying on the plush beige carpet near the hole was a jigging rod rigged with Ray's Hot Mama. Also on the rug were two of the biggest walleyes Osborne had ever seen.

"What do you think, Ray?" asked Lauren as Ray knelt to hoist the fish.

"Twelve, maybe thirteen pounds each—these are trophy fish, girl."

Theurian glanced at the fish then back at his daughter. "Lauren, do you have any idea what time it is? It's nearly ten o'clock at night. I've been looking for you since noon."

Lauren gave her father a sharp look. "That's not true, Dad, and you know it. You didn't even get back to the house until four." The challenge in the girl's voice startled Osborne. He shot a quick glance over at Ray, but his neighbor was on his knees in the far corner of the room, lifting another patch of carpet to examine the flooring beneath.

"So how many holes can you have in here?" asked Ray, trying his best to change the subject.

"If you *had* checked at noon," said Lauren, hands on her hips. "You would have found me down in the basement doing my laundry. And if your *wife* said she didn't know where I was, she lied. She's the one who made me do it. But, Dad, I *told* you I was coming out here this afternoon."

"If you did, I didn't hear you," Theurian said, looking defeated. Osborne felt sorry for the guy. With a highstrung bride and a resentful daughter, he had his hands full. Not even money could buy him out of this pickle.

Lauren kicked at the sofa. "Well, you found me—okay? It's not my fault you never listen."

While the two argued, Nick fiddled with the TV over the bar. "Holy cow, you got cable out here," he said. "HBO, too?" No one heard the front door open.

"Drinking . . . *again*?" Mitten Theurian, a black coat thrown across her shoulders, loomed over the sofa. For such a small woman, she had the presence of a moose.

"I certainly was not," said Lauren, throwing her shoulders back. It was the first time Osborne had seen her stand up straight.

Mitten leveled an accusing finger at a cluster of empty beer bottles on the bar. "What do you call *that*?"

"Those are not mine and . . ." Lauren stopped as if she thought better of what she had been about to say.

"Just how long have you been hiding out here anyway?" demanded Mitten. Lauren didn't answer. Osborne couldn't tell if she didn't remember or was ignoring the question. Mitten waited, her eyes boring into the girl. No one said a word.

"I came out here . . . I guess about . . . three? After I folded my clothes," Lauren said, her voice firm. "I wasn't *hiding*, I told Dad that I was coming out here to fish with this special lure that Mr. Pradt gave me. See?" She pointed to the fish, which Ray had laid back on the carpet. "And I took a little nap—"

"Oh, right," said Mitten with a sneer. "Fishing. Give me a break. Since when do you fish? Tell the truth, for once, young lady. You did this on purpose. Anything to get attention." As she spoke, Lew and Mallory appeared in the doorway.

"And I just hope you're happy—you've almost ruined our party. Now get those damn fish off my rug before you ruin that, too. I tell you, David, she does these things just to annoy me."

Theurian took a step away from Lauren, his shoulders hunched, as if ducking objects instead of words. "Mitten . . ."

"Don't 'Mitten' me—I've had it. She's your kid, you deal with it." Mitten spun around to leave, knocking Lew in the shoulder as she barged out the door.

"Don't worry about Mitten," said Theurian. "She sounds mad but she was worried, too. I'm just glad you're okay, sweetheart." He gave his daughter another affectionate squeeze of the shoulders.

Lauren resisted the hug but offered her dad a slight smile. From where he was standing next to Ray, Osborne could see her face was smudged, her eyes red and glassy. She might have been drinking—or crying—or both.

"I just don't understand how you could nap so long," said Theurian. He walked over to the windows on one side of the room. Opening their shutters, he exposed the main house with all its lights ablaze. "Couldn't you see our party had started?"

"I didn't notice those shutters were closed, Dad," said Lauren. "They must have been closed when I got here."

"Mr. Theurian, a fatigued teenager is capable of sleeping through *anything*," said Lew, walking into the room. "A train could come through here and not wake her up. I know, I raised two."

"That's right. I took a long nap this afternoon myself," said Nick. "We had that layover so long in Chicago and stayed up pretty late at Ray's place, y'know. We were already tired from finals—"

"Okay, okay, let's put this behind us. Just don't do it again," said Theurian, reaching up with his knuckle to give Lauren's cheek a friendly nudge. He had to be close to three inches shorter than his daughter. Osborne found that interesting: Lauren's mother must have been quite a bit taller than Mitten.

But if wife number two was less imposing than her predecessor in height, she more than made up for it. In contrast to her mild-mannered spouse, the woman was a velvet hammer. Still, she was stunning, and opposites do attract. Osborne could see Theurian seduced by her beauty and if his money helped seal the deal—well, it ought to buy something.

As Osborne speculated on Theurian's love life, a soft smile had worked its way out from under the man's moustache. "I suggest you move the fish like Mitten said—but those *are* nice, Lauren. Congratulations. I had no idea you were so talented a fisherman."

"Not me, Dad—Mr. Pradt. He made this lure himself." Lauren dangled the Hot Mama in her father's face. "You should try it, see if it works for you."

"I gotta tell ya, Dave," said Ray, using the mention of his name as a cue to enter the conversation, "this is one heck of a fishing shack." He looked up from where he was bent over rummaging through a cabinet behind the bar. "Got something in one of these cupboards she can put those fish in? Never mind—here's a plastic bag. Dave, you clean fish?"

The look on Theurian's face made everyone laugh.

"Tell you what, Lauren," said Ray, "I'll take these home and clean 'em up for you. You bring your folks down for a fish fry sometime in the next couple days. Would you like that?"

"Dad? Can we do that—please?"

"We'll see. Your stepmother has lots of plans."

"So, Dave, how long have you had this . . . this *house* out here on the ice?" said Ray.

"Couple weeks," said Theurian. "I don't know what Lauren thinks she's doing with that silly thing you gave her, because this place is outfitted with everything an ice fisherman could ever need. Take a look." Theurian turned around to open the doors of a light oak armoire that took up the entire back wall.

"I've got a Vexilar electronic depth finder, underwater cameras, a Strike Master auger for anyone who insists on fishing outside, a dozen tip-ups, and boxes of the best tackle on the market. Oh, and we've got more plastic bubbles up at the main house if you want to open a few more holes in the floor."

He pointed across the room. "That sofa converts to a queen-size bed so you can sleep out here, we put a port-a-toilet out back for the ladies, and there's a generator to run the show." Theurian smiled as he thrust his hands into his pockets, "What more can you ask for?"

"My Hot Mama," said Ray. He raised his right palm in defense. "Just kidding—with a set-up like this you must be one heck of an ice fisherman."

"'Fraid not," said Theurian, shaking his head. "This is for clients, strictly for entertaining. I've got a start-up business to manage—I don't have time. Tell you the truth, my wife put all this together."

"Doc," said Lew, "now that we know Lauren's okay, we should get going. It's late."

"Oh no, you don't," said Theurian, walking around to give everyone's hand a hearty shake. "Before you go, I want you up to the main house, get everyone a hot toddy, some mulled cider—a little something to munch on. We have quite a spread up there."

"I don't know about that," said Osborne.

"Another few minutes won't hurt, will it?" said Theurian. "It's the least I can do to thank you for coming out tonight."

From the expression on Mallory's face, Osborne could see there was no way she would leave now. Even Lew looked interested. Lauren, meanwhile, had pulled on a jacket and was gripping Nick's arm, whispering in his ear.

As she whispered, she turned her back to the group, pulled a small object out of her jacket pocket and offered it to Nick. He studied it for a moment, then shook his head as if to say "no." In spite of his response, Lauren pushed whatever it was into Nick's pocket anyway. Osborne hoped it wasn't what he thought it was.

Ray turned around from the armoire, where he had been examining Theurian's high-tech fishing gear. He held a package in his hand. "You got the Loch Ness Monster in this lake?" he asked.

"'Course not, why?"

"This fishing line is made of steel. You could reel in a sumo wrestler on line like this." Ray tossed the box back into the cabinet. "No way you need five hundred pound test line on a little lake like Firefly. Sheesh, what some jabones will sell ya. Next time you need equipment, Dave, you call me. I can get you top of the line and at an excellent discount, too."

"He will, indeed," said Mallory, chiming in merrily as she pulled on her mitts. "And don't stop with the fishing equipment. You need a burial plot? Ray's your man. He can get you a deal on that, too. Right, Ray?"

A funny look crossed Theurian's face. Rarely did Osborne wish he could put a lid on his daughter like he did at this moment. Razzing Ray was one thing, and, of course, she had no way of knowing what Ray had told him earlier—that Lauren's mother died just over a year ago. Ouch. He tried to send her a warning look, but she was already out the door.

"Sorry about that crack Mallory made a minute ago," said Osborne, hanging back with Theurian as he flicked off the lights and locked up the ice house. "She doesn't know about your late wife . . . she didn't intend anything in bad taste."

"No offense," said Theurian, "but I don't get what she's talking about."

"My neighbor is a man with an unusual career path," said Osborne, anxious to keep Ray's professional profile unblemished. "Even though he is considered by many to be the best fishing guide in the northwoods, it can be tough financially in the off-season or during spells of bad weather—so he takes on odd jobs.

"He shoots nature photos for a local calendar printer, traps leeches for several bait shops, runs a snow removal service during these winter months—and he helps out with a backhoe at the Catholic cemetery in Loon Lake."

"Oh, yeah? Digs graves? How the heck do you do that in weather like this?" asked Theurian, hurrying along in the cold air. He was not wearing a jacket.

"It's a challenge," said Osborne. "But Ray doesn't seem to mind. He made enough last summer and this fall from his grave-digging operation to buy a new ice shanty. Not quite the home away from home you've got, but state of the art for the average guy fishing hard water.

"You know, you really ought to come down with your daughter and let Ray fry up that fish she caught," said Osborne. "You haven't tasted walleye til you've tasted Ray's."

"I'd like to do that," said Theurian, causing Osborne to nearly drop his teeth. "I'll get directions before you leave tonight. Just myself and Lauren. She's right, I've neglected the poor kid. It's been hard since—"

"I know all about it," said Osborne, giving Theurian an

understanding pat on the shoulder as they caught up with the group nearing the dock. "I lost my wife three years ago."

"Lauren," said Nick, as he hopped up onto the dock, "could we . . . would your dad mind if I took one more look at those amazing snowmobiles?"

"'Course not," said Lauren, veering towards the garage. "Dad, we'll be right there."

"I'd like a better look at those, myself," said Ray, following the two teenagers. "Me, too," said Osborne. "Do you mind, Dave?"

"Be my guest, boys," said Theurian, trudging up the path towards the main house behind Lew and Mallory. "Don't take too long, Lauren, I have friends I want you to meet."

"Doc, you know how much these muscle sleds cost?" said Ray, rocking back on his heels in front of the Yamahas. "Take a guess."

"Five, six thousand?" said Osborne.

"Try eighty-five hundred each. Now multiply that by four, add two Hummers and a brand-new SUV, and I kid you not—Dave is loaded big time." Osborne wanted to poke him. Lauren was standing right there.

"Yeah, well, you think my dad spends money? She spent twenty-five thousand decorating that ice house," said Lauren. "But I have to show receipts for every pair of jeans I buy.

"See this," she yanked at the sleeve of an electric blue jacket hanging from a hook behind her. "She dropped fifteen hundred on this snowmobile suit and another five hundred so she could have a stupid matching helmet." Everyone stared at the offending blue helmet resting innocently on a shelf beside the suit. "Yep, five hundred dollars for that goofy thing," said Lauren.

"Hey, Lauren, you're not the first person with this problem," said Ray. "New step-people never get along. It takes time."

"She hates my guts."

"A machine like this will do one-twenty easy," said Ray, pretending not to hear Lauren's remark. "But don't you let me catch you two going that fast. Chief Ferris'll shove you in the slammer if you do over fifty."

"On the lake? Can't you go faster out there?" asked Nick. "I swear I see guys doing a hundred on my grand-mother's lake."

"Lauren, will you be riding one of these?" asked Ray. The girl shrugged, a petulant look on her face. Osborne had a hunch she was more interested in dissing her step-mother.

"If you two take these out, I want you to be very care-ful," said Ray, looking both Nick and Lauren in the eye. "Just because that lake is wide and the ice is thick does not mean it's safe. Two cardinal rules every ice fisherman knows: One, the only vehicle you take on the lake is the one that belongs to your rich uncle—and two, whenever you do drive on ice, be sure you have your doors un-locked and your windows open.

"Same goes for snowmobiles: extreme caution. *Under all circumstances stay away from wet cracks.* If you're going too fast to avoid one, be sure you cross at a ninety-degree angle. Better yet—stay at least thirty feet away. You hear me, Nick?"

"Even when it's this cold? I thought everywhere was safe right now," said the boy, disappointment vivid in his eyes.

"Not true. And of course you know to stay away from the shoreline, right? That's where the springs are. You hit a patch of thin ice over a spring, and you'll be minus one eighty-five-hundred-dollar Yamaha and v-e-e-r-y cold."

"But if you do hit some wet stuff—and we all have," said Osborne, "gun the engine. Do not slow down what-ever you do, or your machine will freeze in place. Worst case is you sink, best is you can't move. Not fun when it's freezing cold in the middle of the night and you're miles from help.

"I know I sound like an old geezer, kids, but the best policy is to stay on the trail. And that's still fun."

Lauren shivered. "I'm not riding one of those ever."

"Oh, c'mon," said Nick, "I was hoping you'd invite me out tomorrow."

Lauren giggled, then her face turned serious. "I was hoping you would stay over tonight, Nick. I'm-I'm just so . . ." she dropped her face into her hands.

Osborne had had it. Raising two daughters had taught him a few things. He rested a hand lightly on the girl's shoulder. "Lauren, are you doing okay?"

The girl burst into tears. Keeping her face covered, she wept deep, heaving sobs.

"Come on now, it can't be that bad." Osborne pulled her close, his arm around her shoulders, her face against his jacket as she sobbed. Nick and Ray looked on, speechless. Then, as quickly as she had broken down, the girl stopped weeping.

"I was in the ice house earlier than I said I was," she managed between sniffles and fumbling in her jacket pocket for a Kleenex as she pulled away from Osborne. "My stepmother came in with this guy . . . she's having an affair on my dad . . . I hid in the closet by the front door. She doesn't know I was there. That's why . . . that's why I didn't want to go to the dumb party."

She wept again. "I don't know what to do. I don't know—should I tell my dad? She hates me so much, she'll say I just made it up. I know he'll believe her. Not me." Lauren's hands were trembling as she wiped the tears from her cheek.

"Are you saying you saw them?" asked Ray.

Lauren nodded.

"Doing stuff?" asked Nick.

Again she nodded. "Yeah. I don't know who the guy is—never saw him before. From the way they talked," Lauren sniffled, calmer now, "he must do some work for her, too."

"Lauren," said Osborne, "if I've learned one thing in life, it's that you don't have to rush the tough decisions."

"Doc's right," said Ray. "Take your time with this. It's Christmas Eve, tomorrow's a big day. Why don't you just let this go until . . . oh, next Wednesday."

"And don't say anything to Dad?"

"Not until you know the right thing to say," said Osborne. "It might help to talk it over with someone who has experience with situations like this. Chief Ferris might be able to help."

He decided not to mention that dealing with domestic upsets and violence was the one part of her job that Lew hated. "Would you like me to arrange for you to have a chat with her?"

Lauren nodded and wiped at her nose.

"Hey, you razzbonyas!" They looked out the open garage door. Lew had stepped onto the deck and cupped her hands around her mouth to shout across the parking area towards them. "Hurry up, you're missing the party."

twenty-five

Fishing is a world created apart from all others, and inside it are special worlds of their own—one is fishing big fish in small water where there is not enough world and water to accommodate a fish, and the willows on the side on the creek are against the fisherman.

—Norman Maclean

"**Who** knew cutting down a Christmas tree could be life threatening?"

As Osborne strolled into the party, he heard his daughter's voice. At the center of a group of young men and women, including Mitten Theurian, was Mallory regaling everyone with a step-by-step replay of their confrontation with Clyde.

"So there we are in the middle of nowhere, and this old guy shoots my dad in the back of the head."

"Now Mallory," said Osborne raising his mug of hot cider, "don't exaggerate. Clyde knew he was far enough away that the worst I'd feel was a scattering of pellets. He had no intention of really hurting anyone."

He smiled down at Lew who had just walked over to stand beside him. "We don't need a good friend of Ray's arrested for high-speed lead poisoning."

"Arrested for *what*?" said Mitten, looking confused.

"Another term for shooting," said Osborne.

"Oh." As Mitten turned her head back towards Mallory, Osborne was surprised to see that even though she held a drink in one hand, she was chewing gum—not just chewing but cracking her gum with her mouth wide open.

Osborne was stunned. He could not believe this drop-dead beautiful woman with her expensive jewelry and lovely clothes would ruin it all chomping away on a hunk of junk that couldn't cost more than a nickel. Jeez Louise! What does that tell you about a person, he thought. Jeez.

"I don't care if he was far enough away not to hurt someone," said one of the men listening to Mallory. "I can think of safer ways to warn someone off your land."

"We weren't on his land, were we, Dad? We were on state property."

"So what the heck made him shoot at you in the first place?" said someone else in the group.

"He thought we were a couple of snowmobilers who've been riding down the streambeds and wrecking his beaver traps. Some blond woman cursed him out when her sled got stuck. He's making sure it doesn't happen again."

"So he shoots first and asks questions later?" said one of the men. "Sounds like the Wild West out there in McNaughton."

"Yeah, tell us again where this happened," said one of the men. "Just so I know where not to ride. Last thing I need is a buckshot haircut."

"Back in by Little Horsehead Lake," said Mallory. "But the day had a happy ending. Dad survived, and we got a great tree. And old Clyde knows to be more careful. He promised Dad next time he'll wait until he's sure it's the blond."

"Well, that's good to know," said Lew. "Clyde and I better have a little chat."

"Does everyone know Chief Ferris, head of the Loon Lake Police Department?" Mallory asked the people standing around.

"Sure, Chief Ferris, you won the muskie tournament a few years back," said one of the men. "I buy my lures at Ralph's Sporting Goods—he told me you're more into fly fishing these days. That so?"

"I'll never give up fishing on water," said Lew, "but I do love the trout stream. Which is why I'll argue Clyde's method but not his intent.

"I don't want snowmobiles off-trail in that region. That's next door to my favorite spring pond where I've caught some magnificent wild trout thanks to Clyde. Trapping is the only way to keep those beaver from backing up the stream and muddying the pond."

"You catch wild trout in a pond?" asked an older man who had just walked over to join the conversation. "By the way, Paul, good to see you. Been a while." He shook Osborne's hand, then Lew's. "Herm Metternich."

Osborne had been surprised to see how many people at the party he knew, most of them well-to-do retirees who had had occasion to drop into his office when needing dental work during their summer vacations. Apparently they all attended the same church: affluent, proper Episcopalians. Mitten had better restrain her gum cracking if she wanted to fit in with this crowd. Maybe she should consider chewing with her mouth closed.

"A spring pond," said Lew, answering Metternich's question. "It's a headwaters for one of the better trout streams. I caught a nineteen-inch brookie last time I fished it."

"*Nineteen inches*? Whoa, I haven't heard of a brook trout that big caught in this neck of the woods since the 1940s," said Metternich. "I know better than to ask for directions—but may I ask what you caught it on?"

"Certainly," said Lew. "It was mid-September, there was a midge hatch that day, and I was using a size 18 Griffith's Gnat."

"Nineteen inches, huh. That is hard to believe."

"So is the fact that Wisconsin has more indigenous trout than any state in the country, thanks to spring ponds—but let's keep that a secret." said Lew with a grin. She sipped her cider and looked up at Osborne. "Doc, we really should head back."

"Okay, I'll find a place to put this," said Osborne, indicating his mug, "and round up Ray and Nick."

He walked over to a nearby table, looking for a good spot to set down his empty mug. The Theurians had put out a spread indeed. Cheeses of all kinds, baskets of crackers, plates of cookies. A platter of sliced tenderloin with tiny egg rolls and horseradish looked tempting, but he was still full from dinner. He found a tray of empty glasses off to the side and set down his mug.

"Doc Osborne? What the heck are you doing here?" asked a familiar voice. Osborne looked around to find himself face-to-face with Craig Kobernot, his wife at his side. Craig wore his usual jovial grin. Not Patrice; she looked tense. Osborne wondered if they had been arguing. But then he remembered. Patrice always looked unhappy.

"Howdy, Mrs. Kobernot, someone spike your cider with an anchovie?" Ray had walked up and wasn't about to let Patrice's dark mood go unnoticed. Osborne ducked his head so she wouldn't see him smile.

"Well, I'll be," said Craig. "What's the Loon Lake contingent doing up here?"

"Enjoying Wisconsin River highballs. And a Merry Christmas to you, neighbor," said Ray, clinking his glass of ice water against the drink in Craig's hand. "So Patrice, did you hear what happened to our milkman the other day?"

Patrice couldn't have looked less interested.

"One of our lovely neighbors ordered thirty quarts of milk for her milk bath. And when the milkman asked her if she wanted that pasturized, she said 'Oh. no—just up to my neck."

"That's an old joke," said Patrice without cracking a smile.

Craig found it pretty funny.

"Do you folks go to the same church as the Theurians?"

asked Osborne, anxious to divert Craig's interest in why he and Ray were there. Since they had driven up immediately after Nick's call, they were still in their dinner party clothes, so they looked like they belonged. He decided it would be just as well to let the Kobernots assume they had been invited.

Before Craig could answer, Mallory rushed up to grab Ray and pull him across the room into a conversation with their host. "Come over here, Ray, I've been telling Dave about your Hot Mama. He said he's been looking to invest in a company that makes fishing lures."

"Are you serious?" said Ray, following her like a lab puppy. That's curious thought Osborne, less than an hour ago when Lauren had tried to interest him in the lure, the guy couldn't be bothered.

Lew walked over as they left, and Patrice's eyebrows just about hit the ceiling. "Mrs. Kobernot," said Lew graciously. "You probably don't recognize me out of uniform but we met the other day. Lewellyn Ferris. Nice to see you again."

"You, too," said Patrice, slamming a swallow from her wineglass as if she needed fortification.

"So what do you think of our new Three Lakes residents?" asked Osborne, making small talk. "Nice addition to the community."

Patrice gave him a strange look. "What do you mean?"

"I understand Mr. Theurian is launching a new enterprise, which the town can certainly use, and Mitten is quite an attractive woman," said Osborne.

Patrice looked like she was about to gag. "Mitten? That's a good one. *Mitten.* You and that Ray Pradt, honest to Pete. You think you're so damn funny." She slammed her wineglass onto the table and huffed off.

Osborne looked at Craig. "What did I say wrong?"

"They're sisters," said Craig. "Around those two, trust me, you can't say anything right. Who knows what upset her. This is a command performance for us—Patrice did not want to come in the first place."

Osborne could guess why: Patrice was one of those women, like his late wife, who coveted things. One look around this huge, beautifully decorated lodge room, the centerpiece of what must be a million-dollar contemporary home, and it was obvious which sister had acquired the most material goods. That would rankle a woman like Patrice.

"Excuse me a moment, Doc," said Lew. "I'm going to find a ladies' room."

When she was gone, Craig raised his hand and pointed his drink in the direction of Ray holding court across the room. Osborne got a whiff of whiskey.

"I don't understand Ray Pradt," he said, slurring his words. "Look at the jerk. His old man was an excellent physician, his brother's a hand surgeon, his sister's a big-shot lawyer in Chicago—they're all successful. What the hell happened to him?"

Osborne studied the physician weaving back and forth on his feet. "I'm not sure what your point is, Craig. Ray made his choices. I know him to be a happy man. Hell of a lot happier than some people I know."

Osborne had had enough of Craig. He wandered over to where Mallory and Ray were in a heated discussion with Dave Theurian.

"I'll tell you, I do *not* understand ice fishing," said Theurian with an enthusiasm that had been missing earlier. "Why go out and freeze your butt?"

"Whaddya mean 'freeze'?" said Ray. "You've got a fully heated house out there."

"You know what I'm talking about. I used to come up here with Lauren's grandfather, and he'd make me go drill those damn holes, scoop that freezing water, stand out there when it's forty below zero. Shoot, every time you catch a fish your fingers fall off. That's no fun."

"*Anybody* can fish when it's seventy degrees and sunny," said Ray. "Ice fishing's a challenge. Some of us enjoy doing things the hard way. Sure, it can be a little un-comfortable—but worth it. The fish taste great. The air, the landscape, it's just . . . pure. You come back after a cold night on the lake, the stars are brilliant, the moon so high and full. You crawl under those warm blankets, let your dogs cuddle in. I tell you winter is heaven."

"You sleep with your dogs?" Mallory was appalled.

"Well, they aren't all dogs," said Ray with a wink. "So, Dave, what's this new business of yours?"

"Cement," said Theurian.

"Oh," said Ray, "construction?"

"Basically," said Theurian. "Would you excuse me, I need a refill." He walked off just as Nick appeared.

"Ray, Doc, c'mon downstairs. You've got to see the setup Lauren's old man has for deer hunting. It's unbelievable."

"Another time, Nick," said Osborne. "Chief Ferris is due back in a minute, and we have to get going." The boy's face fell. "Well, okay, we can take two minutes," said Osborne.

The room they walked into was long, narrow, and bright with fluorescent lighting. Sliding glass doors opened to the outside along one wall, two long steel tables were situated down the center of the room, and a series of drains were set into the dark ceramic tile floor. Opposite the sliding glass doors was a wall of industrial refrigerators and deep, steel-sided sinks.

The room resembled a veterinary clinic. It smelled of antiseptic and something else that Osborne couldn't quite place.

"A hunter's delight," said Ray, pulling open a drawer in one of the long tables. Knives gleamed under the fluorescent lights. "With a setup like this, I bet I could skin and butcher a deer in fifteen minutes."

"We'll have to compete," said a throaty voice from the doorway. Mitten Theurian stood there, drink in hand, still chewing away.

"What's your name, anyway," she said to Ray as she

sauntered into the room. "I noticed you earlier. And where did you get those gorgeous finger-in-the-socket curls?"

Ah, the woman can flirt and chew simultaneously, thought Osborne. Now that takes talent.

Ray walked over to peer outside, then stared down at the floor. "You bring the carcass in through here, I take it."

"Right through those doors," said Mitten, snapping her gum. "Dave got an eight-buck over Thanksgiving. We had friends up who shot two doe and a small buck—butchered, wrapped, and frozen before supper."

Ray headed towards the wall of refrigerators. Mitten stepped forward just as he reached for one of the door handles, causing his hand to brush across her bosom instead of grasping the handle.

"Ohmygosh—excuse me," said Ray turning bright red. For all his bad jokes, Ray was not a total boor.

"Excuse *me*," said Mitten, "my fault." She positioned herself between Ray and the refrigerators. "We keep our venison over here," she gestured towards one long unit, "and the other I use for my berries."

She snapped her gum. "I l-o-o-ve to pick berries. This fall I put up blackberries, strawberries, blueberries."

"Any thimbleberries?" said Ray, his face shading down slowly.

"No, I've never picked a thimbleberry. Maybe you'd take me . . . and Dave sometime."

"We could do that," said Ray.

Mitten turned to Nick and Lauren, who were standing behind Osborne. "Lauren, honey, you tell me next time you want to bring your friends down here. Will you? I try to keep it locked. This is my special little workroom, and I don't always have it quite so neat and clean. I don't know why it was unlocked tonight."

"We have to get going," said Osborne. "Very nice meeting you this evening, Mrs. Theurian." As they headed towards the door to go back upstairs, Mitten took up the rear, pausing near the door to open a small garbage can with her foot and spit out her gum. Holding the lid of the can open, she reached into a pocket in her skirt for another stick of gum, unwrapped it, and shoved it into her mouth.

Osborne shook his head as he went up the stairs. Nothing so classy as a chain chewer. He could just imagine the condition of her teeth. At the top of the stairs, he paused. He recognized that odor now. Mitten's basement smelled like St. Mary's morgue.

twenty-six

At the outset, the fact should be recognized that the community of fishermen constitute a separate class or subrace among the inhabitants of the earth.

—Grover Cleveland

"**That** poor kid," said Lew, after hearing what Lauren had witnessed in the ice house. "She seemed so calm . . ."

Osborne slowed the car to let two does and a large buck cross the road. Even though he knew everyone was anxious to get back to Loon Lake, he was keeping his speed at 55 mph: too many deer on the move.

"She was pretty upset at first," said Nick, "but she felt a lot better after Dr. Osborne told her she should talk to you before saying anything to her dad."

"Oh?" said Lew. She gave Osborne a sharp look. "I'm not sure I can help."

"Let me talk to her," said Mallory. "I know more than anyone needs to know about people having affairs."

"Mallory," said Osborne, shaking his head, "this isn't funny."

"I know it's not funny, Dad. I'm serious. Chief Ferris," said Mallory from the backseat, "I just found out my ex has been seeing one of my closest friends—since *before* our divorce. It really threw me for a loop at first. I had to go running off to see my shrink and, you know, she said something that really surprised me: She knows more people who have affairs not for the sex—but to be listened to."

The car was silent for a few seconds.

"You think Mitten Theurian has a hard time being listened to?" asked Ray. "Her husband, maybe. But the blond torpedo? I don't think so."

"Lauren thinks the man she saw with her stepmom might be involved in her business whatever it is—" said Nick.

"Then *that's* the party who would have a hard time being listened to," said Ray. "Can you imagine working for that woman? If her *husband* can't get a word in edgewise . . . jeez."

"Ray," Nick punched him in the arm, "will you let me finish?"

"Sorry."

"Lauren wants me to help her out," said Nick. "This pager fell out of the guy's pocket when he was getting dressed. She thought I might be able to use it somehow to figure out, you know, who he is or something." He held up a small black case.

"That is not a good idea," said Lew, turning around to look at Nick. "Lauren needs to let her father handle the situation. It's his marriage. I'll talk to her, Nick. That kid should not be putting herself in the middle of what is likely to be an unpleasant situation."

"Fine with me," said Nick. He started to shove the pager back in his pocket.

"Wait—Nick, can I see that for a minute?" asked Lew.

"Sure." the boy leaned sideways to pull it out of his jacket pocket and hand it over the back of the car seat. Osborne was relieved to see that it appeared to be the same object he had seen Lauren pushing into the boy's pocket earlier. Not drugs after all.

"The way they were talking, Lauren said she's pretty

sure he has to be a computer tech or something like that," said Nick as Lew examined the pager.

Osborne flicked on the dome light so she could see better.

"She found it on the floor after they left. She almost got caught, too. Right after she picked it up, she heard his boots in the snow—said she barely had time to hide before he rushed back in looking all around on the floor and under the sofa."

"This isn't a pager," said Lew. "It's a *case* for a pager all right, but . . ." She flipped open the top and gave it a shake. Out fell a metal unit about four inches long and an inch wide. Lew turned the metal object over in her hands, a funny smile on her face.

"Know what this is, people?" She held it up so everyone could see. "A skimmer. Used to steal credit card numbers. I have a picture of one of these up on the wall with all the Wanted posters.

"Very easy to use. It's battery-operated and all you have to do is swipe a credit card through and the skimmer picks up all the account information. One of these buggers will hold anywhere from fifty to a hundred credit card numbers.

"All you do then is download the information into a computer connected to a card encoder and copy all the data onto a blank card. Now you have a counterfeit credit card that you can use for at least a couple days before anyone's wiser.

"But this is the first one I've seen up here. They busted a ring down in Madison last summer that was working through waiters and bartenders who wore skimmers on their belts—right in plain sight—and were paid fifty bucks a number. Before it was shut down, that one ring had used counterfeit cards to buy over thirteen million dollars worth of goods."

"Does this mean we should turn around and go back?" asked Osborne.

"Gosh, no," said Lew. "I need to think this over. For

one thing, we don't know who the man is that dropped this—or even if he's used it. He could be selling these for all we know."

"You'd ruin a nice party if you went back now," said Ray. "Be a little awkward to ask Mitten who she was boinking at two o'clock this afternoon. Talk about putting Lauren in the middle—how would you explain that?"

"And if there is a ring operating up here, then I sure as heck don't want to alert anyone before I know what I'm dealing with. But at the same time, I need to find out if these are being used right now—and alert people. I can't wait too long." The relaxed look on Lew's face was long gone.

"I'm more worried about Lauren," said Osborne, pressing harder on the accelerator. "Credit card companies can survive."

"Chief, remember the bartender out at Thunder Bay—the gal who told me she had customers complaining that someone had stolen their credit card numbers and were accusing her . . ."

"That's right," said Lew, sitting up straight in the passenger seat. "Didn't you say they're open tomorrow?"

"Open at noon."

"Ray, Doc, we have got to stop by Thunder Bay once we've checked out those trail maps Gina downloaded. That okay with you guys?"

"You betcha," said Ray. Doc nodded. Christmas was shaping up to be more memorable than usual. He hadn't planned on spending it in a strip joint. Once again he was struck by how much life with Lew resembled a day of fishing: never predictable.

"Nick," Lew was saying, "when we get to your grandmother's, I'd like you to call Lauren, then put me on the line. I need to talk to that girl as soon as possible. Darn, I wish I had my cell phone with me."

"Wouldn't work out here, anyway," said Osborne glancing out the car window.

"True," said Lew. Cell phone service around Loon Lake was abysmal.

"First thing tomorrow," said Lew, thinking out loud, "I'll put out a notice to all the law enforcement in the surrounding areas. See if anyone knows anything, if they're getting complaints. I think I'll see if Gina can help us find out what Mrs. Theurian's business is and who works for her.

"Once I know that I can probably get a police officer or a sheriff's deputy in that jurisdiction to pretend they found this in a parking lot somewhere, drop by and ask a few questions. That would keep Lauren out of it."

"Incidentally," said Mallory from the backseat, "did anyone besides me notice Mitten Theurian's hands?"

"Only when she was sticking another hunk of gum in her mouth," said Osborne. "I didn't see anything unusual. Why?"

"Her fingernails. She has the same holiday design painted on her nails that I saw on the fingernails of that young woman you found over by the Kobernots' rink. Remember what hers looked like, Dad? Dark blue background with tiny silver Christmas trees painted in the center of each nail and outlined with glitter. Custom nail art—at least thirty dollars a hand."

"That's very interesting," said Lew.

"I asked Mitten where she had hers done," said Mallory, "but all she said was a manicurist out of town. I was trying to get more information, but another guest walked up right then and I couldn't ask any more questions without seeming obnoxious."

Osborne pulled into the circle drive in front of Nick's grandmother's house. The porch light was on, but all the interior lights were off.

"Looks like Grandma's asleep," said Nick. "There's a phone in the guest room where I'm staying. I've got Lauren's cell phone number on my dresser. Shall we call her on that? She keeps it in that little purse she's always wearing."

"Let's hope she has it with her right now," said Lew.

*   *   *

"Lauren," said Lew, exhaling with relief when the girl picked up on the first ring. "This is Chief Ferris. We need to talk, but it has to be a private conversation—so where are you right now . . . are there people around? Good . . . how long do you think they'll be out caroling? Fine, that's more than enough time."

As she spoke, Lew sat on the edge of the bed in the guest room. Osborne waited nearby, ready with a notepad and pen if she needed it. Nick sprawled in a chair across the room, his face averted as he listened. Ray and Mallory were in the kitchen, poised to divert Nick's grandmother should she wake up.

Lew hunched forward over the phone as if that alone could hurry things along. "We need to get together as soon as possible, Lauren," she said, then paused. "Yes, to talk about the situation with your father and your stepmother—but something else you need to be aware of." Talking fast, Lew told her that the object she'd given Nick was not a pager, but a device used in credit card fraud.

When she had finished, she changed the subject: "Nick is under the impression that you overheard some of their conversation. Was there anything said that might help me figure out who that man is? Did she call her friend by name? 'Darling?' And that's all, huh."

Lew listened then said, "Okay, I want to ask you a couple questions about that. Also, I'm going to give you my home phone number in case anything comes to mind after we talk. Does anything you heard lead you to believe that your stepmother knows about the credit card operation? No. That's good. I can't imagine she would, but it helps to know nothing was said.

"Now, Lauren. I'm very concerned for your safety. I do not want that man to know that you found the skimmer and passed it along to me. This is critical, so listen hard: I know you're upset about what you saw. I would be, too. But, please, do not confront your stepmother. *Under any circumstances.* Not until I know what we are dealing with here.

"The given is the man is a crook or is affiliated in some way with a crooked operation or he wouldn't have that skimmer on him. But is he operating alone? Is he dangerous? Until I know for sure, I do not want to risk putting you and your family in jeopardy. Do you hear me, Lauren?

"I know . . . I know how it feels." Lew tipped the phone away from her ear and Osborne could hear the girl crying. "I know, kiddo." said Lew, her voice soothing.

"Now, Lauren, can you arrange to come down to Loon Lake tomorrow afternoon? Set it up so your folks think you're seeing Nick? We could lend him a car to come pick you up. Oh . . . right, I forgot. Christmas. What about Monday? That's better for me, too. So we'll send Nick up to get you. And, Lauren, last question. You did see his face, right? Because I'll have some photos for you to take a look at.

"No, don't do *that*," said Lew. "Don't go poking around. You'll only get yourself in trouble. Lauren . . . Lauren, *please* . . . look, kid, your stepmother is a human being and we all make mistakes. I sincerely doubt she knows the guy is a crook.

"So we're agreed that you will not confront her, and that means you won't say a word to your father about this until we know more. Right? Good. I agree with Ray and Dr. Osborne on waiting until Wednesday. That gives me time to find out what's going on. When we know that, you'll have a better idea what is the right thing to say to your dad. This won't be easy for him, you know.

"And Lauren," said Lew, her tone gentle, "your father loves you very much. When we were searching for you, he was so worried. We need to do our best to help your dad get through this, too. Okay?

"Do you want me to put Nick back on?" Lew handed over the phone.

"What a mess," said Lew, back in Osborne's car. "Keep your fingers crossed that Mitten woman doesn't give Lauren a hard time. The last thing we need is for that kid to get mad and blurt out everything she knows."

"What was she up to that made you say 'no' as hard as you did?" asked Osborne.

"Oh, dear," said Lew. "She was planning to sneak into her stepmother's office. Since she had heard them talking about microprocessor controls and drying cycles, she thought a search through the computer files might lead somewhere. No doubt it would, but if she got caught— ouch."

"I wonder what line of business that woman is in," said Mallory. "She sure doesn't strike me as the corporate type."

"Her husband is in cement, if that helps," said Ray. "Theurian Resources Inc. Dave told me he's got patents pending on a number of new cement products for construction companies. He moved his lab up here in order to test under tough weather conditions. Said he makes his money developing new products and selling the patents to major manufacturers. Apparently, he put six million into that laboratory and warehouse of his.

"In fact," said Ray, leaning forward from the backseat, "he told me not to tell anyone—but I know you guys can keep a secret . . ." He paused for dramatic effect.

Lew rolled her eyes, then cast a dim eye towards the backseat. "Ray . . ."

"Mister . . . David . . . Theurian . . . has offered to help yours truly . . . develop a business plan . . . to market my Hot Mama. We've scheduled a meeting for next week. He wants to see specs and more samples."

"Seriously, Ray?" asked Mallory. "He came through? I can't believe it."

Ray's smile filled Osborne's rearview mirror. "Y'- know," be said, "I gotta tell ya, the guy is something else. He's not all business, that's for sure. Would you believe that man takes time out of his busy day . . . whenever he's needed . . . to do grief counseling for their church? And he's not just going by the book either. Nope—he's looking for new ideas.

"For example, he's very interested in how things are done at St. Mary's. He wants all the details on how we handle burials, our policy on storage and delayed interment—"

"What does that have to do with grief counseling?" asked Lew. "Or *you* for that matter? You dig graves and thaw frozen ground—"

"But I *observe*, Chief. I know how people behave when they're grieving, I know all the different reactions they can have. Keep in mind, the funeral is one thing, interment is quite another. Serious emotions are at play. As Dave pointed out, I'm a professional bystander . . ."

"A *what*?" asked Osborne and Lew simultaneously, locking eyes. Ray did have a knack for the conversation stopper.

"You want my advice, Ray," said Osborne. "Use your head. You better think twice before you get into a business deal with an individual who may be on the verge of a nasty divorce. That's asking for trouble."

"I hear you, Chief, but he struck me as a man who has great respect for the individual."

"Respect for hot blonds and big bucks is more like it," said Mallory. "Dad's right. When he finds out about his wife's affair, who knows what'll happen? Doesn't matter if she's at fault, she still gets half his net worth—and that could be his half of *your* net worth, Mr. Pradt."

"Ah-h-h, wisdom from the mouth of a babe," said Ray.

A loud boo echoed through the car.

"Okay, okay," said Ray, raising his hands. "Just so you know, Dave Theurian is the one talking about putting up money, not me. All I do is provide the design, the field tests, and be willing to have my name on the product. And it's hardly a done deal—we've had exactly one conversation on the subject."

"Ray," said Lew, "even a fish wouldn't get caught if he kept his mouth shut."

"What does that mean?"

"She means you should be careful," said Mallory. "Good ideas get stolen every day. Fact of life in the business world. Personally, based on what I've learned studying for my MBA, I don't like the idea that your Hot Mama is hanging on the end of a fishing pole in that guy's ice house. No patent, no registration of any kind. You've handed over your design. Ray—what does he need *you* for?"

"Me! It's my image that'll help sell—"

"Ray, sweetheart," said Mallory, patting him on the shoulder. "Not to hurt your feelings but it takes more than a good-looking guy with a stuffed fish on his head to break into a tough consumer market. I mean, just for starters you need demographics, focus groups, marketing, sales reps, etcetera, etcetera.

"Launching a new product is very, very difficult. Whether you're selling a Hot Mama or . . . or *cement*, for God's sake, you've got to know what you're doing. Or people will take advantage of you."

Ray looked so wounded and worried, Osborne felt sorry for him.

"So . . . maybe I should get my lure back?" said Ray.

"I sure would if I were you," said Mallory. "And I'd ask that girlfriend of yours to do a Google search on the guy. Find out more about him."

"She's *not* my girlfriend."

"Yeah, right."

As the backseat voices settled into a low squabble, Osborne looked over at Lew. "That was nice, what you said to Lauren . . . about her father—"

"I lied," said Lew, turning her face away. "Kid needs hope."

"Lewellyn, why don't you let your truck warm up and come inside for a few minutes," said Osborne after he ulled into the garage. Mallory was already heading for the house. "I have your gift under the Christmas tree."

"Gosh, I'd love to, Doc, but this has been one heck of a long day."

"Just for a few minutes?"

"Tomorrow morning." Lew laid a hand on his arm. "Please? With everything hitting right now, what I need most is a good night's sleep. Besides, it'll be more fun in the morning when we're both rested. So bring the gift with you to my place—and I'll see you at eleven?"

If her kiss followed through on its promise, the morning might not be bad. Not bad at all.

twenty-seven

There's no taking trout with dry breeches.

—Cervantes, *Don Quixote*

Osborne's car bounced down the rocky lane to Lew's farmhouse. Ice freezing, melting, and freezing again made it a challenge to navigate smoothly. Add to that the treacherous winter sun, so low in the sky that the glare off his windshield made it next to impossible to see.

Osborne raised a hand to deflect the rays. Demolishing one of Lew's treasured Blackhull spruces was all he would need to complete the morning. A morning on which the first mistake he had made was to get up.

Joining Mallory under the tree to open gifts, he had saved the present from Lew for last. Stripping off the ribbons and paper and lifting the lid, what he found inside was not what he had expected.

Mallory caught the look on his face. "What is it, Dad?" He held out the box. "Oh, cool, you've never done that, have you? Don't look so worried, it can't be that difficult." She smiled and turned back to her own pile of presents.

Osborne sat there, staring down at a very expensive and

very unwanted Renzetti "True Rotary" Vise. Nestled alongside the vise was a selection of tools whose harsh names belied their delicate appearance: a Matarelli Whip Finisher, a Griffin Hackle Pliers.

What on earth made Lew think he'd want to tie trout flies? Soft, fluffy, feathery, slippery, garish, squishy, dead-animal-decorated trout flies. Didn't she know he loved hard stuff: gleaming surfaces, pointed edges, gold, silver, porcelain. Wire, not thread; teeth, not feathers. His fingers were made to sculpt and polish, not snip and tie. Fishing with someone else's creation was one thing; fussing with your own quite another.

Looking at the gift, he felt like he had when Mary Lee forced him to accompany her to performances of the Loon Lake Orchestra—three hours in an overheated auditorium on a day ideal for fishing. Right now he felt that same boxed-in dread. Oh dear, how was he going to manage this?

Brunch at Erin's was okay, though she undercooked the scrambled eggs. Things did not improve with the gift exchange: His daughters must have coordinated their purchases with Lew.

From Mallory, he got a two-hour video on tying trout flies, two rooster necks (one brown, one black), three bucktail pieces (red, white, and yellow) and one Hungarian partridge breast. Erin's box held a packet of blood maribou, two wild turkey wings, beaver fur, and the flank of some poor wood duck. Also, gaudy strips of something called "crystal flash" and a hunk of "chenille." All that was missing were directions from Ray on how to shave a dead squirrel.

Osborne knew his daughters needed to feel they had given him something special, so he smiled and smiled. Even when Cody ran over his foot with the left training wheel on his new bike, he smiled. Finally it was safe to leave.

Hurrying home, he pulled on his insulated ice-fishing

pants and parka. They would have to double as snowmobile gear. Fortunately, he had saved the helmet from the one winter, a decade ago, when he had tried to get interested in the motorized sleds.

As a sport, he had never liked snowmobiling. His friends who did were men who loved speed. Not Osborne. He was too cautious, always struggling to keep up. The sled he rode didn't handle curves well, and he found the trails too icy—the hard bumps jarring to his spine. And the noise cut out what he loved most about being in woods.

The sight of Lew's little red farmhouse outlined against the perfect blue sky lifted his spirits. He'd find a way around his disappointment. After all, hadn't she promised they would spend some time together before meeting up with Ray? Osborne checked his watch: he was early . . . maybe . . . and if that went as well as he anticipated—hell, he could learn to tie a million trout flies. He knew, of course, that she would *adore* what he had for her.

But Lew answered her door dressed and eager to leave, the expression in her dark eyes all business. "I called Ray and told him to meet us earlier than planned—he and Gina should be at the trailhead shortly. Do you mind driving, Doc?"

As she turned to shut and lock the door behind her, he slipped the tiny wrapped gift back inside the upper vest pocket of his parka. She was right—later would be better.

"Don't we look like aliens?"said Gina, swinging her arms and walking stiff-legged towards Lew and Osborne as they got out of the car. Osborne laughed. He always forgot what snowmobilers look like to civilians. With their bulbous helmets, padded snowsuits, and fat, insulated mitts and boots—they do look extraterrestrial.

"Wait until you see where we're going," he said. "It's like a lunar landscape out there. We'll fit right in."

"Chief," said Ray, looking up from where he was

kneeling to adjust something on his sled, "maybe we should stop by Thunder Bay first?" Using the wrench in his hand, he pointed across the highway. The trailhead was just down the road from the strip club. "They open in half an hour. No customers yet, if we walk over now."

Lew looked down the road, then back at the two snowmobiles that Roger had dropped off for her and Osborne. "Good idea. We'll take the keys and leave the sleds here."

That suited Osborne fine, he always worried whom he might meet at Thunder Bay. It would sound so feeble to try to explain he was there on official business.

Only one car was parked outside the club, and they had to knock as the door was still locked.

"Come back at noon," said a woman's voice.

They knocked again, and someone looked through the door's curtained window. Then came the sound of the door unlocking.

"Oh, Chief Ferris, sorry. I didn't know it was you. Come in."

The woman backed away, opening the door for them to enter. Laura was in her late forties. She was wearing jeans, a black turtleneck, and a western belt cinched tight at her waist to emphasize her generous bust. Under a head of too-red hair, she had a friendly face.

Osborne knew from his McDonald's pals that her husband had been killed in an industrial accident at the Rhinelander paper mill, leaving Laura with five kids to raise on workman's comp.

"Is this about that Tomahawk rider? I hope you found him—he's a good guy."

"Not yet, unfortunately. This is a separate matter," said Lew, pulling off her helmet and gloves. "Only take a few minutes."

"Oka-a-y . . . but I told Ray everything I know about Eileen when he stopped by before." She walked back behind the bar as she talked, reaching down into a sink of soapy water. "Do you mind if I keep working behind the bar here while we talk? I'm behind already, and this place will be crazy later. What can I do for you?"

"Have you ever seen one of these?" Lew set the skimmer on the bar.

"Sure—that's a card cleaner," said Laura, rinsing two large, glass beer pitchers at a time. "The fella from Hurley who's been picking up receipts since Eileen . . ." she paused, "well, in place of Eileen. He uses one of those."

"Oh yeah?" said Lew, her manner nonchalant. "So you don't have one here right now?"

"He comes down on Wednesdays. I guess they do it then because there's so many people here on karaoke night. He sets it right by the cash register there, and we run every card through. Why?"

"So, you figure he'll be down this Wednesday?"

"Can't imagine why he wouldn't," said Laura. She stopped and rested both hands on the sink. "I miss Eileen, she was much more pleasant than that jerk."

"What's this fella look like?" asked Lew.

"Big guy, chunky. Always wears these funny sunglasses. Dark in here, and he's still got those damn things on." Laura shook her head. "Spiky hair—must spend a fortune on mousse. Makes us call him 'Boss.' That's a crock, but we don't argue."

"What's his real name?"

"Who knows? It ain't 'Boss,' that's for sure—but no one who works here regular calls him anything else. If you want to know, I'd check the Hurley club. He's a bouncer up there. When he's down here, we put up with him, figuring no percentage in being on his bad side. He'd report you and wham—no job."

She waved a soapy hand in the air. "I've seen it happen. The only person who ever gave him grief was Eileen . . . oh." She paused. "Oh, don't say I said anything, will you?"

"What kind of grief?" said Lew.

"Nothing specific, she just gave orders is all." Laura

put both hands on the edges of the sink and leaned towards the bar. "That's really all I ever heard."

Ray, who had taken a place on a bar stool with Gina alongside, gave a low whistle. "Whoa, look at those fingernails. Show Chief your hands, Laura. Now where the heckaroonie did you get that amazing artwork done?"

Laura looked sad as she thrust her hands out so everyone could see. "Eileen did these for me, the day she disappeared. I was supposed to pay her, but . . ."

Osborne stared at the woman's hands: dark blue background, tiny silver Christmas trees edged with glitter. Holiday nails.

twenty-eight

*A lake is the landscape's most beautiful and expressive
feature. It is earth's eye; looking into which the be-
holder measures the depth of his own nature.*

—Henry David Thoreau

Osborne struggled to see through his helmet as their
snowmobiles moved down the trail. Though the sun had
moved higher, every time the trail turned south, the glare
off the snow made it impossible to see.

Finally, right hand on the throttle, he used his left to
shove the plastic face guard up. He'd rather freeze his
cheekbones than blindside another sled at a crossing—or
vice versa. Pushing with his mitt, he was able to nudge his
neck warmer up over his chin.

They'd left Thunder Bay after learning that Eileen had
painted the nails of two other girls, both dancers, working
at Thunder Bay—but not her own. She'd told Laura that
she had trained a friend in Hurley to help her finish hers,
as she could do one hand but not both.

"You don't want to tell Laura about the skimmer? What
if she uses it again?" asked Ray as they walked out of
Thunder Bay.

"Sounds to me like it's only used down here on

Wednesdays," said Lew. "I want to collar that bouncer before he gets word we're onto him. I called in a bulletin this morning alerting all the law enforcement in the region to the potential for credit card fraud. Marlene is checking with the Feds to see who notifies the credit card companies.

"Terry is on duty at three today. I left a message with Marlene for him to get the names of all the employees at the Hurley club—try to avoid alerting our man until we can do some more checks."

"Are you going in later, Chief?" asked Gina.

"I hope not," said Lew, smiling at Osborne. "I have a Christmas turkey in the oven."

"Do you mind if I work in your office for awhile this evening?" asked Gina. "I promised Ray I'd do a computer search on his new business partner before they meet tomorrow."

"You two are meeting *tomorrow*?" said Osborne, turning to Ray. "I thought it was later in the week."

"Theurian called just before we left this morning and said he would be driving Lauren down for her date with Nick. He wants to get a sandwich and talk it over."

"But I agree with Mallory," said Gina. "Ray needs to know more about the guy before he lets him near his Hot Mama. I made him call back and tell Lauren to bring her lure down with her. On the pretense of going fishing—but just to be on the safe side."

"You and Mallory—you're such cynics," said Ray. shaking his head.

They were thirty minutes down the trail, which had taken them to the edge of Little Horsehead Lake, when Ray pulled off to the right and stopped. The lake was surrounded by state land, which meant the shoreline was free of cabins and year-homes.

Not the same for the ice: It looked like a town in miniature. Fishing huts of all shapes and shades dotted the expanse, some in clusters, some off alone. Their confetti colors against the white surface turned the hard water into a giant Monopoly board.

Leaving Gina on the back, Ray walked back to Lew and Osborne, pulling off his mitts and helmet. "Be very, very careful as we cross," he said. "Do not go off the trail—this lake is riddled with deadheads and boulders. One reason the state has claimed all the land around here is they want to keep boats out—too hazardous."

Pushing up the face plate on her helmet, Lew said, "Can you see where we're supposed to leave the trail and make a hard right?"

"Yep," Ray had the map that had been downloaded from the victim's Blackberry in his hand. "Looks like we cross the lake, then off to the right a quarter mile, and keep an eye out for a large boulder to our left."

"Then what?"

"Assuming there's a trail, we follow it."

No trail, but a snaking expanse of white about six feet wide. Again Ray stopped. He walked back to the sleds holding Lew and Osborne, new snow squeaking under his boots as if it were confectioners' sugar. Though three or four inches had fallen over the last forty-eight hours, stiff winds had crimped it into drifts, exposing a crusty surface.

"Up this streambed from the looks of it. And other sleds have been down here, but it's been awhile."

"Are we on a trail?" asked Lew.

"Hard to tell—nothing's very well marked out here. It wasn't easy finding the marker by the lake. But I do know one thing," said Ray. "We're heading back towards Clyde's."

"How far from his place?" asked Lew.

"Third of a mile, I'd say, maybe less. He's off the lake just far enough to save on property taxes."

"Might be wiser if we were to go in from the other side," said Osborne. "Stop by Clyde's place and let him know it's us coming his way."

"Tell you what," said Ray. "Let's go down a short distance to where the map indicates a cabin—then decide."

"I like that idea," said Lew.

Again, they moved forward on their sleds. Even though the sun was already tipping into the west, patches of snow glittered as they glided in and out of the shadows cast by the white pine, spruce, and balsam crowding the stream.

Osborne had lowered his visor now that they weren't traveling directly into the sun. More than one branch slapped hard against his helmet, even as he ducked.

The ride was smooth across the ice, partly because they were off-trail and partly because the police department sleds were new and easy to maneuver. And quiet. Osborne was struck by how less invasive these snowmobiles felt.

He had forgotten that the snowmobile, for all its sins, had one virtue: It took you back into territory where few humans ventured. Not even hunters and fishermen got back here. Fishermen were limited by water, hunters by land, hikers by existing trails. But the sleds could go anywhere: bounce across swampy hillocks, speed down shallow waterways, and shoot across the smothered mounds of underbrush that normally kept humans out.

As they emerged from the streambed onto a broad white plain, Ray slowed his sled. When he stopped, they all stopped. Osborne got off his sled, removed his helmet, and looked around.

The pond was guarded by elegant cedars, tall dowager queens, whose branches sloped earthward, draped with needles dense as velvet. One point of land thrust its way past the ancient cedars to set the stage for a cluster of rogue balsam. Young, stalwart, and swathed with garlands of snow, the balsams swayed in the wind like ballerinas en pointe. And all was silent: a cathedral of peace.

Ray pointed to a dark hole in the ice near the shoreline. Above it a chrysalis of ice hung from the underbrush overhang. Something had been splashing up and out from under the ice. Beaver, perhaps.

"No cabin," he said after doing a 360-degree turn. "But this is where the map ends."

"Doc, this is the spring pond I was talking about last night," said Lew. "I recognize it by that point of land with the row of balsam. Year to year, I'm never sure I'll find it again. But this is it, all right."

"Can't you just wade upstream from the lake?" asked Osborne.

"No way," said Ray. "I've seined minnows in here, and I can tell you that creek has deep holes and spots where the loon poop is five, six feet deep. You don't even hike in here without a compass." Osborne could see why. Between logging and beaver damage the terrain would be in constant flux: woods one day, swamp the next.

"That's why it's got such big brookies," said Lew with a wide grin. "Nobody knows about it."

Ray plunged through the snow toward an opening along the shoreline, his boots breaking through a good foot or more. Once on shore, under the trees, it wasn't so bad. He disappeared for a few minutes then waved them forward.

"Easier by sled," said Lew, hitting the ignition button. Gina climbed into Ray's seat and followed with Osborne taking up the rear.

"Someone's been here recently," said Ray. He was right. Now that they were in shadow, it was easy to see ruts under the new snow that led back into the forest. "Looks like a logging road from way back, because this is pretty good second growth," he looked around. "No one's done any selective cutting in a while, so no loggers have been using this. Maybe some hunters—season's not over until Saturday."

"What do you think, Chief? Shall we keep going?" he asked.

"Excuse me, everyone," said Gina. "I feel the call of nature. Don't leave without me." She marched off down the logging lane.

Osborne had walked back onto the pond, curious to see

what was causing a series of irregular patterns in the drifts near shore. "Looks like someone's been fishing here, Ray. Ouch!" He staggered over a sharp-edged boulder hidden under a drift.

"Wow, be glad you didn't hit that with your sled, Doc," said Lew. "I've had people kill themselves on rocks like that going less than thirty miles an hour. Flip you right over."

"You think someone's been fishing?" asked Ray, walking over to the spot Osborne pointed out. "Looks to me like they got a sled frozen into the ice." Ray looked back towards shore. "Sure—because those tracks look more like a small truck."

"We'll have to ask Clyde if this is where those two sleds got stuck. You know, the ones where the woman read him the riot act."

"Hey! Hey!" Gina came running down the logging road. "Hurry up! Someone's back here." Helmet swinging from one arm, jacket flapping, Gina clutched the front of her snow pants. She hadn't waited to zip.

Gina was wrong. The snowmobile suit that had been flung across the sled so that it appeared to be a body slumped over was empty, although the helmet resting on the hood added to the eerie effect.

"I was looking around and saw the black tarp," said Gina. "When I pulled it back, man, I thought that was a dead body."

They were staring at three snowmobiles someone had stowed under the heavy tarp. "Same type of sleds that those two victims were riding," said Lew. "I want to check the model numbers." She had her cell phone out and was trying to reach Marlene on the switchboard. Three times she tried then shut it down in frustration. "No service, dammit."

"Battery's too cold," said Ray.

"Can't be," said Lew. "I keep it inside my jacket."

"Your friend Clyde's got a phone, doesn't he?"

"Yeah," said Ray. "We're pretty close to his place. Want to head over?"

"Can we keep him from shooting at us?" asked Osborne.

"Ah, he was fooling around," said Ray. "He'd never hurt anybody. Don't worry about it."

"Ray, what do you think of all these tire marks?" asked Lew, waving him over to where she was standing. She had walked about twenty feet down to a clearing. "When we get to Clyde's, tell me if these look like the tracks from the tires on his truck, will you?"

"Just eyeballing it, you've got more than one vehicle backing in here," said Ray. "That's a wide wheel base— you might be better off looking for a van or one of those longer sled trailers. Clyde's got a pickup the size of mine. These tracks are from a bigger vehicle for sure."

Walking back and forth, the icy ruts crunching under his boots, he stooped to brush snow away in several spots, then said, "Been coming and going over a period of time, too. I'd bet someone was here as recently as Friday."

Since Ray was so sure that Clyde wouldn't be patrolling with his shotgun, Osborne made sure that his neighbor led the way. They followed the logging road up to where it connected to yet another lane, which circled around several small, unpopulated lakes. Ray rode with enough authority that Osborne was sure he knew where he was going. Finally, they hit a plowed road.

A few minutes later, at the head of an unmarked drive, Ray pulled his sled over. He set his helmet on his seat and reached into a small compartment on the back of his sled. He pulled out his hat with the fur earflaps and the stuffed trout.

"Probably a good idea I let Clyde see me coming," he said, looking into the rearview mirror on his sled to adjust the hat to just the right angle. "His place is about fifty feet past that curve there. Gina, you stay here with Doc and Chief Ferris. I'll be right back."

"Ladies, be prepared for living quarters like you don't see in the magazines," said Osborne, crossing his arms and leaning back against his sled as Ray ambled off.

"So long as he has a phone," said Lew. "That's my only concern."

"By the way, Doc," said Gina as they chatted while waiting, "you had asked me to check on those snowmobile accidents. Very few occur off trail. Very few. Maybe one a year. Does that help?"

"Why did you want to know that, Doc?" asked Lew.

Before he could answer, Ray came around the corner. This was not the man who had strolled off moments earlier. This was a man much older, a man who put each foot down in a deliberate, defeated way. He didn't even see the branch that knocked his hat off. Nor did he stop to pick his hat up. He just kept coming until they could see the flat sadness in his face.

"Ray . . . ?" Before the word left his mouth, Osborne knew the answer to his question.

twenty-nine

Fly fishermen spend hours tying little clumps of fur and feathers on hooks, trying to make a trout fly that looks like a real fly. But nobody has ever seen a natural insect trying to mate with a Fawning Ginger Quilt.

—Ed Zern, *Field & Stream*

Bending from the waist, Lew straddled what was left of Clyde. She placed both palms under his arms. "Warm enough," she said. "This had to have happened within the last couple hours."

Ray was at the window, as if looking out meant he could refuse to accept what would be confirmed by the end of the day: Someone had used Clyde's own shotgun to end his life.

"Does this place always look like this? I mean, aside from the obvious," said Lew, stepping carefully around the pooled blood to look for the phone. Either Clyde was an unprincipled pack rat or a whirlwind had passed through the spacious one-room cabin. Clothing, papers, dishes, food, and tools were strewn everywhere.

"No," said Ray, squeezing his eyes to keep from weeping. "Clyde . . . um . . ."

As he struggled, Osborne reached out to grasp his friend by the shoulders. "He loves order, y'know. He keeps everything . . . ah . . . everything right where he wants it."

"Then it's been ransacked," said Lew.

That was as much as Ray could manage. Falling into a beat-up, dark brown easy chair near the fireplace where the coals of the last log still smoldered, Ray dropped his face into his hands and wept.

Gina, who had said nothing since entering the room, stood to his side, gently rubbing his back. "Just tell me how I can help," she said.

"The best thing you can do is stay out of the way," said Lew. "The less we disturb the better."

What remained of the afternoon flew by. Lew finally located Clyde's phone, an old rotary dial number, under a pile of newspapers on the counter near the small refrigerator. She asked Marlene to patch her through to Terry at his home.

It took him less than ten minutes to make it into the department and review the files. He confirmed that two of the snowmobiles under the tarp sounded like those belonging to the victims whose legs had been severed.

The other matched the description of the sled belonging to the missing rider, the man from Tomahawk. Lew gave him a description of the empty snowmobile suit and the helmet and asked him to check with the man's family. "Polaris," she said. "It's a red and black Polaris suit with a checkerboard design across the back."

Anxious to have Clyde's body and the crime scene photographed as soon as possible, she tried Bud Michalski, but there was no answer. "What's the point?" She shook her head. "He's supposed to be available at all times. I'm calling Arne tonight—I don't care if it is Christmas."

She reached Bruce at his mother's outside Stevens Point. He offered to head north immediately. Moments after they had spoken, he called back to announce that he had been able to arrange for a pathologist from the Wausau crime lab to drive up with him as well. Lew was relieved, but Osborne couldn't help feeling that Bruce was horning in again. Even his enthusiasm seemed more than a little over the top. After all, this wasn't a party. A decent man was dead.

Lew spent the rest of the afternoon at Clyde's. Both she and Ray refused to leave until Bruce arrived. She assigned Ray the task of going through Clyde's belongings in hopes of finding out if he had any relatives in the area.

Meanwhile, she asked Osborne and Gina to get the snowmobiles back to the trailhead near the Corner Bar. Roger would pick them up there. They then drove Ray's truck and Osborne's car back to Clyde's. After stopping by Lew's farmhouse to pull the roasted turkey from the oven and leave it out on her unheated porch where it could cool safely, Osborne dropped Gina off at Lew's office.

Before driving home, he stopped at Ray's to feed Ruff and Ready, Ray's dogs. He knew without asking that Ray would stay with Clyde until the old man was at rest in the morgue. When he walked in his own back door, it was nearly six.

No one was home. A note from Mallory said she was spending the night at Erin's. Osborne pressed his lips together in an attempt at a smile. Of course she thought she was giving him an opportunity to spend an evening alone with a dear friend. Not necessary now. Hell, he'd even forgotten to leave his gift at her house.

Osborne made himself a sandwich from the leftover roast beef, but he wasn't very hungry, so Mike got half. He wanted to be in Wausau by seven the next morning. The Dental Society annual meeting panels usually started at eight. That would mean getting up by five. He decided to turn in early.

At nine-thirty, he tried Lew at home. No answer. He called the office, but Marlene said she was still with Bruce and the pathologist. She also said that Lew had asked if he could help out in the morning. Osborne asked Marlene to remind her he had the Dental Society meeting and would call as soon as he got back.

A final call to Ray went unanswered.

The drive south in the morning dark didn't help his spirits. He was so preoccupied that he almost forgot to bring along the dentures he'd found in the forest. By the time he parked, he had decided to cancel his reservation for dinner that night.

He was worried about Ray. Clyde might have been an eccentric and stingy with his recipes, maybe even smelled bad, but he was a close friend of Ray's. At a time like this, his neighbor would need him.

"Paul Osborne, you razzbonya," a deep voice over his left shoulder so startled Osborne that he spilled half his coffee into the saucer, "how the heck you doin'?" Rob Kudla had ten years on Osborne but was still practicing in Stevens Point. He was one of the reasons Osborne enjoyed attending the annual event even though he was retired. No better time to catch up with old friends.

"Well, pal, since you asked," said Osborne, and proceeded to give Rob a full report. He started with the fly-tying dilemma and ended with poor old Clyde.

"Certainly not boring up there, is it?" chuckled Rob. "I got a suggestion for the fly tying. This *is* a gift from a woman, right? So you can't return it."

"Both statements are accurate," said Osborne.

"Think pink squirrel," said Rob. He sat back, fingers laced over his chest and a look of infinite wisdom on his face. A skinny man, his brown hair white now, Rob had a sharp nose and black brown eyes that were always laughing. Had been laughing since Osborne met him in dental school at Marquette forty years earlier.

"Forget that—I haven't had a drink in two years," said Osborne. "Can't stand ice cream drinks anyway."

"My pink squirrel is not a drink," said Rob. "You do

what I tell you—whoever she is will be convinced you're a master fly tyer—and you'll only ever have to learn to tie one damn trout fly in your entire life."

"Sure. And if I buy that, what else can you sell me?" said Osborne.

"I am dead serious." Rob scooted his chair forward. He pulled out a pen and started sketching on the back of the program he was holding.

"The pink squirrel is my signature trout fly. I can guarantee it'll catch bluegill, bass, trout, steelhead, perch, crappie, sunfish, suckers—even carp. I'll bet you I've tied four thousand over the years. It's the only fly I ever tie—I can do twenty an hour.

"Once I teach you a double whip finish, you'll look like a pro. All you need is a couple hundred #12 Mustad hooks from Cabella's, some brass beads, a pile of coral pink chenille pills, and some toilet ring seal wax. If you can afford it, I prefer a #14 scud hook, but they're pretty expensive. Tell you the truth, the Mustad 3906 works fine."

"Toilet ring seal wax?"

"Yeah, you mix that with beeswax and stick it in a Chapstick container. Real easy to use. I'll write down all the directions for you. See me at lunch."

"And that's all you ever tie—a pink squirrel?"

"That's all I ever fish with! Sounds crazy, I know, but I got twenty years of pink squirrels to prove it. Works under all conditions. 'Course, you still have to read your water, steal along quietly enough and make a decent presentation. Trust me, you will always catch fish . . . and the girl, too.

"Paul, you gotta give it a try. I'll be in your neck of the woods for some ice fishing next weekend. If you want, I'll stop by your place and tie a few up to show you how."

"Toilet seat wax, right?"

"Toilet *ring* seal wax. I'll give you a list and the directions at lunch."

The day was looking brighter. "Say, before you go, Rob—what do you think of these?" Osborne unwrapped the dentures. "Not porcelain, these are human. Would you believe I found them out in the woods?"

"Know who you should show these to? Remember Ed Wallace from our class? He's working on a history of dentistry for the National Dental Society. See what he thinks. He's here with his wife somewhere."

Osborne knew Ed well. He was retired from a practice outside Milwaukee, but he had grown up in Rhinelander where his parents owned a small resort. They'd hunted and fished together often when they were in their mid-twenties. Even now, Ed's wife, Maddie, made sure Osborne always received the Wallace family Christmas card.

Draining his coffee after Rob left, Osborne checked the morning program. He choked, spewing coffee across the table. One of the early panels was titled "Using Allograft Tissue in Your Dental Practice." He checked his watch. He had ten minutes. A fresh cup of coffee in hand, he hurried down the hall.

Ninety minutes, a slide presentation, and two handouts later, Osborne was convinced Gina Palmer was right, Bruce was wrong, and Lew had something more sinister than credit card fraud on her hands.

According to the tissue expert conducting the panel, the cadaver femur was in great demand. More and more dentists were using products made from the shaft: cortical bone was ground into powder or gel form and used for grafting tissue into the mouth during periodontal surgery. Even a skin-based matrix could be used in dental surgery. One of the dentists in the audience mentioned hearing that these procedures were proving to regenerate bone growth.

The first handout listed the key panel points, but it was the second handout—the one citing allograft tissue sources—that stunned Osborne. High on the list of providers of cadaver femur products was a firm with which he was familiar—Theurian Resources Inc. The man was in cement all right: bone cement.

thirty

Inspired by the beauty of trout, Franz Schubert composed the "Trout Quintet."

He didn't have to search far for Ed and Maddie Wallace. They were six people ahead of him in line for the Holiday Inn luncheon buffet.

"Is this seat taken?" He beamed down at Maddie. She was darn cute in her twenties when they had first met, and time had been good to the petite brunette—the brunette might be fading to white, but she was still easy on the eyes. Ed was looking good, too. Age spots aside, his face was as fine-boned as ever, his eyes kind, and the set of his shoulders firm.

Osborne felt a touch of envy as he set his plate down next to Ed's. The Wallaces were one of those rare couples who had weathered well together. They exchanged a few pleasantries, then Osborne reached into his pocket for the dentures, which he placed with care a decorous distance from everyone's lunch. "Rob Kudla suggested I show you these, Ed."

"You've got to be kidding me," said Ed, fork poised in the air. "Where did you find those?"

Osborne told his bird hunting story. This time, for Maddie's benefit, he included the wolf. "So there I was running to beat hell—gun in one hand, dentures in the other."

"They were stolen from the dental school at Marquette University," said Ed. "You remember Harley Fruehauf? He was a lumber Fruehauf, family money from the old days. He endowed a permanent exhibit that I helped set up and where these were on display."

"Heard the name often," said Osborne. "Wasn't he kind of a strange one? An orthodontist, if I remember right."

"I wouldn't call him 'strange,'" said Ed. "He was unique."

Maddie sputtered at her husband's choice of words. "Oh, Ed. He was as nutty as they come. Be honest."

"Well . . . okay. Harley was a bit extreme." said Ed, "I have to be careful because he left money to the state dental society, and a grant from that endowment is funding this history that I'm writing."

"He collected lightbulbs," said Maddie. "Does that tell you anything? What do you do with sixty thousand lightbulbs?"

"Take it easy, honey," said Ed with a chuckle. "We all have our quirks."

"Tell Paul what he did with his quirks," said Maddie, stabbing a fork into her lettuce.

"Quite the collector, Harley, and a very generous man," said Ed. "He displayed his bulbs in a room in the basement under his office that he called The Fruehauf Museum of Incandescent Lighting.

"But," Ed waved his index finger, "before you poke too much fun, I want you to know the man was a pretty bright bulb himself. When it came to the science of dentistry, Harley was no slouch. Right up to when he died.

"Not only did he specialize in orthodontics, it's my opinion Harley set the standards for prosthodontics. That man knew more about the art and science of creating dentures than anyone of our generation, Paul. I got to know him pretty well the last few years of his life. They were members of our church in Fox Point, and he asked me to work with him on the exhibit.

"That's why I recognize the dentures you've got there. Harley had collected those teeth over the years and was using them to experiment with remineralizing. He was convinced that by putting minerals back into the teeth, you could repair early decay.

"But why go to all the trouble of getting teeth from so many different people?" asked Osborne.

"Two reasons. First, he wanted to test on smooth surfaces and, second, because we know all teeth decay at different rates and for different reasons. He figured that using teeth from different individuals could telescope the time involved.

"At least that's the theory he shared with me. He died before this set disappeared, thank goodness. The theft would have broken his heart. Irritated the heck out of me.

"Still can't believe it happened, but we had no security to speak of. So when two busloads of teenagers from a summer camp outside Rhinelander came through one day—and we found the teeth missing the next—I was convinced some smart aleck kid swiped them.

"In a way, it was a self-fulfilling prophecy. I don't know if old Harley had had stroke or what but he wasn't easy to work with in his later years. Just obsessed that someone was going to steal his ideas. That man didn't only have a lock on every door—he locked every damn *drawer*. Some days it would take thirty minutes to find your files, not to mention pens and pencils.

"When the dentures disappeared there was nothing we could do. How do you allege theft of human teeth in this day and age?"

"Biohazards," said Osborne.

"You got it. Rather than let it become a big joke, we dropped it."

"You're right about the kids," said Osborne. "I happen to know from one of my daughters that the stump where I found them is located in an area they call 'the Horsehead Hollow,' a favorite spot for keg parties."

"Stinkers. I'd like to crack a few heads," said Ed. "Well, thanks, Paul. The ghost of Harley Fruehauf will be happy these are back where they belong."

"It's quite an amazing set of dentures, Ed. I had to use a magnifying glass to be sure they weren't porcelain. And the gold in those posts. You can't buy that anymore."

"That's Harley all the way. Who else would spend money on gold of this quality?"

"Or buy sixty thousand lightbulbs," said Maddie. "Those people had money all right—for all the good it did them. Paul, did you ever know Jane and Harley's daughter, Eve? Now there's a sad, sad story. Mary Lee may have met Eve, she knew Jane from the Garden Club."

"Probably so," said Osborne. Ready to finish his lunch and get a call in to Lew about the handout mentioning Theurian Resources before the afternoon panels began, he was listening with half an ear. He nodded and nodded as Maddie chattered on, paying more attention to her cheery eyes than to what she was saying.

". . . It was only five years ago that Jane died of cancer," she was saying, "then Harley had his heart attack and . . . what was it, Ed? Two years ago that Eve committed suicide? And her daughter so young. I felt so sorry for little Lauren. Of course, she's not so little anymore. Last time I saw her, she was taller than her mother. And much better looking."

Osborne looked up from his coleslaw. "Little *who*?"

"Now, Paul, you must know the story. The Fruehaufs' summer home isn't far from you—just outside Three Lakes. Don't you remember the year Mary Lee was cochair and the Garden Club featured the Fruehaufs' on their annual garden tour? That is one amazing house—as wacky as old Harley."

"He designed it," said Ed. "Did a lot of work on it himself. He just loved the place. If I remember right, it belonged to his grandfather. He loved to hunt and fish, but even then he was paranoid. He butchered his own deer, because he swore the local butchers would mix up the animals so you never got your own back."

"Maddie . . . Ed . . ." said Osborne, "you two wouldn't be talking about Lauren *Theurian* by any chance?"

"Yes, Lauren," said Maddie. "She's sixteen or seventeen now."

"I met her just the other day," said Osborne. He explained the circumstances, then said, "She's having some difficulties adjusting to the new stepmother."

"Oh my God—and have you met *her?*" Maddie slapped both hands on the table, her eyes wide.

"Mitten Theurian? She's quite . . . attractive," said Osborne, deciding not to say too much.

"Mitten?" said Maddie. "*Mitten?*" She used the same inflection that he had heard in Patrice Kobernot's voice at the Christmas party when he had somehow managed to insult her.

"Isn't that her name? That's what her husband calls her."

"David Theurian, the grieving widower, waited three months from the date of his wife's death before he married Karin Hikennen. You think that wasn't a scandal in Fox Point? And you know who Karin Hikennen is—"

"That I do know," said Osborne. Whatever he knew didn't stop Maddie.

"Her grandmother ran a chain of brothels and strip clubs from Hurley, Wisconsin, all the way up into the upper peninsula of Michigan. I hear she owns them now."

"Karin Hikennen?" Osborne was flabbergasted. "Tell me again. How did Lauren's mother die?"

"Supposedly she stuck the barrel of a 12 gauge in her mouth. In the laundry room of their Kansas City mansion," said Maddie. "But there isn't a woman among her parents' friends who believe that for a second."

"Whoa, wait a minute," said Osborne. "How . . . had . . ." He didn't know where to start, he had so many questions.

Maddie patted his hand.

"I've heard this story many times," said Ed. "if you'll excuse me a moment, I'll find the gentlemen's room."

"Jane never liked Eve's husband," said Maddie as Ed walked away. "She and Harley were over for dinner once, and she said she always worried that he had married Eve for the family money. But Eve adored him. She wasn't the prettiest girl, you know. Quite shy. But always very well dressed. She might not have had beauty, but she had exquisite taste.

"They met in law school and got married, then moved to Kansas City where he joined his uncle's law firm. Everything was swell at first, they were social, they had little Lauren. Then Dave started coming up to Three Lakes in the winter with a group of men to snowmobile. We think that's when he met Karin—at one of her clubs.

"Now, I don't know any details, but there was word that there had been some shenanigans at the uncle's firm, like embezzlement maybe. I don't know the details. But what I do know is this, Paul. The day that Eve was shot, Dave called her best friend first. Before he called the police, anyone—he called Marcy, and she rushed right over.

"Well, when Dave married that woman so soon after Eve's suicide, Marcy called one of Jane's best friends in our church. A good friend of mine. And do you know she is convinced—this is Marcy, Eve's best friend—she is convinced that Eve was murdered. Her reason? When she got to the Theurians' that morning . . . when she saw Eve dead, she saw something else. Something only her best friend would notice . . ."

Osborne waited as Maddie savored her moment. "Eve was wearing curlers in her hair."

Osborne must have looked disappointed because Maddie grabbed his hand and pumped it as she talked. "Marcy said that Eve was so fastidious—she would *never* have killed herself with curlers in her hair."

*   *   *

Osborne headed back to Loon Lake doing six miles over the speed limit, as fast as he knew he could go without getting a ticket. He had taken one look at the afternoon panel subjects—dental spas, the New Age of the Whiter Smile, invisible teeth aligners—and decided that getting Dave Theurian's personal history to the Loon Lake Police Department was more important.

Maddie's story ended with the fact that friends of the Fruehaufs had hired a private detective to look into Marcy's allegation, but he had been unable to convince the Kansas City police that there was proof enough to classify the suicide as a murder.

"You know, Paul," Maddie had said, "Dave Theurian was well connected in legal circles. Lawyers protect their own—we all know *that*."

He wanted Lew to know that, but when he called the office, Marlene said she was out grabbing a late lunch with Bruce. He left the news about Mitten's real name, then tried Ray, but there was no answer.

Not until he was in the car driving north did it occur to him he should have called Gina. She was working at the *Kansas City Star* when they met—before taking the job in Chicago. She would know reporters who could give them more information on Dave Theurian.

Dave and Eve. With both parents deceased, Eve would have inherited the Fruehauf money. No doubt Dave now had a sizable chunk of that money. If Eve's parents had not liked him, however, they might have taken precautions to see that Lauren's inheritance was protected. But if Lauren were to die . . .

Osborne pressed down on the accelerator. He could risk seventy.

thirty-one

. . . not everything about fishing is noble and reasonable and sane. . . . Fishing is not an escape from life, but often a deeper immersion into it, all of it. The good and the awful, the joyous and the miserable, the comic, the embarrassing, the tragic, and the sorrowful.

—Harry Middleton, *Rivers of Memory*

"Looking for digital needles in haystacks of data, Doc," said Gina in answer to Osborne's rhetorical "How are you doing" as he hurried into Lew's office. Lew's desk was empty, and Gina was perched on her stool, the laptop open.

She swung around to look at him. "Chief Ferris was quite surprised to get your message on the Hikennen woman. She's trying to find Ray and see if he can hustle up to Hurley for a list of employees of hers. Take his mind off Clyde, which would be good. I've never seen him so down."

"Did he meet with Theurian, do you know?"

"Yes—and do I have news for you," said Gina.

"I got a few pieces of information on the family myself," said Osborne, pulling one of the chairs from in front of Lew's desk around so he could face Gina.

"You first, Doc. I can listen with one ear while you talk," she said, her fingers moving on the computer keys. "Need to finish this search on Chief's new coroner, we got so distracted with the Theurians today."

But Osborne wasn't more than two sentences into recounting what Maddie had told him when Gina stopped typing, picked up a long, narrow notebook, and began jotting notes as he spoke. When he had finished, she turned back to the computer.

Osborne watched over her shoulder as she pulled up the archives of the *Kansas City Star* and searched for Eve Theurian's name. "Yes! I saw this before, but I assumed it was just the obit," said Gina. "Now I see there's a longer story. Will you look at that . . ."

She scanned the story faster than Osborne could. "Excellent—it's an in-depth profile of Theurian and his late wife . . . and all the sad things that happened. I'll get a printout for you, Doc.

"And I know that reporter. I'm going to e-mail him right now that we need to talk. See if I can't reach him tonight. I want to know what he knows that didn't make it past his editors. That guy's good, he'll have his notes still. Now let me tell you what we found.

"You said you saw Theurian's company listed on that handout? He's been in the allograft business for about year. And he has been making purchases from funeral homes across the state, including the one run by the Michalskis in Armstrong Creek—which helps explain why your new coroner is so interested. Theurian products are all derived from human bone. Mainly femurs. And when he told Ray he was in cement—by golly he is. Specializes in powders, putty, and gels.

"And he appears to be totally legitimate. Chief Ferris and I are making an unexpected visit over there first thing in the morning. Just to see what the warehouse and lab looks like. It has become much too coincidental to have two victims with their legs severed—so close to a bone tissue processor."

"He can't be that stupid," said Osborne.

"You just told me he's suspected of killing his wife. Trust me, Doc, after twenty years of investigative reporting, I cannot tell you how stupid bright people can be. Now wait till you hear what else I learned this morning.

"Remember I promised Ray I'd do a search on Dave Theurian before he entrusted him with the Hot Mama? So, I got started. First thing I see is Dave listed as president and founder of Theurian Resources Inc. I go to the Web site. Very professional with details on all the freeze-dried products. And the equipment: cold rooms for product storage, screening units for size classification, mixers for product blending, drying chambers with microprocessor controls for biological products. Yadda, yadda.

"Back on the search under his name, I see some interesting history. Now we find out from newspaper stories that he was put on leave by his uncle shortly before Lauren's mother died for suspected embezzlement from client trust accounts.

"After his wife's death, the embezzlement was no longer suspected—he made it a fact. He stole five million dollars from trust accounts, converted it to hundred dollar bills, packed the money into suitcases in his car, and drove across Missouri, staying in cheap motels, until the cops caught up with him.

"At that point, he alleged having had an emotional breakdown. They put in him jail, he pleads insanity. And he gets off. The money is returned, he leaves the firm. Shortly thereafter he marries Karin Hikennen."

"The man is crazy."

"Crazy like a fox. I made a call to the *Star*'s business desk after I saw all this and reached one of the editors on the story. I was trying to figure out how Theurian made the transition from law to allograft tissue. I mean, where does that come from?

"Interesting answer. Shortly after moving to Kansas City with Eve, Dave Theurian was invited to join the board of one of the big hospitals there—surely thanks to

Fruehauf family connections. That hospital is a pioneer in using allograft tissue. And they had their own small scandal when they caught one of their chief administrators making deals on the side with tissue processors."

"Kickbacks?" asked Osborne.

"Yes—and they had several close calls with infections. But that's where Dave Theurian did his R&D on allograft tissue. So when Chief Ferris and I go out there tomorrow morning, one of my questions will be how he learned about the business. Should be interesting, don't you think?"

"How did Ray take all this?"

"He doesn't know yet. Chief Ferris and I are damn sure Theurian's just using Ray to get in with the funeral directors in Loon Lake, but we don't want to come out and say that. Not yet anyway. Poor Ray. He's so upset over Clyde's death. We didn't think it could hurt to let him meet with the guy."

"So they had their meeting."

"As far as I know, yes."

Lew walked into the office. "Doc, I'm glad you're back. Did Gina tell you what we found out about Dave Theurian?"

"She certainly did, and let me tell you what I heard."

Again, Osborne told Maddie's story. When he got to the allegation by Eve's best friend that she was convinced Dave had had a hand in his wife's death because she died with curlers in her hair, both Gina and Lew nodded thoughtfully.

"You don't marry a woman like Karin Hikennen, a.k.a. Mitten the sex kitten, within three months of losing your wife without some history of hanky-panky," said Gina.

"It's the curlers," said Lew.

"I don't get it," said Osborne.

"A man wouldn't," said Lew, "but a woman who puts curlers in her hair is a woman planning ahead."

thirty-two

. . . until a man is redeemed he will always take a fly rod too far back.

—Norman Maclean

"Sounds like quite the day," said Osborne. Gina had turned back to her computer, and Lew seemed ready to chat for a few minutes. Together they walked over to fill their coffee mugs.

"Hell of a day," said Lew. "One thing after another. Started with young Lauren. We had a good talk, Doc. I think I've got her settled down and willing to give her dad some time to find out things on his own.

"Then she took some time with mug shots we've got in of some local no-goodniks, but no one looked like the man she saw with her stepmother.

"Around ten this morning we got a call on a nasty collision at one of the trailheads. I had to send both Roger and Terry out. Six people injured. Two snowmobiles came over a rise and plowed right into a group stopped down below. I'll bet those riders were doing a hundred. No one killed, thank goodness. But we had to call in EMTs from Minocqua and Eagle River."

Back at her desk, Lew collapsed into her chair. "If you

ask me, Doc, when the holidays are over, I'll need a vacation from vacation."

"Oh," she sat forward suddenly, "did Gina tell you what they found at Clyde's?"

"Didn't want to steal your thunder, Chief," said Gina from her perch.

"I sent Ray out to help Bruce this morning," said Lew. "First they went over Clyde's cabin inside and out. They found some tire marks in the drive and went over to see if there might be a match to the ones over where we found the snowmobiles. They got a match all right—and found a strongbox, shoved down between the snowmobiles, with a hundred and seventy five thousand in small bills."

"Are you serious?" Osborne was dumbfounded.

"I want to put a watch on the location. The only possibility I have is Bud Michalski and I'll be damned if I can find that guy. I'm beginning to think he went to Vegas or somewhere. I finally located Arne—he's at a family wedding in Milwaukee. Meanwhile I am really shorthanded. Roger and Terry have their hands full policing the highways and the snowmobile trails."

"Bruce around?" asked Osborne.

"Right now he's back in Wausau with that empty snowmobile suit. Wants to see if they can get some DNA off it. The girlfriend of the missing Tomahawk man identified it as belonging to him."

"Doesn't that make the DNA test redundant?"

"Well, someone had to remove it from the victim and could have scratched themselves or left traces of skin. Bruce is planning to go over it very carefully along with the two suits from the earlier victims.

"That was something else, by the way. I had those poor people, the girlfriend and the parents, here all morning. The parents brought over their son's insurance records, so we were able to confirm that it is his snowmobile that we found.

"I'll tell you, there's one thing worse than dealing with people who have to claim a body, and that's family that knows the worst but have to live in a limbo of not knowing where and how someone died. I made it a point to stay with them as long as they needed me."

Osborne sipped from his coffee. Lew had lost her only son when he was a teenager. The framed photo on the bookshelf by her favorite chair showed a boy who inherited his mother's dark and lively eyes, though he was tempered with his father's bad behavior. She had loved him, and the hurt that the Tomahawk family had to be feeling she would know well: Her child, too, had been murdered.

"And how's Ray? Is he doing any better?"

"I think. I'm keeping him busy, that's for sure. He stopped in after his get-together with Theurian. Your message on Karin Hikennen had just come in, so I asked him if he'd run up to Hurley and see what he could do about getting me a list of her employees—formal or informal.

"That might take his mind off Clyde. He was so downhearted this morning. He went through the old man's papers and still couldn't find any sign of family members. Until we find someone, we have no one to release the body to."

"Don't let your new coroner close to Clyde," said Osborne with a wry smile. "If he so much as touches the old man, Ray'll turn that jabone into horsemeat."

"Speaking of Bud," said Gina from behind Osborne, "why don't you two come over here for a minute. I've got some more information on his references, the funeral directors he interned with in Rice Lake. You know, the ones that were murdered . . ."

"The best reference is a dead reference," said Lew. "Why does that seem appropriate for Mr. Michalski, who, by the way, is still not answering his phone. I would have loved to have him photographing the scene of that snowmobile accident instead of Terry."

"Dock his pay," said Osborne.

"Wish I could, but technically he doesn't start until the first of January."

Mugs in hand, Lew and Osborne crowded in behind Gina.

"So what's this we're looking at?" Lew said.

"This is an interview in the *Rice Lake Gazette* with one of the widows," said Gina, scrolling slowly through the text. "She is quoted as saying that her husband and his partner had no business difficulties or personal problems she was aware of that might have led to the killings.

"But here she says that when she went in to do the bookkeeping after her husband's death—and she was the bookkeeper for the business—she found records missing and some that had been handled incorrectly."

"Huh," said Lew. "Did they ever arrest anyone for the murders?"

"No record of that in the newspaper," said Gina.

"If the widow was the bookkeeper, she may have known Bud," said Osborne.

"That is one reference I would very much like to check," said Lew.

"My mother's family is from Rice Lake; why don't I make that call, Lew," said Osborne, checking his watch. "It's only four, I might be able to catch up with the widow today. I'll work out of the conference room."

"If you'll wait one minute," said Gina, "I've got the name, we know the town and . . ." she hit a few keys, "there you go . . . here's the phone number you need, Doc."

Reticent at first, Margie Dondoneau warmed up the minute she heard that Osborne's Métis grandmother was from Rice Lake. "My father is Métis," she said with pride. "I'll bet they knew each other."

"I'm sure they did," said Osborne. "And those were days when you didn't always say you were Métis either. Took courage."

"You better believe it," said Margie.

After explaining that he was a retired dentist and a part-time deputy helping out with forensic dental IDs and ran-

dom administrative duties, Osborne added that he was a
widower and his duties as a deputy helped to fill the
empty hours.

Margie clucked with sympathy. "You don't have to tell
me, Dr. Osborne. It's not easy being alone. So what do
you need to know about Bud?"

"Just confirming a few things on his résumé. Says here
that he worked in Armstrong Creek before his internship
with you folks."

"That's what he told us," said Margie. "His uncle gave
him a glowing report, but as it turned out, he wasn't as ex-
perienced as we expected. Don't misunderstand—he was
a nice boy. It's just that my husband got a little frustrated
with him at times. He wasn't *careful* enough. Before
Bert's death we were expanding our business with several
companies in the health care field—"

"Oh, sure, the tissue processors," said Osborne, his tone
matter-of-fact.

"Yes, you know about those? My husband and his partner were pioneers in the field, you know. Ours was one of
the first funeral homes in the state to establish an ongoing donation service. With transplants becoming more
and more critical to the health care field, we were quite
proud to be able to help families feel better about their
loss.

"But those donations have to be handled very carefully,
and Bud needed more than a little training in that area."

Using what he had learned during the morning panel
about the use of bone and skin-based matrixes in dental
surgery, Osborne couched his questions in a way that led
Margie to assume he knew more than he did. And she
seemed relieved to talk to someone who didn't find the
subject abhorrent.

"Tendons and ligaments were what we trained Bud to
help with," she said. "But between you and me, that boy
has a hard time with detail. Before I took over the bookkeeping for the business, I taught high school English.
Well, I tell you, the day Bud told me his favorite book

was *How to Kill a Mockingbird* I just about died. That was the one time I suggested to my husband that we find someone else.

"The problem, Dr. Osborne, is you have to harvest quickly and under the most pristine conditions. We couldn't count on Bud to do that. Now, as a coroner he should be fine. All ours does is draw blood, take photos, and keep the records straight. Everything else is turned over to our local pathologists. As a coroner, I would expect Bud to do just fine."

"Margie, I'm glad to hear that. By the way, did I read somewhere that you had problems with records?"

"We got that all cleared up." Margie's voice tightened.

"Do you mind telling me what kind of problems? I mean, was it anything Bud might have handled? Accuracy in record keeping is an essential responsibility for the coroner in this jurisdiction."

"Like I said, we got it all cleared up. Although . . . in fairness to the memory of my husband, I'll be honest. Bud was involved. Again, it was simple sloppiness. The problem was limited to two families who were under the impression that they had approved organ donations only to discover a serious misunderstanding."

"In what way?"

She sighed heavily. "They asked for a private viewing before the burial and found that more than the approved donations had been taken. It happened on Bud's watch, and I think he just wasn't paying attention to the fine print. He explained to us that he thought once a donor contract was signed that all tissues in good condition were available for use. That's what I mean when I say he's not the best when it comes to details."

"Oh dear," said Osborne. "How did you handle that?"

"It wasn't easy, I'll tell you. People were quite upset. The families filed lawsuits but we reached a financial settlement that they're happy with. Thank the Lord I was able to keep the details out of the paper. My son-in-law is taking over the business, and that would have killed it."

"How fortunate it was only two families."

"Yes, indeed." Margie had paused just long enough for Osborne to sense she *hoped* it was only two.

"Good," said Osborne reassuringly. "Probably just a co-incidence those were the records that were missing."

"Oh no, the missing records were hard copies of my invoices to the processors we supply. I'm old-fashioned, and I like paper—in case of an electrical outage, you know. You know, the more I think about it, I must have done something with those myself."

"You've been such a help, Margie, thank you," said Osborne. "I'm so sorry for your loss. Any news on who they think may have—"

"Yes and no. They arrested a young man on the Minnesota border who's been breaking into veterinary offices and funeral homes—looking for drugs. The police are convinced he killed Bert and Jeremy during an attempted robbery. Personally, I doubt we'll ever know."

Osborne picked up his notes from the conference room table and made his way down the hall to Lew's office. Just outside her door, he could hear Ray's voice.

"Our new coroner's got an interesting day job," Ray was saying. "Did you know he's been working for the last six months as a bouncer for Karin Hikennen?"

thirty-three

. . . bluegills . . . ounce for ounce, there is no better scrapper in fresh water.

—Elmer Ransom

As Osborne walked into the room, Gina jumped off her stool, Bud Michalski's résumé in her hand. "How can that be? Says right here he's been working the call center at that pet supply place over in Rhinelander. I checked it out, Ray. He does a three-day twelve-hour shift with four days off."

"Did I say 'day job'—I meant nights," said Ray, throwing his parka over the chair in front of Lew's desk. "He works nights at either the Cat House or Thunder Bay, Wednesdays and weekends."

Lew looked so stunned, Ray raised his hands in defense. "I'm not lying. You can chalk it all up to some bad bluegills, but I got the scoop, folks. I think everyone better take a seat."

And for a change he talked fast. As he recounted the events of the afternoon, Ray was as focused and determined as a man with a loaded gun. No joking around, no wasting anyone's time.

"I walked in and recognized the guy right away," he

said. "Remember the Japanese fella I said was at Thunder Bay last summer? The one who was leading karaoke one of the nights I chatted with Eileen. Well, he was at the bar when I walked into the Cat House today.

"So I took a seat and asked how the fishing was. He said he didn't fish, and I said too bad 'cause I just caught a nice mess of bluegills. He said he hated bluegills—'god-dam marauding foreign invaders' he called 'em.

" 'Come on,' " I said. 'How can you say such a thing about my favorite piscator.' And offered to buy him a beer, of course. So he told me. And when he finished telling me why he hates the lovely bluegill, I did what any self-respecting American would do. I offered to buy him another beer.

"Only this round we left the Cat House, went next door. I mean, this is a town with thirty-one bars for a population of eighteen hundred, so I suggested we sample the local culture. That's when he told me he was celebrating due to the fact that he had just quit his job at the Cat House due to the fact that last night the owner shoved a dancer's head in the toilet. He figured he's next on her list . . ." Ray could not resist a pause.

"You have our full attention, Ray," said Lew. That was understatement. Both Gina and Osborne were hunched forward in their chairs.

"The gentleman I was talking to? His name is Keni-churo Fujimoto—Ken for short. Real nice guy. Grew up in Oshino, Japan, and came here for college. He's trained as a lab tech in freeze drying pharmaceutical and biological products.

"Dave Theurian hired him right out of school to work for Theurian Resources. Only when he got here Dave told him because it's a start-up business, he only had a couple days' work a week for him. That's when Mrs. Theurian offered him the job running karaoke nights at three of her clubs.

"He said it was fun at first. He would work Monday to

Wednesday at the lab, then have his days off and work nights. Fun until he discovered what was going on.

"That's kinda how he met Eileen. She came to work for the Theurians at the same time he did and found out, like Ken, that the job opportunity she had been promised—in her case it was the dancing contract—wasn't gonna happen. At least not right away. Like Ken, she was assigned another job, which was basic bookkeeping—paying bills, handling invoices, ordering supplies. And driving around with Ken to collect receipts.

"He said about a month into working the clubs, he and Eileen started to notice things. On the few occasions Karin showed up at one of the clubs, which was only when she was angry about something, she didn't hesitate to abuse the staff. A bartender got her fingers slammed in the cash drawer. The dancer whose head was shoved in the toilet? That was because the girl held out ten bucks in tips. An in-house legend says when Karin was a teenager, a boyfriend thought he could dump her: she ran over him with his own car. Yep, according to Ken, the people who work for Karin Hikennen work scared."

"Did he know anything about the credit card—" Lew couldn't help interrupting.

"Hold your horses . . . I'm getting there. This fall Eileen told Ken she was getting calls from club patrons, not locals but people from the cities, who said their credit card statements showed unauthorized cash advances—always *after* they had used their cards at one of the clubs. They accused someone connected to the clubs of putting those through."

"That fits," said Lew. "I called around. No recent complaints of credit card theft in the county, nor the neighboring counties. If tourists had a problem, they would call their card companies direct—and the police in their own districts."

"Now it so happens that Bud Michalslci started working as a bouncer right last summer—"

"And you're sure it's Bud?" asked Lew. "Were you able to get names of the other people working there?"

"Oh, yeah," Ray said, reaching into his back pocket, "Ken wrote them down. He's been there long enough to know everyone at the Hurley club. Bud's was one of the first names he mentioned, because everyone working there noticed how he and Karin seemed to get along real well. Real well.

"At first, Ken assumed it was a status thing. Bud bragged how his family had so much influence when it came to tax assessments, shoreline regs, that kind of stuff. Now he's sure there's something going on between those two. Bud acts like a sick puppy when she's around.

"Keep in mind Ken is still working part time for Dave and something real curious happens. Early last week, Dave Theurian was out of town on business. Ken drove out to the warehouse to see if there had been any deliveries that needed processing. Driving in, he passed Bud driving out.

"Didn't think too much about it until he started work in the lab and found that someone had been running the freeze-drying equipment, someone who didn't realize the computer recorded all operations. This was odd. Supposedly Ken and Dave are the only two with keys to the warehouse—but the computer showed the units had been used during Dave's absence. And Ken knew he sure as hell hadn't been there.

"He said something to Dave about it, too, because whoever had used the equipment didn't seem to know what they were doing. Any tissue processed might have been compromised and shouldn't be shipped. He's not sure Dave heard him—the guy seemed to have a lot on his mind. Ken's main worry was covering his own ass."

"What about Eileen—did he say anything about her death?" asked Lew.

"Oh, yeah. That's when he made up his mind to quit. He was so bummed. They had become good friends, and he's positive Karin had something to do with it. Eileen had confronted Karin about something the day before her body was found. Right in the office, which is located at the back of the Cat House, so everyone heard the shouting.

"Ken heard Eileen slam out and watched her drive off. That's the last he saw of her. Karin left a little while later.

"And that skimmer? I described it to Ken. He was told it was a card cleaner. Didn't think much about it. As far as he knew, Bud would set it by the cash register on karaoke night and badger the girl tending bar if she forgot to use it."

"I need to get your friend in here," said Lew. "I guess he'll be surprised to find out you're a deputy, huh?"

"No," said Ray. "When he was halfway into telling me all this, I figured he better know. I also told him to get his butt out of town."

"What did he say to that?"

"He was already on his way. When I ran into him at the bar, he was only there because he was saying good-bye to a couple of the girls. He gave me his new phone number, Chief. He starts a new job at a hospital in Minneapolis. They're doing ACL transplants and offered him double what he's been making for Dave and Karin."

"I hope he knows not to say anything to anyone who might alert Bud or Karin—"

"Can't imagine he would. Not only is he leaving town today, but he said Bud hasn't been working the club the last few days—hasn't been around at all."

"Ray, you done good," said Lew. "I'll put in for double time for you. Be sure to make out an expense report for your gas and all the beverages."

"Thanks, Chief, but one more thing I want to mention. It's about Dave Theurian." Ray leaned back in the chair, a look of regret on his face.

"That guy's not interested in my lure. We had our get-together over at the Pub, and I could tell he wasn't paying attention the way he should have."

The room was quiet as Ray spoke. "You know what he

really wanted this morning? He wants me to introduce him to Joe Terzinski and Mark Stiles. I could see why after Ken explained that Theurian Resources' cement isn't exactly what you want to use in a sidewalk. Then it made sense. Grief counseling? Baloney."

"We were planning to give you the details this afternoon," said Gina.

"So everyone here knows?" Ray looked at Osborne, who nodded.

"Who are the two men you just mentioned, Ray?" said Gina.

"Joe owns the funeral home used by the Catholics around town, and Mark is the manager for St. Mary's Cemetery—the guy who hires me to run the backhoe." Ray gave a rueful grimace. "Never thought my sideline as a gravedigger could make me so attractive."

"Not a gravedigger—a *cemeterian*," said Gina. "We gotta upgrade your title, Ray. Who knows, the tissue trade could change your life."

Ray waggled a finger at her and broke into a half smile. "Yeah, well, the only cheeks I plan to fillet are the ones I find on walleyes."

"Ray, that is so gross!" said Gina, slamming the papers in her hand on Lew's desk. "That is a totally inappropriate remark."

"Honestly, Ray," said Lew. But she caught Osborne's eye to share a look of relief: inappropriate for sure, but good to have Ray back to his old self.

"One question, Ray," said Osborne. "You said you and this Japanese fellow bonded over bluegills. What the heck was that all about?"

"Oh, I'll tell you, he hates those fish. To hear Ken talk, it's a criminal situation in Japan.

"Years ago Mayor Daley of Chicago visited Tokyo and as a thank-you he sent Emperor Akihito some bluegills to put in the Ushigafuchi Moat at the Imperial Palace. The moat was famous for its seventeen native species and now they put in the bluegills, okay? Over time, those bluegills have eaten every one of the native fish. When Ken calls our beautiful bluegills 'marauding foreign invaders,' he's not kidding.

"Yep, ol' Ken was in the mood to chat. All it took was one bluegill to get that dude started."

Gina unhooked her computer. "I think I've covered the bases for you, Lewellyn," she said as she shoved her laptop into its case. "I have a call in to that *Kansas City Star* reporter who wrote the feature story on the Theurians. He has my number and the number at Ray's place, so if I hear anything critical I'll give you a call. But he could be taking the week off."

"What's that?" asked Ray.

Gina waved a hand. "Oh, I've got more to tell you that'll make you just as happy you aren't in business with that man. Chief, do you mind if I corral Ray to take me fishing in the morning?"

"Heck no," said Lew. "Please, do that. You both deserve a break."

"Are you sure, Chief?" asked Ray. "I'm still trying to locate Clyde's family."

"If I need you, I'll call. Now get out of here—both of you!"

"What about you, Lewellyn?" said Osborne, pulling on his parka. "You need a break. Can I at least buy you a burger over at the Pub? Mallory is having dinner with friends, so I'm baching it . . ."

"I can't, Doc, I have paperwork up the wazoo. I need a warrant to search Thunder Bay and more paperwork to persuade my colleagues up in Hurley to search the Cat House. I have to find Arne Steadman—this situation with Bud is driving me nuts.

"But if I can take a rain check," she walked towards him as she spoke, "you are invited to my place for New Year's Eve."

"Just me?"

"Just you." She reached up and he reached down.

So the wind didn't seem too cold as he bounded out to his car, frisky as a sixteen-year-old. Plus he had plans for breakfast. Ray's last words as he held the door for Gina were to invite his neighbor down for a classic ice-fishing breakfast: wild rice pancakes, local maple syrup, and sautéed walleye.

thirty-four

The fish are either in the shallows, or the deep water, or someplace in between.

—Anonymous

The long-forecast snow started during the night. Six inches of the white stuff forced Osborne to put all his weight against his back door in order to open it far enough to let the dog out. And it was good snow—not too heavy, not too light—ideal for cross-country skiers and snowmobile trails. It was the kind of snow that smelled like money to the Loon Lake Chamber of Commerce.

A hollow howl of wind tossed the tops of the Norway pines lining the lane down to Ray's, and a scrim of falling snow obscured the lights in the trailer windows. Osborne loved days like this.

He'd awakened with a plan: breakfast with Ray and Gina, then a quick trip to town for coffee with his pals at McDonald's. On to Lew's office to deliver her Christmas gift, then back to his own cozy living room. Once home, he would set the fly-tying vise on a card table in front of the fireplace and tackle the damn pink squirrel.

*   *   *

Lauren had called shortly after midnight, reaching Nick who was just falling asleep. She kept breaking down in tears as she whispered that even with her door closed, she could hear her father and stepmother screaming at each other. Nick did his best to calm her down, then called Ray.

"She's one jumpy kid," said Ray, standing at the stove in his long underwear. He was lifting and turning one slice of bacon after another, the gas as always on low. Ray was a firm believer in slow cooking. Too slow sometimes, but just right this morning.

"Can you blame her?" said Osborne, sipping his coffee from where he sat at Ray's kitchen table. It might be blowing snow and twenty-three degrees outdoors, but inside the trailer was cozy. Glancing into Ray's living room, he saw a suitcase open in one corner but no other evidence of Gina sleeping on the sofa. Not that it was any of his business.

"Nick wasn't sure if I should call her back or not. I tried—but no answer. Nick said he would keep trying until he could reach her. If not, he'd call back. I didn't get any more calls, so things must have settled down."

"Knowing what I know now about her father, I worry about that girl," said Osborne. He had filled Ray in with all the details from Maddie Wallace.

"Yep," said Ray. "On the other hand, because so many friends of the family suspect Dave of having a hand in his wife's death, don't you think he would be doubly careful to see that nothing happens to his daughter?"

"You're right about that. He'd be in the hoosegow so fast."

Gina came walking down the hall in a pair of bright red sweatpants and a matching turtleneck, her head down as she rubbed at her hair with a towel.

"Where's my coffee, guys?" She plopped into the chair beside Osborne and inhaled deeply. "Life doesn't get much better than this, doncha know."

"That's my line," said Ray.

"You better believe it," said Gina.

The phone on the wall near the stove rang. Ray cradled it between his ear and his right shoulder as he lifted crispy strips of bacon from the pan and laid each carefully onto a paper towel.

"Uh-huh," he said, turning off the gas under the front burner. "Yep, where is she? When she calls back, you tell her to stay right where she is until she sees Doc's car in the driveway . . . no, we can't take the time, Nick. I'll call you when we get there."

Wiping his hands with a towel, Ray turned around to face Osborne and Gina. "Lauren just called Nick on her cell phone—she thinks her father is dead. She heard noises in the driveway, looked out her bedroom window, and saw her stepmother and the boyfriend carrying his body. Just now."

"Where is she?" asked Osborne, jumping to his feet.

"Holy shit," said Gina, rushing into the living room and grabbing clothes from her suitcase.

"She's locked herself in her bedroom. They don't know she saw them."

The phone rang again. Ray listened, said "Okay," and hung up. "They just left in one of the big cars—but without the body."

While Ray and Gina scrambled to pull clothes on, Osborne reached Lew at home. It wasn't even six-thirty yet.

"I'll meet you at the fire number in front of Theurian's drive," she said. "I have to call the sheriff's office. Theurian's property is outside my jurisdiction. He may want to go in with us. Call Nick back and give him the emergency number. Tell him to keep us updated if he hears more from Lauren. I'll alert Maureen to patch him through to my radio or the cell phone."

The two cars, Doc's and Lew's cruiser, fishtailed and skidded their way up Theurian's drive and around to the back of the house. Ice was building under the snow, making it difficult to maintain traction. Since the last call from Lauren indicated she was still alone in the house, Osborne pulled his car off to the right, alongside the garage. Lew 's cruiser hit ice as she stopped in front of the stairs leading up to the deck, her left front fender nearly taking out the railing.

The county sheriff had given Lew the okay to go in without him. He and his deputies were working a three-car, four-fatality pileup caused by a jackknifed semitrailer. The accident had closed Highway 17 south of Rhinelander, and traffic was backing up.

"You need me to uncase the shotguns?" asked Gina from the backseat.

"I don't," said Osborne. Driving in, he had noted no new tire tracks in the snow, so he felt confident only Lauren was inside. He hated carrying guns around people.

"What about you, Ray?"

"Yeah." Ray reached for his gun as he got out of the front passenger seat.

"Back me up, Ray," said Lew, dashing up the stairs, her SIG-Sauer drawn. Ray followed, twelve gauge ready. Osborne and Gina stayed by his car, crouched low behind the passenger door.

As Lew knocked, Ray shouted, "Lauren—it's Ray, we're here. Open up." They waited. Lew knocked again. Again Ray shouted.

Still no answer. Osborne backed off towards the garage. He tried the knob on the door and pushed it open to peer inside.

"Lew, *both* Hummers are gone," he called. The snow was so heavy he could barely see her standing on the deck.

At that moment, Lauren threw open the door. "Hurry," she cried. "My dad's downstairs but the door is locked. I've been trying and trying . . ." She burst into tears as Osborne and Gina ran up the stairs to the back foyer.

Ray was already pulling at the drawer where he knew Theurian kept the keys, but it was locked. "Lauren, what about the key to your bedroom?"

"On my dresser—"

"Go get it—we'll meet you downstairs."

Lauren ran down the hall towards her room, as the rest of them crossed through the main hall past the darkened living room and down the stairs, stopping at the door to the room where Mitten said they processed their berries and butchered their deer.

They waited for Lauren. She came rushing down the stairs, the key in her hand. Ray grabbed it.

"They had this big fight last night, see—"

"Who's 'they'?" asked Lew, keeping an eye on what Ray was doing. Sitting on the stairs, he held the key against his left knee. In his right hand was the file he kept in the pocket of his parka for filing down fishhooks. Twice he swiped at the key, then tried it in the door. No luck.

"My dad and Mitten. She started it. All of a sudden screaming at him to stay out of her business. I heard like a slap, then he said she was doing her best to ruin his operation—that anything she did reflected on him.

"They just kept at each other. It was so awful. That's when I called Nick. I kept thinking, I should break into their room and tell my Dad what she's been doing—but Nick kept saying that was a really bad idea."

"Which it was; you would not have helped. You could have been hurt, too. So then what?"

Again Ray tried the key in the door.

"Then this morning . . ."

"Ray, what is it you're doing with that key?" asked Gina in a low voice. "Why don't you just blow a hole in the damn door."

"Give him two more seconds," said Lew. "He'll get it."

"How do you know that?"

"Ray's first misdemeanor," said Lew, raising her eyebrows slightly. "When he was in high school, he managed to find a key to the boy's gym and turn it into a master key that unlocked every door in the school—perpetrated mischief for months before he got caught."

"Any kid who takes shop knows the secret," said Ray,

as he gave another careful swipe with the file. "If there's a master key to a building, all you need is one of the other keys and a file and you'll find your way in.

"Okay, let's try again," he said. This time the door opened. Lew was the first to enter, though slowly. Dim light through the sliding glass doors gleamed off the two steel tables in the center of the room. The room was empty. Even the counters were bare.

"Footprints," said Lew, pointing at puddles of grit and water on the ceramic tiles. "Someone's been here but—"

At the sound of tires crunching in the driveway, everyone turned to look towards the windows. "That'll be the sheriff," said Lew.

"I'll go meet him, show him where we are," said Gina, running up the stairs. She was back in less than a minute with an odd expression on her face. Before she could say anything, Dave Theurian walked into the room, amazement on his face.

"Daddy! But I thought—" Lauren burst into tears and flung herself at her father.

"Hey, hey, Lauren, take it easy." Theurian looked over the head of his sobbing daughter. "What are you people doing here?"

"Chief Ferris, Loon Lake Police. We met the other night," said Lew, stepping forward. "What are *you* doing here? Your daughter reported you missing."

"*Missing*? For heaven's sake, Lauren, I had business appointments in Madison starting at noon but the roads are so bad, I turned back at Stevens Point. Lauren . . ." Theurian grasped his daughter by the shoulders, pushing her away until he could see her face. "I know I told you I would be gone overnight."

"Yes, Dad, you did but—" Lauren threw her hands up. "Oh, Daddy, I was so scared . . ." Theurian pulled her close as she shuddered, sobbing, into his shoulder.

thirty-five

Of course, folk fish for different reasons. There are enough aspects of angling to satisfy the aspirations of people remarkably unalike.

—Maurice Wiggin

"Theurian Resources is highly technical in its methods and our product line is considered quite innovative within the health care field," Theurian was saying. "We are fully vested with all the proper licensure."

They were sitting around a table that doubled as his desk in the spacious room that Theurian referred to as "the lab" and that took up half the warehouse. Ray and Lauren were at the main house. Lauren was calling to assure Nick she was okay, while Ray, at Lew's request, was alerting the sheriff's office to the false alarm.

It was Gina's prodding about his company's role as a tissue processor that had prompted Theurian to invite Lew, Osborne, and Gina into the warehouse for a quick tour of his operation.

"Let's dispel any negative connotations right off the bat," he'd said as they walked across the driveway through the blowing snow. "Boy, am I happy I turned back. We must be getting an inch an hour."

But if he was good at reading snow, the man was a failure with bright women. Theurian made no effort to hide the fact that it required his level best to explain the complicated science behind his company to the chief of the Loon Lake Police and Gina Palmer. No matter that Gina had been introduced as a 'technical services deputy,' he answered her questions as if she had just graduated from a voc-ed school.

Describing his company in words so simple they bordered on condescension, he didn't improve matters by bracketing various remarks with—"And you understand, of course, Dr. Osborne"—his tone implying that only a medical professional like himself or Osborne could hope to grasp such sophisticated concepts. Each time he said it, Gina winked at Lew.

Osborne sat quietly, as the man talked at the two women. It was like watching a fly fisherman cast a dry fly so poorly that it presented with a splash loud enough to hasten the good humor of a lurking trout.

And when Theurian had completed "Class 101 in Tissue Processing," it was Gina's turn to grill: Where did he find trained staff? Who were his suppliers? Who inspected the operation and how frequently? What were the most common complaints received from purchasing hospitals?

If the caliber of her questions came as a surprise, Theurian didn't flinch. Only a slight shaking of his fingers whenever he reached to pull a sheet of paper or a brochure from the file cabinets behind his desk gave any hint of stress.

"The documentation is all here," he said over and over, ready to prove his point with a blizzard of paperwork. "I welcome anyone—anyone with credentials, that is—to examine everything in this building except my database of suppliers and accounts. Those lists are confidential. I'm sure you understand."

"Is the Michalski Funeral Home in Armstrong Creek one of your suppliers?" asked Gina, ignoring his remark. Osborne was beginning to understand what she meant when she said she was good at "confrontation interviews." The woman was relentless.

"Never heard of them." Theurian's response was so immediate and abrupt it had to be true. Nevertheless, Gina made a note on the pad she was carrying.

"Getting close to the end here," said Gina with a pleasant smile, "how's business? Are you doing well?"

The silky voice, the stone face, the façade faltered. Theurian's shoulders drooped. "Up to a point," he said, "up to a point. Never easy starting a business from scratch. I've got suppliers and state-of-the-art processing capacity, but two of my major accounts got some bad press recently. They put a freeze on purchasing. Sorry," he winced, "poor choice of words there. But business will pick up. Always does." If Theurian was trying to sound positive, he failed.

"I have one favor to ask," he said. "My daughter isn't well informed on what I do. And I would like to keep it that way until the company is on its feet. Do you mind not sharing with Lauren what we've discussed here? It's rather a grim business for a young girl to understand."

But if he was concerned about Lauren's understanding of his innovative and pioneering business practices, Dave Theurian had been nowhere near as considerate of her understanding of his relationship with her stepmother.

"All you saw was Mitten getting some help from the chief maintenance engineer for her properties, which she has just put up for sale," he had said while they were still in the basement of the main house.

"That was plastic sheeting over some building supplies—not a body, for heaven's sake. You've been watching too much television. And how did you get in here, anyway? Mitten keeps this room locked."

Theurian turned to Lew. "My wife is the hunter and the gatherer for the family. She grew up north of here and loves to hunt, pick berries, that kind of thing. This is her place for dressing her wild game and her morels and her berries. Some women want privacy in the kitchen—this is Mitten's little nest. Off limits unless invited."

"Really," said Lew. "She told us you shot the buck this fall."

"She did, huh. Yeah, well, it was a nice one." Theurian was less than convincing.

"Nest?" said Ray. "You call this place a 'nest'?" Ray jerked his head towards the stainless steel tables and countertops, the stainless steel doors on the refrigerated lockers lining the walls. "Little short on cozy, doncha think?"

"It's how my wife wants it," said Theurian. He walked over to the door. "Did you break the lock? She's going to be furious—"

"I have some questions for Mrs. Theurian on a separate matter," said Lew, interrupting. "When do you expect her back?"

"Late this afternoon sometime. She has business up north, meetings with the real estate group brokering the properties for her." Theurian looked relieved to have the father-daughter bickering behind him.

"In that case, perhaps you can answer my questions. I believe your wife's legal name is Karin Hikennen. Is that correct?"

"Yes, she kept her maiden name after our marriage for business reasons."

"But you call her Mitten?"

"I know that sounds silly, but from the day we met I've called her Mitten, and she calls me—"

"She didn't call you very nice names last night, Dad," said Lauren, a sullen arrogance evident in the thrust of her chin. She straightened up to her full height, her shoulders back.

"Honeybunch, all couples have disagreements—but they don't kill each other."

"A *disagreement*? Is that why she's been boffing that . . . that maintenance—whatever the jerk is—out in the ice house. I saw them the afternoon before your party,

Dad." Lauren waited, daring her father to contradict her this time.

So brief was the flash of rage across Dave Theurian's face that Osborne wasn't entirely sure he'd seen it. If there was any vestige of emotion after Lauren's statement, it was only a slight pulsing of a vein along his jaw.

"Lauren, we'll discuss this later. You are very out of line."

"Your wife's properties," said Lew, warning Lauren with a look that she had said enough. "I assume you're referring to the strip joints?"

"She inherited several businesses, of which a chain of gentlemen's clubs happens to be one," said Theurian. "Part of her grandmother's estate and, as I just said, she is in the process of selling those off."

"Is Patrice Kobernot in the business, too?" Osborne couldn't resist asking.

"No, Karin's sister asked to be bought out of her share back when the estate was settled."

"And when was that?"

"I'm not sure," said Theurian, sounding exasperated. "End of November, maybe? A family squabble I had no interest in. You need to understand one thing: Mitten and I make it a point to have nothing to do with each other's business interests. That's how we keep our marriage on an even keel."

Lauren snorted.

"Most of the time," said Theurian. "What Lauren heard was a modest misunderstanding."

"No, it wasn't, Dad. You were shouting last night. I heard you say she was going to ruin you. Didn't you say that?"

"Lauren . . ." The man paused. "In the heat of discussion people often say things they don't mean. Now, please. Will you accord me some respect as your father and stop airing our personal family matters. This is embarrassing both of us."

Osborne marveled at how, in spite of his daughter's ac-

cusations, Theurian managed to keep his voice to a soft
purr and a light, kind expression in his eyes. Hallmarks of
an excellent lawyer, a talented persuader.

Only Lauren wasn't buying. She edged away from her
father, her shoulders rigid, arms folded tight across her
chest. Was it the look on his face? Or the oily tone? Had
she heard him speak to her mother just that way? Whatever the reason, Lauren's body language signaled that
trust had left the room.

Back in the warehouse, after acknowledging the tissue
processing industry was proving to be a tougher market
than he had expected, Theurian resisted Gina's request for
a demonstration of how allograft tissue is processed.

"I'm not sure how to operate the microprocessors. I
leave that to my lab tech. He's off today."

"I understand," said Gina, "but maybe you could just
walk us through. You know, give us a brief rundown on
the process."

"Dave, I'd like to see your operation, too," said Osborne. "A number of my colleagues in the dental profes-
sion are using allograft tissue. Bone powders in the
periodontal field in particular. How 'bout just a brief
overview of the processing—nothing too detailed. Something I can bring up at our next meeting, encourage the
board to invite you down to speak."

"Well . . ." Theurian checked his watch. "I have a conference call at ten with the client I had planned to meet—
but I can take a few minutes. You don't mind if it's
short . . ."

"Not a problem," said Osborne.

"Freeze-drying allows a biological product to maintain its
original size and shape with a minimum of cell rupture,"
said Theurian, explaining as he walked them quickly
through the lab area of the warehouse.

"Not only will the products maintain their color and
texture but they are shelf-stable for six months to three

years if properly stored. Degradation occurs only if the product is exposed to oxygen.

"I explained to your friend, Ray, the other night that I have patents pending on my proprietary freezing equipment, which are those units over there," he said, pointing to a wall of steel cabinets outfitted with dials and gauges. "In addition, the warehouse contains six cold rooms for product storage and processing at temperatures as low as minus forty degrees Centigrade and twelve drying chambers with over fourteen thousand square feet of freeze-drying capacity."

"That explains the size of your building," said Lew.

"This is a major investment that you're looking at, believe me," said Theurian. Again he pointed. "On that side of the room are low-temp granulators, screening units for size classification, and mixers for product blending."

He paused at a door to a small office but made no move to open the door. "That room holds the microprocessor controls that keep each chamber running at peak efficiency. Also in there is our central computer where we collect chamber operating data, store that data on hard disk, and dump it to tape after the cycle completion to provide permanent validation.

"And it is that validation that is critical to the hospitals and other health-care providers that we supply." He looked at Gina. "All the documentation I showed you earlier? That is generated here."

"And finally . . . follow me, folks," said Theurian as he walked towards a door at the back of the building. "To be sure we maintain control of the product every step of the way, we have two vans specially outfitted for shipping . . ." He opened the door and stepped into a small garage-like area and looked around. "That's odd."

"What's wrong?" asked Gina.

"Oh, nothing. I guess my lab tech is using one of the vans is all. I forgot about that, I guess." Theurian looked at the three of them. "If there are no more questions, I need to get on with that call to my client."

"One last thing," said Lew. "Going back to our earlier discussion of your wife's business—what was the name of that gentleman who was here this morning? The chief maintenance engineer?"

"I have no idea. I left the house at six this morning, and my wife was still asleep. And as I said several times, *I have no interest in my wife's business.* I don't know who works for her, I don't know what she makes, I don't know jackshit about those clubs. And I don't want to. That's one reason she's selling the damn things.

"Sorry, I don't mean to sound upset but . . . I am." He dropped his voice, "I didn't want to say this in front of my daughter, but Lauren has been sent to boarding school for a reason. She's getting help for what you might call an active imagination. She's too sensitive, she imagines things. She always has, but it's been worse since her mother died. Very sad, really. I mean, would you believe she went through a stage of believing I caused her mother's death? Can you believe that?"

He looked each of them in the eye, expecting sympathy.

"Hmm," said Lew. "I can see that being a problem."

As they left the warehouse, Theurian kicked his way through the snow towards the garage where an overhead door was still open to the stall where he had parked his Hummer. He stopped and looked around, hands on his hips, then turned back towards the house, a puzzled look on his face.

"Something else missing?" asked Lew, walking towards the garage.

"My snowmobiles," said Theurian. "Lauren must have left them down in Loon Lake when she went riding with her friend Nick."

"If you mean yesterday," said Gina, "the kids rented sleds. I happen to know that Ray helped them arrange the rentals." Osborne walked over to the garage and looked in. He checked the stall to the right where he had seen the sleds two days earlier. It was empty all right.

"But I was sure that Mitten said . . . oh well, I must be wrong. I'll be glad when the holidays are over. It's obviously I'm getting things mixed up."

But before Theurian hit the switch to close the garage door, he scanned the hooks along the wall in the empty stall. Osborne followed his gaze. Also missing was a neon blue woman's snowmobile suit with its five hundred dollar matching helmet.

Ray and Lauren were standing by the rear passenger door to Osborne's car. Lauren had a backpack slung over her shoulder.

"Lauren, I want to see you up at the house," said Theurian.

"Later, Dad, I'm going ice fishing with Nick and Ray. We can talk when I get back, okay?"

"No, it's not okay. I want to talk to you now."

"Dad, I have plans—"

"You heard what I said."

"Tell you what, Dave," said Ray, opening the car door and shoveling Lauren in as he spoke. "How 'bout I take the kids fishing and have her back here by three this afternoon. That works for you, doesn't it?" He slammed the car door closed.

Osborne watched Dave Theurian in his rearview mirror as he pulled around to follow Lew down the long drive, the slight figure, shoulders slumped, hands thrust deep in his pockets, staring after them as they disappeared into the haze of snow. He didn't wave.

thirty-six

A jerk on one end of a line, waiting for a jerk on the other.

—Classic folk definition of fishing

Once they were outside the entrance to the Theurian's drive, Lew pulled her cruiser over off to the side of the road. She walked back to Osborne's car.

"Doc, Ray, let's talk for a minute. I just checked in with Marlene, and something's come up. Gina, you wait here with Lauren, okay?"

"What did you find?" she asked Ray after the two men had climbed into the backseat of her cruiser. She crooked an elbow across the back of the front seat to listen, her eyes dark with worry.

Oh, thought Osborne, so that's what Ray was doing while they were listening to Theurian. He should have known.

"What you thought I might," sai Ray. "A grim experience, might I add."

"Tagged with supplier names and dates? Poly-bagged?"

"No. Not an iota of identification. Unprocessed tissue wrapped in heavy-duty plastic. At least it isn't Saran Wrap. I'm sure it's what Lauren saw early this morning."

"Doc, Dave Theurian was careful to point out that every harvested unit of tissue is tagged, dated, and catalogued. This sounds more cavalier."

"This sounds like you have cause to shut down Theurian Resources until some questions are answered," said Osborne. "If what Ray is describing is what I think he is, I can't help but speculate someone is obtaining tissue samples illegally. Yet Dave Theurian comes across pretty darn straight."

"I agree," said Lew. "All my years in police work, I consider myself a good judge when it comes to people lying. I didn't get that vibe as he talked about his business. About his wife maybe, about shooting a buck, yes—but not about his business. And if he had something to hide in those basement lockers, why wasn't he concerned about Ray being in the house on his own?"

"He was more worried about his wife's *reaction* to our getting into that room," said Lew. "And he didn't lock the door behind him when we left. He didn't behave like a man with something to hide—not in the house anyway."

"That leaves the lovely Mitten, doesn't it," said Ray. "The family hunter and gatherer. Well, folks, I can pretty well guarantee you her quarry ain't venison."

"Guessing or you're sure?"

"I've butchered enough deer to know the difference."

"You didn't touch anything did you?"

"Nope, did not disturb a thing. Just opened the doors and looked in. Oh, no berries, by the way—just more of the same."

Lew stared out the window in silence.

"Why are we so calm?" asked Osborne after a moment. "Think about what Ray is telling us he found down there. Shouldn't we be sick to our stomachs? Out vomiting in the road?"

"We could," said Lew. "But what good would that do?" She kept her eyes fixed on the falling snow, thinking.

Finally she said, "As I came down the drive, Marlene radioed that Arne Steadman is demanding to see me in my ffice *with* his grandson at eleven. Or as he put it to Marne—'Tell that idiot woman she left me six goddam hone messages and that's five too many.'"

Lew managed a weak grin. "So that's another priority or the moment, though with all this snow even the high-ay is going to be slow going. I'm not sure I can make it y eleven."

"We could get stuck," said Ray.

"Nah, if I'm going to get anything accomplished I need at meeting with Arne . . . and Bud."

"What do you want us to do about the situation here?" sked Osborne. "Surely you don't want Lauren going ack in there, do you?"

"Hell, no. Let's get back to Loon Lake," said Lew, her oice suddenly brisk with plans. "I'll call the sheriff on y cell phone and explain why I have good reason to sus-ect exceedingly unpleasant circumstances here. And I'll ave Marlene get in touch with Bruce. Let him know we eed him up here ASAP. At least the county can pay his ill this time."

"My advice," said Ray, "be sure it's Bruce who opens hose lockers down there, not Sheriff Kopitzke. Know vhat I mean? You don't need old Kopitzke having a heart ttack on your watch."

"It's not pretty, huh."

"Chief, this is *raw*—"

"I hear you, Ray."

"I'm worried about Lauren," said Osborne, "what do ve say to this kid? You think she'll want to stay in a ouse where—"

"I know, I know," said Lew, "that's another problem 'm mulling over as we drive back. Doc, will you swing y my office when we get into town? Hopefully, I'll have few minutes before my meeting with Arne, and we can ll sit down with her together . . ."

"What about Theurian? You think it's okay to leave him ere right now?" said Ray. "What you got in there is vorse than—"

"Jeez, Ray, think about it, will you?" Lew banged he steering wheel in frustration. "I've got a limited numbe of authorized personnel and even less time. At least thi snowstorm buys me a window. And we're due to get an other foot before morning. I don't see Theurian goin anywhere and that science project in his basement sur isn't walking. If things go halfway decently, I ought to h back here with the sheriff in a couple hours."

"I never got any breakfast," said Ray in a tiny voice.

"Out!" said Lew with a mock swipe of her hand. "An Doc—drive slow. The last thing I need is one of us in th ditch."

Half a dozen fender benders around Loon Lake an enough snow to force traffic to a crawl delayed everyone including Arne Steadman. While Lauren was using th ladies' room, the adults gathered in Lew's office for quick debate. It was decided that Gina would deliver th news.

"Lauren, come over here and sit by me," said Gina, pat ting the seat of the chair beside her as Lauren walked int the room. The girl loped over and plunked herself down.

"Can we call Nick?" she said.

"In a minute, hon," said Gina.

Ray and Doc, steaming mugs of coffee in hand, pulle over two more chairs. As they were settling in, Lew' phone rang. She hit the speaker button. "What is it, Mar lene?"

"Michalski's on his way back to your office. I told hin not to interrupt your meeting, but he said his grandfathe is stuck and he can't wait, he has to be somewhere—"

Before Marlene could finish, there was a quick knock and the door to Lew's office opened. Bud Michalsk poked his head in, "Sorry, Chief Ferris, but I have to leave. Grandpops was supposed to tell you that I can' start work until after the first of the year . . ."

Lauren was on her feet. "That's him! That's the man

aw with my stepmom. He's the guy who was in the ice
ouse. He was at our house this morning—"

Ray was fast. He tackled Bud in the hall. But the man
icked back, his boot slamming into the bridge of Ray's
ose. Ray cursed and grabbed at his face, blood spurting
hrough his fingers. Lew had her gun out and was shout-
ng, but Bud scrambled down the hall and through the
nain doors. A cluster of people filling out accident reports
n the front foyer made it unwise to get off a shot.

Lew dashed through the doors after Bud, but he must
ave parked on a side street. There was no sign of him in
he unplowed lot serving the department. With the snow-
all limiting visibility, it was impossible to see past the
arking area.

"Dammit," said Lew. She hurried over to Marlene at
he switchboard. "Where's Roger? Where's Terry?"

"Accidents all over town—they're working the bad
nes."

t took half an hour to get a license plate number from the
)MV for the car registered to Bud Michalski. Spelling
vas a problem for the clerk on duty. Once Lew got it, she
ut out an APB for a black Chevy Blazer—as well as a
ed Hummer, license plate unknown.

Lauren drove Ray to the emergency room in Osborne's
ar, while Gina and Osborne worked the phones. A call to
)ave Theurian for help in locating his wife went unan-
wered. Sheriff Kopitzke said he didn't care how many, if
ny, body parts were involved, it would be at least an hour
efore he could get to the Theurian home. He had six
nore accidents on county roads.

"How about getting some *live* people to the hospital
irst," he said before hanging up on Lew.

She stared at the phone in her hand. "That man *is* going
o have a heart attack."

She reached Bruce at the crime lab in Wausau, and he
said he would be happy to help out, but Highway 51 south
f the exit for Highway 17 was closed due to three jack-

knifed semi-trailer trucks. As soon as the roads opened, he
promised to be on his way. With the wind whipping the
snow to near-blizzard conditions, Bruce's arrival time was
pushed back to early evening.

It was one-thirty when a state trooper radioed in that
Bud's Blazer was parked at the Thunder Bay Bar on
Highway 47.

"Don't approach, I'll take it from here," said Lew.

"Chief Ferris, these roads are bad," the trooper said.
"We've got motorists stranded from here to Hurley. You
make sure the guy is worth it before you risk your life in
this weather."

"Doc, I'd like to take Michalski by surprise if I can,"
said Lew, "but I've got Roger and Terry out for at least
another half hour."

"Surprise?" said Osborne, jumping to his feet without
hesitation. "Driving up in your cruiser isn't what I'd call
surprise. We'll take my car."

"No, I have a better idea . . ." A quick check with Marlene confirmed that Roger, slow out of the gate as usual,
had not yet picked up the department snowmobiles. They
were still parked at the trailhead near the Corner Bar, one
half mile from Thunder Bay.

"We'll ride up just like any customer. But, Doc, your
helmet and clothes—don't tell me they're back at your
house?"

"Still in my trunk from the other day." Osborne was on
his way to the parking lot as he spoke.

"Doc, I want you armed. We don't know what to
expect . . ."

"I'm no good with a handgun, Lew. My twenty gauge
is in the car. I'll get that, too."

Within five minutes, they were sweating as they finished pulling on the heavy snow pants and thick boots.
They had just zipped their parkas and grabbed for helmets
and gloves when Arne Steadman blocked the door to the
office.

"Out of the way, Arne," said Lew. "Emergency. We'll talk later."

"What's this about my grandson?"

"I *said* we'll talk later."

"Paul," Arne shook a thick finger at Osborne, "what do you know about this?"

"Sorry, Arne," said Lew, shouldering her way past the old man. "Doc's working on city time right now. You heard me—later."

Osborne and Lew hurried outside. Even though it was only mid-afternoon, the falling snow so darkened the day it looked like the sun had already set. Lew paused at her cruiser. "Maybe we should take yours instead. That way someone driving up Highway 47 won't see mine and get spooked." They climbed into Osborne's car.

Lauren and Ray had returned it after getting his nose taped. He decided it would be safer to walk Lauren and Gina over to the Pub for a late lunch. With all the excitement, no one had yet taken the time to tell the teenager why—if Ray's assessment of the contents of Mitten Theurian's wild game lockers was correct—her father and stepmother were soon to be arrested.

The drive to the Corner Bar was excruciating: a forty-minute crawl along the highway instead of the usual fifteen. But once they were on the snowmobiles, it was less than five minutes to the Thunder Bay parking lot, where Bud's Blazer was one of two vehicles parked in front.

Laura, the bartender they had spoken with the day before, had the door open before Lew touched the handle. "I'm closing," she said.

"Not yet you aren't," said Lew, pushing past her. The darkened interior was empty.

"Where's Bud? Whose car is that parked next to his?"

"That's my car—he's gone. Left about fifteen minutes ago. He left with the boss. Her car's out back. She brought the sleds, and they took off on one."

"Which way?"

"To the east, I think. Sounded like, anyway."

"Did you say they're on one sled?"

"Yeah, he couldn't get the other one started."

"But they didn't say where they were going?"

"Did that guy do something wrong?"

"Credit card fraud. Laura, tell the others this bar is closed." The bartender put a hand to her throat. "I had noth—"

"Don't worry, you're not under arrest. We're after Bud and Karin Hikennen. If there's anything you can say that will help us . . ."

A crafty look came over the woman's face. "Chief, I couldn't tell you this yesterday. I didn't dare even tell you his name. I couldn't risk losing my job, y'know."

"Make it fast, Laura." Lew's voice was kind but firm.

"When that rider from Tomahawk—the one that's missing . . ."

"Right."

"The night he was here, Bud and him were talking about some kind of party Bud was taking him to. Bud kept calling it a 'real party,' that the girls were more fun and the booze was free. Told the guy where to meet him—"

"By snowmobile?"

"Yeah. I couldn't say anything before. I mean, if that was just a party and Bud knew I said something that got him in trouble . . ."

"It's okay. That helps."

"Anything else, anything that Bud or Karin might have said before they left . . ."

"She has a really foul mouth and was going bananas waiting for him. When he finally got here, he kept trying to calm her down. I couldn't really hear what they said, y'know. I just wanted to keep out of their way."

"Was she chewing gum?" asked Osborne.

"Doc, we don't have time," said Lew, giving him a funny look.

"Shit, yes, like a huge wad."

"Bear with me, Lew," said Osborne. "She didn't happen to spit it out while she was here?"

Laura gave him a strange look. "Couple times—right in that ashtray. I emptied it in the trash."

"Good. Save the trash for us, would you please?"

Back in the parking lot, Lew pulled out the trail map they had used the day before. "We've got a good chance of catching them, Doc. Two people on a sled—especially a guy the size of Bud. They can't go that fast." She looked at him sharply. "You okay with your gun slung that way? The trails could be bumpy . . ."

"It's comfortable. I'm more worried about finding our way. This snow is deep."

"I got it down," said Lew with assurance. "Remember, I know that spring pond. You follow me."

She paused before she pulled down the face shield on her helmet. "Won't they be surprised to find the money missing."

thirty-seven

*A man may fish with the worm that hath eat of a king,
and eat of a fish that hath fed of that worm.*

—William Shakespeare

Osborne stayed close behind Lew's sled, hoping the high beam from her headlamp would help him anticipate the twists and turns in the trail. But the snow not only reflected the light, it blew straight into his face shield. While he could manage the straightaways, at every turn he was driving blind.

Lew stopped once at the junction of two trails to check the map, then pushed on. To Osborne's relief, she didn't drive much over forty-five, but then she had to have limited visibility, too. Finally they reached a long narrow stretch of trail. As he grew more confident on the sled, Osborne's mind wandered. He couldn't help but speculate on the two riders in the dark ahead.

Unaware their money was locked away in the Loon Lake Police Department evidence room, they must be planning to pick up their cash, then make their way north by sled. At Hurley, where the storm belt ended, they could grab a car—or more likely Theurian's missing van—and make the Canadian border before midnight. After all, who ould expect them to travel off-trail, much less to a well idden spring pond.

Of course, they were about to discover that if Bud had hecked his phone messages from his new employer . . .

Lew's sled disappeared just as Osborne felt his pitching orward. Before he could brake, everything went black.

Ie woke to such acute pain from his shoulders down that nat his first reaction was to recite the Act of Contrition. 'wo lines into the prayer he knew he wasn't dying. He nust have blacked out when he hit, landing so hard on the lat of his back he had the breath knocked out of him.

As the pain in his chest subsided and he could breathe, .e felt to each side with both hands. He was on a cushion f snow, legs splayed. No sled. No gun.

He heard a low moan.

.ew was lying facedown in the snow at the bottom of the orty-foot embankment. Her sled was tipped sideways, inning her lower legs. Her upper body was twisted away t an angle. Osborne realized he had been thrown clear of iis sled, which lay on its side, a silent hulk in the shadows wenty feet away.

"Lew!" Yanking off his helmet, he threw himself on his nees beside her head.

"My arm . . . my neck." Her words were muffled by her elmet, which was facedown in the snow. "Hard to reathe."

"Hold on." Adrenaline spiked with grim determination gave him the strength to heave the machine forward and off. He dropped to his knees again.

"I'm going to dig the snow out from under your face shield to give you some air—but without moving your head." Mitts off, he dug with his fingers, never feeling the cold. He cleared a pathway near her breath reflector. "Is that better?"

"Yes." Her voice was clearer. "I don't know if it's my neck or my shoulder—but I hurt."

"How are your legs?"

"They feel okay—but I don't want to move."

"I don't want you to move." Osborne got to his feet and looked around. Through the falling snow, he could make out a forty-five degree angle to the hill—way too steep for a snowmobile. Lew must have missed a trail marker.

He crouched near her head. "Did you bring your cell phone?"

"In the travel pack on the right-hand side of the sled."

Fortunately he had tipped the sled onto its left side. He found the phone—it was on. He punched in 911, hit "send" and waited. And waited.

"No service, Lew. We're in a gully here, which doesn't help. Now don't you worry. Can't be too long a walk for me to get help. But before I go, I want to see your head and neck better supported."

Again, he dug. This time, he pulled off his parka, rolled it up and maneuvered it into place under the face shield of her helmet, taking care not to move her neck or head. She was lying on her left arm, the one that hurt.

"Lew . . . how's your right arm and hand?" She could wave from the elbow down.

"If I move any more, the shoulder hurts. But, Doc, how can you go without your jacket? You'll freeze."

"I'm fine, this is a heavy sweater I have on. Now here's what I'm going to do. I'm going to walk out a short distance and see if I can't figure out where we are. I'll be right back, okay?"

"Can you use one of the sleds?"

"The runners on both are pretty smashed up."

"Do you have a compass?"

"No, think there's one in the sleds?"

"Should be." He checked the travel packs on both snowmobiles but there was no compass. Walking back to Lew, he spotted his cased shotgun in the snow where it had flown off as he fell. He stood it up against a clump of brush. "Okay, I'll be back in a few minutes."

"Doc . . ."

"Yes, sweetheart . . ."

"Are *you* hurt?"

"I'm fine, I just need to find us a way out of here."

He hadn't gone more than a hundred feet when he knew that was impossible. The scrim of falling snow, not to mention that the snow cover was hip high in spots—and all with no idea which direction was right. Retracing his footprints, he found his way back to Lew.

"Are you warm enough?" he said.

"I'm feeling a little chilled—but I'm okay for now. Any idea where we are? I don't think we can be that far off the trail." He gave her the frustrating news, then stretched out long beside her, his body shielding hers from the blowing snow. Neither of them said anything for long while.

"Doc . . . what are you thinking?"

"That this is bullshit."

Lew's body shook slightly. "Don't make me laugh, it hurts."

Osborne raised himself up onto one elbow. "I wasn't trying to be funny."

Either the snow eased or his eyes had adjusted. "Hey, I can see better . . . the moon . . ." He looked up. Something was moving in the dark at the top of the hill.

The cloud cover broke. Light from the half moon glinted off topaz eyes. The wolf stood still, watching them. Then he was gone.

"Wait a minute—" Osborne scrambled to his feet. The moon threw enough light for him to see the trail, which wound down through trees along the side of the hill. The snow was not so deep there, an easy jog to the top of the hill. Once there he found the trail marker that Lew had missed. It was barely visible under a three-foot drift.

From the top, he could see over the trees below to a vast white expanse: lake. Had to be Horsehead Hollow. He looked off to this right—sure enough. He could see the tamarack, towering over the balsams. The tree that marked the famed "beer bowl" of Mallory's teenage parties.

Osborne hurried back down the hill.

"Lew, I can see now. We're not far from Horsehead Hollow. I'll make it across and up to Clyde's place. If we're lucky, his phone hasn't been shut off. But if it has, shouldn't take me more than ten minutes to the main road."

"Take my cell phone," said Lew. "You might get service once you're over there."

"Now here's the only thing I worry about . . ."

He told her about the wolf, then uncased the shotgun and placed it on its canvas case near Lew's good hand. "This is a side by side, remember? You've got two shells loaded and the safety is off. All you need is a warning shot, Lew, enough to scare him off."

"Why don't I use my pistol?"

"Because you're lying on it, and I don't want to move you."

"Oh. Well, heck, don't worry so much—wolves don't attack humans."

"You're right, you're right," he patted her good arm gently. No need to remind her: They prey on the weak.

As he set out, he prayed the snow would continue to abate. He bargained with the clouds for glimmers of moonlight. When he reached the lake, he decided to head straight for the tamarack. Shallow troughs between high drifts made it easier to walk. He stepped nimbly around the deadheads poking through the ice.

Halfway across the lake, he saw a cluster of fishermen, sitting on their pails around a fishing hole. Odd, he thought. No bonfire, and why are they all fishing the same hole? As he got closer, one moved away—on all fours.

Osborne stopped. Three wolves were feeding. And the one that moved off to the side . . . that must be the male, the one with the topaz eyes.

He circled around, anxious not to disturb them. When he had gotten to the far side of the pack and could look back, he swore he saw neon blue. Whether it was cloth or fiberglass, he couldn't tell—only flashes of color as clouds skidded over the half moon.

They never could tell who had been driving. Most likely it was Bud who decided to take a shortcut at high speed—doing eighty or more straight across the lake towards the streambed leading up to their cache.

A three-foot high boulder wrapped in a snowdrift was the fatal surprise. The sled flew into the air. Even after the wolves had taken their share, the pathologist was able to determine that they died instantly: blue helmet of a broken neck, the big guy of a massive subdural hematoma caused by landing forehead first on the ice.

The lock on Clyde's door gave easily. And the phone, thanks to Ray's reluctance to close down the old man's place, still worked.

Two EMTs went in on sleds, Osborne riding on the back of one. The shotgun was unfired, the snow light, and Lew was alert. Two of her ribs and her left shoulder were broken. Her collarbone had a nasty bruise, and her left wrist was sprained.

"Other than that, I'm fine," she said woozily as he kissed her on the forehead before leaving the hospital.

Osborne started home, heart bruised from worry, the back of his head aching from his fall. Driving by St. Mary's Church, he pulled over on impulse, left the engine running, and tried the front doors. One was open.

No Act of Contrition this time. He knelt, collapsed forward to rest his forehead against the wooden pew, and gave thanks for Lew, for himself, and for topaz eyes.

thirty-eight

The last point of all the inward gifts that doth belong to an angler is memory.

—*The Art of Angling*

Mallory shook him awake. "Dad, Chief Ferris is on the phone."

"What time is it?"

"Seven-thirty."

"Lew?" Osborne struggled up on one elbow, phone to his ear.

"Doc, Dave Theurian is dead."

On the way to the hospital, he stopped to pick up a small bouquet of daisies. He selected a small vase in the shape of a frog. Lew wasn't exactly the flower type but this might work.

"Don't you look fully recovered," he said, walking around the hospital bed. She was sitting up, a sling holding her left arm and shoulder.

"I would be out of here today," said Lew, her voice strong, "but they want me to see the physical therapist. Were you able to reach Bruce?"

"Saw him on my way over here. He'll stop by with a

full report later this morning. Said to tell you he's still negotiating with Kopitzke, but he thinks he can get two-thirds of his bill picked up by the county."

"Terrific. Doc, help yourself to some coffee there. Now tell me everything he said."

"I hate to steal his thunder . . ."

"Forget it, I can't wait."

"Well, the best news is that even though they haven't completed a full inventory of the lockers in the Theurians' wild game room, the forensic team has enough evidence to say with confidence that all four victims died at the hands of Michalski and Hikennen.

"They ran a postmortem urine screen on the victim from Tomahawk, and the initial results show traces of either valium or flunitrazepam—just like the first two victims. Bruce is willing to put money on the latter. That they'll confirm by Friday."

"So that's why Arne requested that autopsy report—he didn't want it, Bud did. He wanted to know if we had an inkling of what really happened to the first two. I'll bet Bruce is feeling a little foolish, huh," said Lew, shifting carefully in the bed. "So much for *his* early take on why those gentlemen lost their legs."

"Yeah, but once he realized he was wrong, he kept an open mind—"

"Which is a hell of a lot more than I can say for how that lab has treated me in the past," said Lew. "Good for Bruce. Does he agree with our theory?"

"You betcha. Bud lured the men into the woods with the promise of meeting up with him for a ride to a wild and crazy party with lots of girls. On the drive north, he would give them drinks spiked with roofie. By the time they reached Theurian's ice house, they were out cold. With Karin's help, Bud would strip the bodies and suspend them in water through the hole cut in the floor for fishing until they were dead—"

"Which wouldn't take much more than half an hour in this weather."

"Bruce figures Bud did the harvesting. He's looking to confirm that by comparing the cutting patterns with the knives found in the basement. He figures they stored the harvested parts until Dave Theurian was away on an overnight business trip. That's when Bud would run the processing equipment—remember the lab tech saying he knew someone had been fooling with the microprocessor controls?"

"How far did they get with all this, can Bruce tell?"

"As of this morning, he's ninety-nine percent sure they never made their first delivery."

"So Dave really wasn't a part of this, was he?"

"Apparently not. Gina got into Karin's computer late yesterday. She found a database of middlemen brokering to the hospitals—probably stolen from that funeral home in Rice Lake. She and Bud were moonlighting. They were convinced they could hand off a few femurs here and there, pick up a nice fee and no questions asked. What with being the coroner and the connection to his uncle's funeral home, Bud had all the right credentials. I wouldn't be surprised if those two weren't planning to steal processed tissue from Theurian Resources as well."

"I'll bet ol' Bud had plans to 'flush it out' to where he could make his full $272,00 on someone someday," said Lew.

"Yep," said Osborne. "My guess is the only reason they didn't do it this time is they knew they could get a quick turnaround and payment by working Theurian's client list."

"Too bad Bud grew up in Milwaukee, Doc. If he'd been a local boy, he would have dropped those bodies elsewhere. Had they surfaced in the spring—no one would have been the wiser."

"He was lazy. He found some open water, shoved them under and figured they would sink."

"Take one that's lazy and not all that bright—and add sheer arrogance," said Lew. "Sure as hell runs in Karin's family. That grandmother of hers was as nasty as they come. I was looking through the department records a few months ago. Back in the forties and fifites, when the old lady was alive, there were more drunks rolled and left to die out in the cold. Coincidentally in a neighborhood not far from the Cat House or one of her other joints. For Karin—this was family tradition."

"Don't you wonder what possessed her to choose Bud Michalski of all people?" asked Osborne. "Wouldn't you think she could find a smarter operator?"

"Women like Karin know who they can con. She recognized Bud as a pup who would take orders—not to mention abuse. And she knew how to keep him happy: a little sex and commissions off the take from the skimmers. That was easy money until Eileen started to hear complaints."

"And confronted Karin?"

"Or Bud. She probably thought it was Bud and went to Karin to blow the whistle. Poor kid."

"Poor Dave—he should have known better."

"Maybe," said Lew. "On the other hand, we'll never know the extent of the collusion between him and Karin when it comes to his wife's death." Lew took a sip of her coffee. "Maybe he deserved to go the way he did."

Sheriff Kopitzke had arrived at the Theurian home shortly before Bruce. When no one answered the front door, he went around to the back. Still no answer. He tried the warehouse and found that door open. Dave Theurian was at his desk, asleep. Or so Kopitzke thought until he got closer.

Like Eileen, Dave Theurian had been surprised by death. A Phillips screwdriver shoved in from behind had pierced his heart. "Bruce doubts he even knew what happened."

"Bud?"

"Oh, no, he's hoping to prove that was Karin's work. Gina's checking phone records later this morning. We won't be surprised to find Dave calling his 'Mitten' after

Lauren's little bombshell—that encounter she witnessed in the ice house.

"Who knows what was said. Dave Theurian put it all on the line for Karin Hikennen: his family, his business, everything. He may have threatened divorce, he may have threatened to expose the credit card scam, maybe he was in a position to finger her as his wife's killer. Whatever— a call from him after we were there would have triggered Karin's response."

There was a knock at the door of Lew's room, and a nurse appeared with a food tray. "Mid-morning snack," she chirped, as she placed the tray in front of Lew. Osborne reached into his pocket for a small box, which he set on the tray beside the cup of yogurt.

"Belated Merry Christmas, Lewellyn Ferris. Do you know how long I've been carrying this around?"

"I know, I'm sorry," said Lew, surprised and pleased.

"Do you need help unwrapping it?"

"I can manage." She worked the ribbon off carefully, then the paper and opened the tiny box. "O-o-h, gosh . . . a Megan Boyd trout fly." She raised her eyes to his. "Doc, these are so expensive."

"And hard to find. Ralph scouted eBay for weeks. But we got a good one—"

"Boy, you don't have to tell me. This is the Atlantic Salmon pattern that's named after her—the Megan Boyd. Oh, Doc, it's lovely." Lew held the delicate blue and black wet fly carefully between two fingers. She brought it closer to the light. "A size 18 treble?"

"Um—hmm, and that's blue cock hackle over blue seal fur. Did you know she never charged more than a buck fifty for one of her trout flies?"

"You paid a lot more than that, I'm sure. She tied flies for the Prince of Wales. I never thought I'd *see* one of these, much less own one . . ." She set the trout fly back in its box, then looked at Osborne, a worried expression on her face.

"I got you the wrong present, didn't I. When Ralph told

me you were asking all kinds of questions about famous trout fly patterns, we both thought you wanted to learn how to tie some."

"I was trying to figure out which Megan Boyd I wanted to get you."

"So you weren't planning to tie flies?"

"Not to worry, Lew, you gave me a wonderful gift."

"It was a choice between that vise and a pair of breathable waders. Would you rather have the waders?"

"Tell you the truth . . ."

"I wish you would."

And so he did. A new pair of waders beat a thousand Pink Squirrels any day.

Late that afternoon, Osborne sat down at his kitchen table with his magnifying glass and three Ziploc bags containing wads of chewed gum.

One he had retrieved from the snowbank the night they found Eileen, and Bruce had since returned it to the evidence room. Osborne hated to admit it, but the guy was as efficient as he was pushy. Another was pulled from the trash and dropped off at the police station by Laura, the Thunder Bay bartender. And the third one he had fished out of the wastebasket in the Theurians' wild game room on Christmas Eve.

Bruce might have the advantage when it came to high-tech forensic science but some things never change: the uniqueness of bite marks. Osborne hitched his chair forward, eyes and hands eager. He just knew he was about to reel in a big one.

Satisfaction reigned: The tooth marks were identical. He reached for the phone. "Craig, do you have a minute?"

Craig Kobernot was alone. "The boys are down on the rink, and Patrice is in town finalizing the arrangements for her sister," he said after opening the door to let Osborne in. "Someone had to do it. Patrice is the last of the Hikennens.

"This way to the kitchen, Doc. Can I offer you a beer?"

Osborne declined the beer but accepted the proffered chair.

"Does Patrice know about your relationship with Karin?" asked Osborne.

Craig looked whiter than snow. "That was over last year. How did you find out about that?"

"I meant the arrangement she made to provide allograft tissue to the hospital through your medical group."

"Oh," said Craig.

"Sugar-coated sin, that woman," was Lew's comment when he shared the details of Craig's long-running affair with his sister-in-law. "He's lucky we caught up with her before they had any business transactions—or his career would be over."

"It may be," said Osborne. "I hate to admit it but Bruce was right about Eileen's severed tongue."

Their conversation had ended with Craig insisting he wanted to call a lawyer. That was fine with Osborne. What happened next had to be handled by the chief of the Loon Lake Police Department anyway.

Craig was sure to deny any knowledge of his lover's various business activities—until it could be proven otherwise. And the unpleasant message left in his snowbank that night implied he knew more than he should.

He would, in fact, need two lawyers—another for the divorce. Patrice had long been willing to overlook his philandering for the amenities of being a doctor's wife. But she drew the line at her own sister.

thirty-nine

*I fish because I love to; because I love the environs
where trout are found, which are invariably
beautiful . . . and, finally not because I regard fishing
as being so terribly important but because I suspect
that so many of the other concerns of men are equally
unimportant—and not nearly so much fun.*

—Robert Traver

Mallory and Gina decided to drive down to Chicago in
tandem—driving separate cars but stopping to have lunch
together. They were leaving early Sunday. Nick and Lauren had late afternoon flights returning to school later that
same day.

So Ray scheduled his memorial service for Clyde on
Saturday: ten-thirty at his place with brunch to follow.
Due to space limitations, the number of guests had to be
limited to Clyde's friend and six of that friend's friends,
not including Ruff and Ready.

"Time to leave," said Osborne from the kitchen. Mallory
was still in the bedroom, and it was already ten-fifteen.
"Mallory?" No answer. He checked his watch, then
knocked on the bedroom door. "Ready, hon?" A sound

familiar to the father of daughters reached his ear. He opened the door.

She sat in the chair at the vanity that had belonged to his mother. Elbows propped on the vanity, face in her hands, she was dripping tears onto the doily covering the cherry tabletop.

Osborne sat down on the bed. He listened for a brief moment, then said, "Do you want to tell me about it?"

For the last two days, he had been aware that something was bothering her. At first, he wondered if it had to do with Ray. But he discounted that when he saw Mallory and Gina getting along like the best of friends during Friday night fish fry at the pub. How that happened, he had no idea. Ray had an uncanny ability to keep all the women who wanted him happy—with him and with each other. Not even Lew could figure that one out.

He remembered that Mallory had mentioned meeting an attractive young surgeon in her AA group. Was he the source of her distress?

"Whatever the problem is—you've not been drinking, Mallory. I hope you're giving yourself credit for that."

He waited. She pulled two Kleenex from a box and held them tight against her eyes. "It's all my fault . . ."

Osborne heard a light knock at the kitchen door just as she spoke. That would be Lew.

"What's all your fault?" He could hear the kitchen door open and close followed by footsteps.

"Clyde," she sniffed. "He's dead because I told my stupid story that night." She pressed the Kleenex tighter as more tears squeezed through. Lew poked her head around the door and Osborne motioned for her to stay back. "I feel so bad, Dad, I feel . . . I feel haunted. If that woman hadn't heard *from me* that he saw her, *from me* that he knew her face. Oh God, it's all my fault."

"No, no, sweetheart . . . come here now," he pulled his daughter over to sit beside him, his arm around her shoulder. "You're not being fair to yourself. For one thing—if you hadn't told that story, I might have. It's a good story.

A funny story. Not your fault at all. Clyde . . . poor Clyde was doomed the moment he showed up to help those people. Story or no story—once they knew he could identify them—"

"Excuse me," said Lew from the doorway. "I couldn't help overhearing. Mallory, telling that story may have had nothing to do with Clyde's death. When Bud lured the rider from Tomahawk back to that area upstream, Clyde took a shot at him—just like he did your dad.

"Now I'm not positive exactly when it happened, but I think they killed that old man because they knew he would find the money and the snowmobiles they were hiding not that far from his place.

"And, believe you me, they never expected anyone to find his body so soon. They thought they were doing away with an old recluse nobody knew. Which was a good guess up to a point. They never bargained on Ray."

"Really, you think that's the reason?" Mallory wiped at her face. "You don't know how worthless I've been feeling. Just awful."

"Worthless," said Lew. "Get over that, will you please? Aren't you finishing up your MBA this spring?" Mallory nodded. "With a major in marketing? That's what your dad told me." Mallory took a deep breath as she nodded again.

"The reason I'm asking is because I need a marketing plan if I'm going to run a successful campaign in the fall."

"What!" said Mallory and Osborne simultaneously.

"Kopitzke told me this morning—he's planning to retire. I want to run for sheriff. Then I don't have to listen to bullshit from razzbonyas like Arne Steadman. Who, by the way," said Lew turning to Osborne, "has already reinstalled his wife's cousin."

"You're kidding."

"I wish I was, but—using the excuse that the creep has agreed to work for half his former salary—Pecore's back in the office."

She looked back at Mallory, "So I was thinking as

Roger was driving me out here a few minutes ago that with help from you and Gina, I could put together a pretty good campaign. You advise me on marketing and Gina on how to work with media."

"Get Erin to be your campaign manager—she's great at that stuff," said Mallory.

As the three of them walked through the sunlit snow down to Ray's trailer, Lew and Mallory arguing about whether or not to launch the campaign in the summer, Osborne couldn't help feeling like the luckiest guy on Loon Lake Road.

"I can't believe you had Clyde cremated," Gina was saying as they entered Ray's trailer. "Isn't that bad for business?"

"Clyde would rather be out and about than stuck in the dirt with a bunch of jabones he never liked," said Ray, putting the finishing touches on his table. "Keep those coats on, folks," he said to the new arrivals. "When the kids get here, we'll be stepping outside for a few minutes."

"Lauren is coming?" asked Mallory, surprised.

"Nick is worried about her," said Ray. "Kid's pretty darn fragile—he doesn't want to leave her alone any more than necessary."

"Before Lauren gets here, I have a question for the women in the group," said Osborne. "I've been trying to figure Karin Hikennen out. She had a wealthy husband, she had cornered the market on booze, karaoke, and sex from Thunder Bay Bar north to the Upper Peninsula. What more could a woman want?"

"Hold on there, Doc. Things were not as rosy as they might have appeared," said Lew. "I learned just yesterday that Eve Theurian's father put all his money in trust for Lauren—so Dave Theurian got very little out of Eve's estate. I am sure that came as a shock to Karin."

"And I had one of my colleagues review the financials on his business," said Gina. "Theurian Resources was not

ooming. Recent media coverage like our series put a
reeze on the allograft tissue industry—at least for the
me being. He was carrying a lot of debt on his building
nd equipment."

"But Karin's biggest problem was that she made a bad
usiness deal with her sister," said Lew. "She bought
'atrice out for major dollars at a time when the Internet
as put sex just a click away. Her club business was way
own. Both Theurians were financially stressed. And I'm
onvinced that if Karin and Bud had made it to Canada,
l' Bud would have found himself 'flushed out' pretty
arn fast."

The door banged open as Nick and Lauren arrived. As
he women swooped towards the girl, arms extended, eyes
listening, Ray stuck out an arm to hold them back.
Later, folks. Right now, everyone outside."

tanding on the ice with the sun high overhead, they gath-
red behind Ray, who was facing west into the wind. He
eld a small black box, which he handed to Nick. Then he
upped his hands to his mouth. Some men are honored
vith a bugle wailing "Taps," some with Schubert's "Ave
Maria," but Clyde would have been pleased with his coda:
he haunting wail of the wild loon.

Dropping his hands, Ray reached for the box. "My
riend loved to fish hard water, and he loved the shouting
vind," he said as he shook the contents of the box into the
ir. A swirling breeze caught the old man's ashes, sweep-
ng them up, up into the arms of the white pines.

"And now," said Ray, turning around, "I know Clyde
vould appreciate a good wake. Let the party begin."

3ack in the trailer, music was blasting, ". . . if the trailer
in't level, ain't nothin' right . . ."

"Who are we listening to, Ray?" asked Gina.

"My Christmas present from Nick. *Trailer Park Trou-
adours.* Great rockabilly."

"Never heard of them. Are they on Amazon?"

"I order off their Web site," said Nick. "Hey, did Lau ren and I tell you? We're helping Ray design his own Web site, and during spring break we're gonna get him set up to sell his Hot Mama on eBay."

"Yep, I'm making lures like crazy," said Ray. "I'll be ready."

"Yeah, eBay," said Lauren. "Ray's gonna be a Power Seller, you wait and see."

"How come I didn't hear about this." asked Gina with a pout. "I can help."

"You've been in town working all week," said Ray.

"Nick and I got him started yesterday," said Lauren. "First, we signed him up for Internet service, then I gave him one of my dad's computers . . ." She paused. The table was silent, forks poised over the first course of fruit salad.

"Excuse me." Lauren pushed her chair back and headed down the hall to Ray's bedroom. Concerned looks passed around the table.

"Kinda hits her at odd times," said Nick. "Think she'll be okay?"

Lew started to get up, but Osborne put a hand on her arm. "Let me try," he said, laying his napkin by his plate.

"Good luck, Dad," said Mallory.

"Lauren, I cannot begin to imagine how you feel . . ." He spoke softly from the doorway. Lauren had thrown herself across the bedspread, her face buried in one of Ray's pillows.

"I hate my father. Why couldn't my dad be normal? Like you."

"Me? Me?" said Osborne with a chuckle. "I will spare you the grisly details, kiddo, but you are talking to a man who nearly killed himself with alcohol. Nearly drove my daughters away forever."

Lauren pulled her head up from the pillow to stare at him. Osborne sat down on the edge of the bed. "Yep, after my wife died, I went a little crazy. Started drinking heavy

y—and behaving so badly—that I ended up in rehab
ver in Minnesota."

He reached over to give Lauren's shoulder a gentle
queeze. "You want to know what becoming an adult is
ll about? Forgiving your parents. Seeing the good, for-
iving the bad. Some of us are just worse than others."

"Not as bad as my dad."

"Lauren, you can forgive a father . . . even a bad
ather . . . terrible things. Who knows—if he had lived, he
ight have changed. I did. I changed, and I continue to
hange. We all do, sweetheart. That's the only thing cer-
in in life: change."

"Maybe you're right," said Lauren, sitting up. "It's
ist . . . it's hard not to hate the fact that I am his daughter.
 mean . . . how much of his awfulness is in *me*?" The
ook in her eyes was heartbreaking.

"Lauren, are you forgetting that you are your mother's
aughter *and* the grandchild of Harley Fruehauf? He was
 brilliant man. Brilliant. Both those people loved you
early, and their goodness is in you."

"Grandpa was weird."

"Right—so you have a family tradition to uphold. You
ave the potential to grow up brilliant . . . and weird. And
s talented as your mom." He could see her thinking that
ver. "C'mon, our eggs are almost ready. Can't keep the
ook waiting too long, doncha know."

As Lauren walked back to her chair, Gina piped up,
Lauren, we've been discussing your new status as an or-
han."

"I'm not exactly an orphan," said Lauren, sitting down.
Mr. and Mrs. Wallace, friends of my grandparents, are
oing to be my guardians for the next two years. Dr. Os-
orne, you know Ed and Maddie, don't you?"

"Certainly do. Very nice people."

"It's just . . . well, I barely know them," said Lauren, a
orlorn look crossing her face.

"Ah ha!" said Gina. "Then hear this—while you were
ut of the room, Mallory, Chief Ferris, and I had quite an

argument—we were forced into a compromise. *Forced* for the record. So you'll just have to deal with the fact w declare ourselves your three big sisters."

"And when you're not in school—our homes are you homes—with plenty of advice whenever you need it, said Lew.

"On anything," said Gina, waving her fork. "Just as and if we don't know, I'll do a Google search."

"Before you agree to accept this new family of yours, said Ray from the stove, where he was carefully breakin eggs into the frying pan, "do you see any redeeming valu to knowing the three bad influences sitting across fro you?"

Lauren looked shyly at each, then said, "They laugh lot?"

"I'll drink to that," said Gina, raising her orange juic in a toast.

"Did you hear the one about eighty-two-year-old Walte who went to see his doctor for a regular checkup?" aske Ray, as he set a plate before each of them: two eggs frie to perfection and sautéed walleye cheeks—framed wit strips of crisp Neuske's bacon.

"Keep it clean," warned Lew. Ray gave her a dim eye.

"A few days later, the doctor saw old Walter out walk ing with this gorgeous young lady on his arm. So whe the doctor saw him for his next checkup, he said, 'You'r really doing great, aren't you?' 'Just following orders Doc,' said Walter. 'You told me to get a hot mama and b cheerful.' I didn't say that, said the doctor. I said you'v got a heart murmur. Be careful.'"

Lauren laughed. "Nick, we *have* to put that on his We site."

When everyone was served, Ray took his place at th head of the table. He picked up a glass pepper shaker, and tapping it with his right index finger, he slowly, slowl peppered his eggs. Everyone watched, waiting for him t take the first bite.

Instead, he took a slice of toast, slipped an egg onto it, added a strip of bacon and covered it with another slice of toast. With a cheery grin, he looked around the table then said, "In memory of old Clyde . . . I'd like to remind everyone . . . never forget . . . to take the time to appreciate . . . every . . . sandwich. Amen."

Walking back to Osborne's place later, Lew crooked her good arm through his. "You haven't forgotten our date this evening . . . New Year's Eve. I promised."

"You sure you're not too tired? Shoulder hurt?"

"Heavens, no. I'm planning on it—I've got the fly fishing videos all set to go . . ." She cut her eyes sideways. "Just kidding.

"Oh, smell that fresh air," she said, inhaling happily as they walked. "You know, Doc, when I'm with you . . . everything is good."

The Lighthouse Inn mystery series
by
TIM MYERS

Innkeeping with Murder

**When a visitor is found dead at the top of the lighthou~
Alex must solve the mystery and capture the culprit
before the next guest checks out.**

0-425-18002-6

Reservations for Murder

**Innkeeper Alex Winston discovers a new attraction at
county fair—a corpse.**
0-425-18525-7

Murder Checks Inn

**The inn is hosting guests gathered to hear the reading o~
scandalous will. But the reading comes to a dead stop wh~
Alex Winston's uncle is murdered.**
0-425-18858-2

Room for Murder

**Alex's two friends are finally tying the knot. Now Alex ~
some loose ends to tie up when the bride-to-be's ex turns
dead on the inn's property.**
0-425-19310-1

**AVAILABLE WHEREVER BOOKS ARE SOLD OR
TO ORDER CALL: 1-800-788-6262**

M 7072-C

24   TN